The shadowy move

As if conjured, an old woman suddenly appeared out of the shop's back room. She was not very tall, and the long purple robe she wore gave her body a shapeless quality. A turban in a violent shade of red covered her head. But most startling of all were her milky, opaque blue eyes—Patrice realized with a jolt that the woman was blind.

"I am Madame Voisin," she said in a rhythmic Creole accent. "You seek help, no?"

"We thought you might be able to tell us about something I've run across in my work." Patrice glanced over at Alan, wondering if this was a dangerous mistake.

Patrice lifted her briefcase onto the table and opened it. Madame Voisin's gnarled hand began to paw its contents. The bony fingers closed over the voodoo doll like a bird of prey grasping its hapless victim.

"I feel hatred. Much hatred." Madame Voisin's long fingers plied the doll. "A killing hatred."

"You mean the doll is evil?" Alan asked, his voice tense.

"Doll only rag and dust. *Person* evil." She cackled dryly. "Full of evil."

ABOUT THE AUTHOR

A native of Little Rock, Arkansas, Laurel Pace attended New York University and the School of Visual Arts in New York City. She worked in advertising as a producer of radio and television commercials before turning to professional writing. She now makes her home in Atlanta, Georgia, with her husband and their five very loving cats.

Books by Laurel Pace

Blood Ties

Laurel Pace

Harlequin Books

TORONTO • NEW YORK • LONDON
AMSTERDAM • PARIS • SYDNEY • HAMBURG
STOCKHOLM • ATHENS • TOKYO • MILAN
MADRID • WARSAW • BUDAPEST • AUCKLAND

Many thanks to Barbara Matheny
for enlightening me about snakebites

Harlequin Intrigue edition published October 1993

ISBN 0-373-22247-5

BLOOD TIES

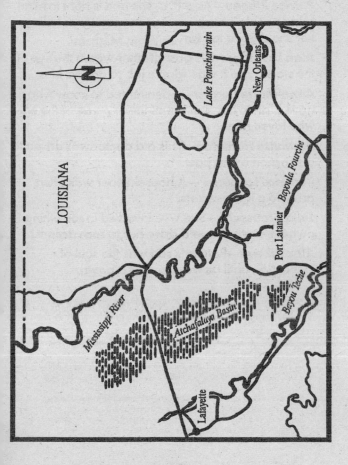

CAST OF CHARACTERS

Patrice Ribeau—As a P.I., she had a right to mind other people's business, but someone was telling her she'd gone too far.

Alan Lowndes—His grandfather was in the eye of the storm, and it was Alan's job to protect him.

Anne-Marie Bergier—She wanted to know who gave birth to her, but not at the expense of the ones who loved her.

Alphonse Hamilton—This old doctor was driven to distraction by his past.

Berniece Lacourier—A housekeeper was often privy to a lot of secrets.

Julia Broussard—She was involved in something awful, but what would drive her to such actions?

Alex Ribeau—Patrice's son was the soul of innocence, until he was used as a pawn.

Prologue

From a distance, the cemetery resembled a tiny village clinging to the edge of the bayou, row after row of faded white cottages divided by paths laid out in an imprecise grid. Like dwellings among the living, the crypts varied in size and ornamentation according to the earthly importance of their occupants. The mansions among them stood in the center of the place, great alabaster monuments shaded by ancient live oaks. Statuary and marble work abounded among these great houses of the dead, winged cherubs, baroque tangles of fruit and vines, curved ripples and swirls that circled the tombs like bands of soiled lace. Crowded nearer the road were the crypts of lesser souls. Weeds flourished freely here, while angels and urns were rare. A few of these humble tombs listed to one side slightly, shoved off balance where thick roots had corrupted the earth beneath them.

Julia Broussard glanced away from the cemetery to check the clock on the Mercedes's dashboard. She had left the house too early, arrived in this somber, desolate spot with too much time to kill. Julia absently twisted the large rings banding two fingers of her left hand, chafing the knuckles. When she could no longer stand the anxious sound of her own breathing, she climbed out of the car.

Julia started at a sudden, piercing cry from the swampy forest flanking the other side of the road. Looking up, she saw a blue heron lift itself above the trees, flushed from its roost, no doubt, by the sound of the car door slamming. She rubbed her arms irritably, annoyed with her own edginess.

She, and not Alonzo, had been the one to choose their meeting place those many years ago. At the time, the cemetery had seemed a perfect location, secluded and seldom visited. Here, only the dead would witness the ritual she was doomed to perform for the rest of her life.

Julia's eyes darted among the crypts, pursuing an elusive shadow. Alonzo rarely followed the footpaths, preferring to chart his own course through the cemetery. Julia was never sure exactly how he reached the cemetery or by what route. He simply appeared at the appointed time. Sometimes when he emerged from behind a crypt, he gave Julia the fleeting impression that he had stepped *out* of the tomb. It was not hard to imagine Alonzo Finch as something inhuman, not entirely at home on this earth.

She straightened herself when she recognized his gaunt figure limping toward her through the grove of live oaks. He was not a particularly tall man, but his prominent bones and the knobby joints holding them together gave him the appearance of height. Alonzo's skin and hair and eyes shared the same dull, sallow color, distinguished only by intensity of hue. A thick stubble covered his chin, dwindling to a few odd hairs sprouting from his bony neck.

He cleared the rusting iron picket fence easily, not taking his eyes off Julia as he hobbled up the embankment to the road. Regardless of the many times she had met Alonzo here, the sight of him never failed to fill her with revulsion. Julia could not control the slight chill running through her, as if someone had laid a bloodless hand on the back of her neck.

They exchanged no greetings, Alonzo only watching while Julia performed the now-familiar ceremony. His dirty yellow eyes followed her hands as they removed the letter-size manila envelope from her handbag. She held it for a few seconds, reluctant fingers testing its bulk and weight, and then thrust it into his outstretched hand.

"It's all there," she said, although by now they both knew she would never cheat him, even by the smallest amount. The unholy pact that bound them was enough to insure her honesty.

Alonzo nodded, and for a moment their eyes met. Julia gazed into the tarnished gold eyes, held by a perverse attraction, like the impulse to stare at the face of a corpse. Only when she recognized her own rigid image sinking into the reflection did she abruptly look away.

Julia's damp hand grabbed the handle and wrenched the car door open. She gripped the keys still dangling from the ignition, willing herself to be calm as she ground the engine. Nothing could ever change the terms of their relationship, but she hated to show any weakness in front of him, could not bear revealing how much he had made her hate her life, filled it with anxiety, shadowed it forever with fear.

The powerful sedan lurched forward, spewing clots of black bayou mud from beneath its wheels. Julia was grasping the steering wheel so tightly her rings gouged her fingers. She forced herself to relax her hold, stretching the fingers stiffly. When she had driven far enough to risk looking back, she glanced into the rearview mirror.

Alonzo was still standing by the side of the road, ill-fitting khakis draped around his fleshless bones like rags hanging on a scarecrow. Despite the distance now separating them, Julia avoided his eyes. Even so, she could tell he was watching her. His unshaven jaw tightened as his lips slowly curved into a smile. The sight of those incongruously white, efficient teeth sent a shuddering cold through Julia, as if all the blood had suddenly been drained from her body. Tearing her eyes away from Alonzo's mocking face, she shoved the accelerator to the floor and sped away.

Chapter One

"I'm... I'm glad you could make time to see me today." Anne-Marie Bergier glanced uncertainly around the tiny, cluttered office, as if she had been caught somewhere she didn't quite belong.

"It's my pleasure." Patrice Ribeau scooped an armload of file folders off the Haitian-cotton love seat to make room for her visitor. She gave Anne-Marie an encouraging smile. "Please have a seat."

Anne-Marie perched on the edge of the love seat, clutching her shoulder bag protectively to her chest.

"Coffee?" Patrice indicated the carafe smoldering on a hot plate on the credenza.

Anne-Marie shook her head, then just as quickly reconsidered. "Yes, that would be nice. Just black, please," she added, anticipating Patrice's next question.

Patrice selected a mug from the credenza cabinet, one embellished with the New Orleans Saints logo, filled it and her own cup with thick chicory-laced brew, and then turned to the desk. She placed the mug within Anne-Marie's reach before easing into her own chair.

As Patrice took a sip of the coffee, she regarded the nervous young woman seated across from her. With her shoulder-length brown hair and fresh, scrubbed-face prettiness, Anne-Marie had always reminded her of the models fashion magazines favored for their back-to-college issues. Until today, however, she had not realized how much the no-nonsense nurse's uniform Anne-Marie usually wore counterbalanced her youthful appearance. The casual skirt and cotton sweater she had chosen for their meeting made her look very young. *Far too young to need the services of a private detective,* Patrice thought, placing her cup on the stained phone pad she used for a coaster.

Ordinarily Patrice had no trouble getting down to business with a potential client, regardless of how uneasy or anxious the person might be. After all, in the private-investigation business, uneasiness and anxiety went with the turf. Anne-Marie was different, however, someone she not only considered a friend, but also to whom she owed an enormous personal debt.

Patrice would never forget the days following the terrible crash on the interstate four years ago, when she had sat half-dazed by her son's bedside, clinging to the faintest shred of hope. The doctors and staff had given Alex expert medical care, but it had been Anne-Marie who had helped heal their souls, as well, coaxing Alex through his difficult convalescence and consoling his widowed mother. If Anne-Marie now needed help, perhaps Patrice could repay in some measure the young nurse's kindness.

"You said you wanted to discuss a problem?" Patrice began, tugging a legal pad from the standing file.

"I want you to find my mother," Anne-Marie blurted. She tightened her hold on the shoulder bag, as if it were a big leather teddy bear. "My birth mother, I mean," she added, clearing her throat. "You see, I'm adopted."

Patrice nodded her understanding.

"You do that sort of work, don't you?" Anne-Marie scooted forward on the love seat as far as she could without standing up.

"I handle all kinds of investigations," Patrice assured her. "Why don't we discuss your situation and see how much we have to go on? Then you can decide if you want me to pursue the case." She gave Anne-Marie a soothing smile, resisting the urge to clasp the young woman's shoulders and gently ease her back onto the love seat. "Okay?"

Anne-Marie reached for the mug of coffee, signaling her agreement.

"First of all, have you done any research on your own? Can your family give you any leads?"

Anne-Marie frowned. "My parents are both totally opposed to my search. I guess it's not uncommon, but every time I've tried to talk with them about this—" she hesitated, groping for words adequate to her complex feelings "—this *need* I have to know where I came from, it's like running up against a brick wall with Mama and Daddy. I've tried to explain to them that they'll always be my real parents. They adopted me when I was a baby, gave me the only home I've ever known. They're wonderful parents, Patrice." Her luminous blue eyes seemed to plead for understanding.

For a moment, a smile relieved the tension in Anne-Marie's earnest young face. "Nothing could ever make me love my parents less," she insisted. Her slender shoulders rose in a helpless shrug. "But the subject of learning about my birth mother really upsets them, so I've decided it's best not to mention it to them anymore."

"Parents often don't know any more about an adopted child's background than the child does," Patrice consoled her. "What about getting a court order to gain access to your adoption records? Have you given that any thought?"

"Yes, I even consulted a lawyer," Anne-Marie told her. "He seemed convinced that a judge wouldn't consider my reasons compelling enough—whatever that means—to rule in my favor. I suppose you have to be in need of a bone-marrow transplant or something equally desperate to get a court order. That's why I've come to you. I remember reading in the paper about that little boy you located, the one who had been kidnapped."

"Actually, it was a parental-custody battle that got out of hand," Patrice put in. "As it turned out, the child's father was the kidnapper."

"But you found him," Anne-Marie insisted.

"Yes, I did," Patrice conceded.

"I want you to help me, too."

"I'm not a miracle worker. And we don't have much to go on." Much as she wanted to help Anne-Marie, Patrice felt obligated to be meticulously honest.

Anne-Marie's face brightened. "Actually, I do have a birth certificate."

Patrice clamped her fingers over the edge of the desk, pushing her chair slightly to one side. "An amended certificate?" she guessed.

Anne-Marie nodded, loosening her hold on the shoulder bag enough to fish an envelope out of its snap pocket. Opening the envelope, she removed an official-looking document and handed it to Patrice. "Mama gave it to me so I could get a passport a couple of years ago."

While Patrice examined the amended birth certificate, Anne-Marie went on. "I tried to get in touch with the doctor who signed the certificate. I've gotten involved with a support group for adult adoptees, and that's one of the techniques they suggested."

Patrice glanced up from the amended birth certificate. "Any luck?"

Anne-Marie's delicate mouth pulled to one side in disdain. "Not really, although I did locate the physician who signed it."

Patrice wrinkled her nose over the scrawled signature. "Dr. Alphonse Hamilton?"

"That's right. He's retired now, lives in Port Latanier. Finding him didn't do me much good, though. He refused to talk with me. Or rather, his housekeeper refused for him. I left my telephone number and address in case he changes his mind, but so far he hasn't."

Patrice noted the information on her legal pad. "May I make a copy of your birth certificate?"

When Anne-Marie nodded, she wheeled her chair within reach of the personal copier. Rolling back to the desk, Patrice slid the birth certificate across the desk blotter to Anne-Marie.

"So you'll take my case?" Anne-Marie's expectant voice carried an edge of urgency. "Will you look for my birth mother, Patrice?" she repeated.

"If that's what you want."

"I do," Anne-Marie replied, almost impatiently.

"I'll need you to sign a contract so that I can legally act in your behalf."

Normally blunt and matter-of-fact with her clients, Patrice felt apologetic introducing hard-nosed business matters in this case. She gave Anne-Marie an estimate of the time involved in this type of investigation, as well as the cost of incidental expenses, deliberately omitting the advance payment she usually required. Anne-Marie provided personal data and then eagerly signed it. Patrice countersigned the contract before presenting Anne-Marie with her copy. As she tore the sheet of notes from the tablet, she frowned over the depressingly sparse information.

"Can you think of anything else that might be helpful?"

Anne-Marie looked down at the big bag locked in her arms. *If she doesn't have a bombshell hidden in that bag, my knack for sizing up people is on the blink,* Patrice thought. Watching Anne-Marie fumble with the bag's clasp, she tried to guess what the young nurse would lay on the desk in front of her. A letter accidentally discovered among the Bergiers' personal papers? A photo, clipped from a newspaper, showing a face that mirrored Anne-Marie's nose or eyes? When Anne-Marie produced a chunky, tissue-wrapped bundle, Patrice leaned across the desk, eager to inspect its contents. To her surprise, Anne-Marie kept one hand clamped on the mysterious object.

"I don't really have any proof that this is connected with my search for my birth mother." Anne-Marie hesitated, and her slim fingers flexed anxiously around the bundle.

"May I see it?" Patrice hinted gently.

Anne-Marie said nothing as she slowly peeled away the layers of tissue. In spite of herself, Patrice tipped her chair, straining for a better look. She started, almost causing the chair to slide out from under her, when she caught sight of the grotesque figure swaddled in the tissue.

"A voodoo doll?" Patrice regarded Anne-Marie quizzically. "Where on earth did you get this thing?"

Anne-Marie licked her lips and then pressed them together tightly. "Someone mailed it to me at my apartment a week ago."

Patrice gingerly lifted the doll from its nest of crumpled tissue. One thing was certain: whoever had constructed the stuffed figure had not wasted much effort on lifelike reproduction. Scratchy feed-sack material had been cut into two identical pieces and then sewn together with long, uneven stitches. Its creator had dispensed with such niceties as joints, fingers and ears, preferring to stick to the basics. The crude abstraction of the human form reminded Patrice of a chalk outline drawn around a homicide victim. Except for two *X*s stitched in heavy black thread where the eyes should have been, the doll lacked any features. A wicked-looking hat pin pierced the ugly figure's upper torso.

Patrice twisted the pin and then withdrew it from the doll's body. Hat pins had disappeared from common use a good sixty years ago. To judge from the rust speckling this one, it was either a thrift-shop find or a carelessly stored castoff. Patrice squinted over the voodoo doll, locating the tiny hole pricked in the rough cloth, before replacing the hat pin exactly where she had found it.

"This came with it." Anne-Marie's voice was hoarse with tension. She held out a scrap of brown paper, clasping it between two fingers as if it were contaminated.

Without thinking, Patrice mimicked Anne-Marie's reluctant grasp on the paper. Her brows rose as she read the message printed in awkward soft-lead pencil strokes.

The ghosts of the past rest uneasily. Do not awaken them.

"Do you think the ghosts refer to my birth parents?" Anne-Marie's tense tone suggested that she did.

Patrice placed the note next to the doll and then slumped back in her chair, folding her arms across her chest. "They could, but I don't want to draw any premature conclusions," she cautioned. The worst thing you could do for a client was to inflate the importance of some vague but intriguing clue. "Do you still have the package this junk came in?"

Anne-Marie looked embarrassed. "I'm afraid I threw it away. I know it was stupid, but at the time I was so upset, I guess I wasn't thinking clearly."

"I can understand that," Patrice said before Anne-Marie could berate herself further. "Did you happen to notice the postmark?"

"It was mailed from here in New Orleans. I don't remember the date, but I received it on April 5." Anne-Marie's eyes followed Patrice's hand jotting the date on the legal pad. "That was exactly one week after I tried to reach Dr. Hamilton in Port Latanier. I remember the date because I marked my calendar."

"You don't have any practical-joker friends who might have sent you the doll, someone with a warped sense of humor?"

"Not that warped."

"Just checking," Patrice remarked dryly. "Okay, Anne-Marie. I think I have everything I need to get started. I'll be reporting to you every week or so, to let you know how the investigation is going. In the meantime, if you think of anything else, you know how to reach me. Oh, and do you mind if I keep this stuff?" Her hand indicated the voodoo doll and its companion note.

"Please do." Anne-Marie sounded more than happy to oblige.

Patrice escorted Anne-Marie to the front door. "I'll call you as soon as I have the investigation underway," she repeated, giving her a smile. She was pleased when the young woman managed a smile of her own before slipping into the elevator.

"Say hi to Alex for me," Anne-Marie said, holding the elevator doors open. "Tell him I'm going to come watch him play basketball someday, so he'd better be practicing."

"Have no fear on that count," Patrice assured her. "And try not to worry," she added, but the closing elevator doors cut short her admonition.

As Patrice returned to her office, she sensed the faint aura of tension left in Anne-Marie's wake, like the persistent ghost of a too-heady perfume. Of course, anxious clients were no oddity in her line of work. People intent on documenting the escapades of wayward spouses or conniving business partners were rarely in a laid-back frame of mind. Anne-Marie Bergier, however, had been such a bundle of nerves, she had even managed to infect Patrice with her apprehension.

Then again, opening up this nasty little present would get to anyone, Patrice thought as her eyes fell on the doll lying in the middle of her desk blotter. Perching on the corner of the desk, she studied the obscene mockery of a human figure and the makeshift stiletto piercing its breast. She tried to imagine Dr. Alphonse Hamilton, a retired physician, probably bespectacled, certainly white haired, interrupting his daily routine of golf and gardening long enough to stitch up a voodoo doll and compose the little bon mot to go with it. It was certainly possible—four years of professional investigative work had taught Patrice never to underestimate the improbable contortions of the human psyche—it just didn't seem likely.

Patrice reached for her briefcase and hoisted it onto the desk. Unlatching the lid, she shuffled papers, carving out a spot large enough to accommodate the voodoo doll. On the surface, it was such a hokey gimmick, like a chain letter or a fraternity Halloween house of horrors. And yet there was a palpable evil to the doll, a whiff of its creator's malicious intent clinging to its shapeless form. Patrice took one last look at the crude figure lying, empty eyed and motionless, in her briefcase. *Like a little corpse in its coffin.*

Frowning, Patrice routed the disturbing comparison from her mind and slammed the briefcase shut. After stowing it beside her desk, she reached for the file she had just opened on Anne-Marie. She removed the photocopy of Anne-Marie's amended birth certificate and surveyed the terse facts it provided.

Place of birth: Port Latanier, Colley Parish, Louisiana. Date of birth: July 6, 1967. Attending physician: Alphonse M. Hamilton, M.D. The name of the hospital had been omitted, but Anne-Marie could well have been born at home. Propping the certificate on the desk's pen set, Patrice rang directory assistance for Port Latanier. The operator offered a residential listing for Dr. Hamilton, which Patrice jotted on the margin of the photocopy.

She punched in Hamilton's number and waited for the call to go through. It was answered quickly.

"Hello." The man's voice was level and precise, characteristics one might expect in a physician. Unfortunately, he also sounded about thirty years too young to have delivered Anne-Marie.

"Dr. Alphonse Hamilton, please." Short, sweet and to the point.

"Who's calling, please?" The voice's even tone never wavered, but something in it suggested a protectiveness.

"Patrice Ribeau."

The man was silent for a few seconds, no doubt trying to place the name. "I'm sorry, but Dr. Hamilton isn't available."

Patrice decided to ignore the stock brush-off. "I can hold. I'm calling long-distance, and I'd appreciate your letting Dr. Hamilton know I'm on the line."

"Unfortunately, Dr. Hamilton can't come to the phone," the man told her with studious politeness.

"That's funny. A minute ago, you wanted to know who I was so you could announce my call." Patrice paused, giving her barb a chance to make the man uncomfortable—not an easy task, if his unflappable phone manner was any indication. "With whom am I speaking?" she asked in an effort to turn the tables.

"I'm Dr. Hamilton's grandson."

Patrice waited a few seconds, long enough for her opponent to get uncomfortable and start volunteering information. It took some moments to realize none was forthcoming. "When would be a good time to call back?"

"I really can't say. Dr. Hamilton has suffered a series of heart attacks, and his physician has severely restricted his activity. Including his phone calls," the man added with finality.

A good investigator can recognize a lost cause. "I understand. Please give Dr. Hamilton a message for me, will you? Tell him that Patrice Ribeau would like to talk with him about a baby girl he delivered on July 6, 1967." She gave Dr. Hamilton's grandson her phone number. "Do you have that down?"

"Yes, I do."

And I'm the reincarnation of Elvis, Patrice thought to herself. "Thank you. Oh, and please wish Dr. Hamilton a speedy recovery," she added. "I'm looking forward to talking with him."

ALAN LOWNDES paused at the door opening onto the sun room. For a moment, he stood back, his eyes resting on the thin figure seated in the wicker fan chair. It seemed like only yesterday that he and his grandfather had played their two-man games of softball on the wide lawn spreading out from the sun room. His grandfather had been a tall, healthy man then, with a robust laugh that carried over the yard as he shared the secret of his merciless knuckleball with the gangly boy. In those days, Alan had believed that his grandfather could do just about anything, and Granddad had never shaken that belief.

"Who called?" his grandfather asked without turning.

Alan smiled to himself. Even after two heart attacks and a triple bypass at the age of eighty, Dr. Alphonse Hamilton's ears were as sharp as ever.

"Someone named Patrice Ribeau. Does the name ring any bells?" Alan walked across the sun room to join his grandfather.

The elderly man shook his head, betraying the slight jerkiness that now characterized his movements. "No, but then, my memory isn't what it used to be. What did she want?"

"Something about a birth certificate you signed back in 1967. I jotted down her telephone number if you'd like to get in touch with her after you're feeling better." Seeing his grandfather flinch, Alan frowned. "Is something wrong, Granddad?"

"No, no, nothing." A twitch contorted the pale lips, giving them a will of their own.

Alan leaned over the wicker chair and rested a hand on his grandfather's shoulder. Beneath the loose-fitting seersucker robe, he could feel the bones, as fragile as spun glass. "You're sure?"

"Of course I'm sure!" His grandfather looked up at him, and for a moment the bright blue spark flared in his eyes as it so often had in the past when anyone tried to tell him what to do.

Alan chuckled. "I guess if I can still get a rise out of you, I don't have that much to worry about." His hand tightened briefly on the knobby shoulder. "Can I do anything for you before I head back to New Orleans?"

When Dr. Hamilton shook his head, Alan could tell he was making a labored effort to control its trembling. "Lucille's already cooked dinner, and she'll stick around until Mrs. Bates arrives for the night. You needn't drive down every day, you know. It's quite enough to stop by on the days you work at the clinic."

"Is that a roundabout way to tell me I'm wearing out my welcome?" Alan joked, as he often did to ease his grandfather's eroding sense of independence. As a doctor himself, Alan could appreciate how hard it must be for the elderly man, after years of caring for others, now to be on the receiving end.

"Go on with you!" The aging physician's laugh still retained a ghost of its once-hardy tenor.

"I'll see you tomorrow," Alan called from the sun room door.

Alphonse Hamilton watched his grandson jog down the driveway to the dark blue Saab convertible parked beneath the magnolia tree. He waved shakily as Alan threw up his hand before climbing behind the wheel. He waited until the car had disappeared before reaching for the walker tucked discreetly behind his chair. With painfully slow steps, Dr. Hamilton made his way to his study.

He sighed as he eased himself into the chair angled behind the big desk. Adjusting the green glass shade of the pharmacy lamp, he channeled the light into a bright pool that spread across the leather desk blotter. Dr. Hamilton lifted his glasses, letting his eyes drift out of focus as they gazed at the note the housekeeper had given him two weeks ago. The penciled words were illegible now, an assortment of meaningless letters. Even his own hand clasping the note looked hazy and indistinct, the papery skin and age-thickened nails obscured by the airbrush of myopia. Sometimes it was a blessing not to see too clearly.

His hand shook slightly as he lifted the receiver from the desk phone. His physician attributed these tremors to his weakened condition, but Alphonse knew better. He slowly dialed the old-fashioned phone, listening to his own labored breath rasp into the mouthpiece.

"Hello?" Julia Broussard answered the phone herself.

Alphonse hesitated for a moment, overcome by the sheer weight of the years he had lived and all the folly that had gone into them. "I've had another call today, Julia," he said. "About the child." He was surprised how much effort simply keeping his voice steady now required.

He could hear Julia swallow on the other end of the line. "Was it the girl again?"

"No." With that one brief word, the burden of his entire life seemed to accumulate on Alphonse Hamilton's shoulders, threatening to crush the brittle bones into a handful of dust. "Someone else knows, Julia. Our secret isn't safe any longer.'' He waited what seemed an eternity for Julia to say something. When she did not, he drew an uneven breath, summoning courage. "I've been thinking a great deal about the past, Julia. At one time, I was certain that we had done the right thing, but now..." He broke off to lick his dry lips. "Perhaps keeping our secret does more harm than good. Perhaps it's time to let the truth come out."

"No!" Julia's agitated voice vibrated in his ear. "Can't you see that they would only use it against us, that they would destroy us?" She was panting now, struggling to regain her composure. "No one must ever know, Alphonse. No one!"

Chapter Two

"Who's ahead?" Patrice smiled as she scooted from behind the steering wheel.

"I am!"

The grinning little boy charged past the car to take a jump shot at the basketball hoop mounted over the garage door. The ball bounced off the backboard with a hollow thump. A man with curly hair whose color matched his gray sweats snatched the ball before the youngster could retrieve it.

"And the old guy comes in for the rebound." Patrice's father mimicked a sportscaster's rapid-fire commentary. "Whew! I could use a breather. Thank goodness, it's halftime." Tucking the ball under his arm, he winked at Patrice.

"We just had halftime, Grandpa! Remember? We're in the third quarter." The little boy's flushed face grew earnest.

"Oh, yeah. Well, then, time-out." Tony Lafon passed the ball to his grandson before forming a *T* with his hands. He gave Patrice a pointed look. "Maybe I can put your mom in on my side and even things up a bit."

Patrice hefted a bag of groceries from the trunk of the Honda Accord and thrust it into the man's hands.

"You'll need more than me to even out the odds," she remarked dryly, propping the second grocery sack on her hip.

"Yeah, but at least I won't lose alone." Patrice's father smiled at her. "C'mon. We'll even give you time to suit up and put on your tennies."

"That's very gracious of you." Patrice gave both basketball players a wry smile. "Okay," she conceded. "Alex, please help your grandfather put away this stuff while I change clothes."

"Sure, Mom."

The little boy bounded up the front steps to hold the door for them. Patrice deposited her sack of groceries on the kitchen counter before heading up the stairs. From her bedroom, she could hear the shuffling of boxes and cans, punctuated by the refrigerator door's slamming. Dumping her stirrup pants and sweater on the bed, she pulled on jeans, a long-sleeved T-shirt and a pair of tennis shoes.

She had to be the worst basketball player in the world, a fact Patrice managed to confirm every time Alex and her dad conned her into a game. Today, however, she was looking forward to the exercise. She felt strangely keyed up, and shooting a few baskets was a good way to work off tension.

Patrice eyed her briefcase, resting innocuously beside the dresser, and a faint twinge of apprehension prickled beneath her skin. She was overreacting to that damned voodoo doll. Regardless of how twisted the person who had sent it might be, the doll itself was just an ugly lump of rag and sawdust. Its powers were only as strong as a superstitious person wished them to be. In spite of these sensible arguments, Patrice could not entirely shake the feeling that she had brought something poisonous into the house, secretly stored in her briefcase.

When she went downstairs, she found her teammate and her opponent waiting for her on the driveway. Alex gallantly offered her the ball to put into play. After passing it to her father, Patrice tried to guard her wily son. True to form, she let Alex slip right past her to catch her father's rebounding ball. By the time the game was over—something largely determined by Alex's appetite for dinner—she had missed enough shots to assure her team a sound defeat. In the process, however, Patrice had worked up a good sweat and succeeded in consigning the disturbing voodoo doll to the back of her mind.

While Alex set the table and her father tossed a salad, Patrice boiled water for spaghetti and thawed a container of homemade meat sauce in the microwave. At least once a week, Patrice's father picked Alex up from school and then joined them for dinner. It was a custom they all cherished, especially Alex, who looked to his grandfather for the male companionship and guidance a father normally provided. Patrice suspected that her father, too, welcomed the excuse to leave the rambling old house he now shared with only his memories and participate in their family's simple activities for the evening.

Family. What a complicated, quirky concept that common word harbored! As Patrice glanced around the table at her two companions, talking and laughing over their dinner, her thoughts returned to Anne-Marie and the young woman's struggle to sort out the intricate meaning of family for herself.

Patrice tried to put herself in Anne-Marie's place as she watched her father tease Alex. He had kidded her that way, too, when she was small, making her giggle uncontrollably when she was happy and cajoling a smile out of her when she was feeling down. Certainly those memories—and so many others like them—would now glow just as warmly in her heart even if she had been an adopted child.

Yet despite that truth, the blood relation between them represented an undeniable bond. Every time Patrice looked at her father, she recognized the source of her own curly dark hair and eyes the color of bittersweet chocolate. By the same token, she had passed a good share of Lafon traits on to Alex: a neat, straight nose, an incorrigible set of dimples, and the short, compact build that would forever doom his NBA aspirations. On the other hand, Alex's reddish brown hair and amber-toned eyes came straight from his father. At the thought of Gerry, Patrice winced, stabbed by a pain that remained sharp after four years of widowhood, and she quickly refocused her attention on Anne-Marie's case.

"Something on your mind, honey?" her father asked while they were clearing the table. With thirty-five years of detective work on the New Orleans police force behind him, Tony Lafon was quick to clue in to people's moods, especially his daughter's.

Patrice nodded as she returned the cruet of salad dressing to the refrigerator. She lowered her voice, out of Alex's earshot. "I talked with Anne-Marie Bergier today. I hadn't realized that she was adopted, but she wants me to find her birth mother."

Patrice's father rinsed the pasta bowl before placing it on the dishwasher rack. "Those kinds of cases can be tough. Lots of confidential stuff to get around."

"Mmm."

Her father leaned against the counter as he dried his hands on a checked towel. Patrice could tell he was watching her, taking his time rolling down his sleeves and buttoning the cuffs. "There's something weird about this case that's bothering you, isn't there?"

Patrice shook her head and chuckled. "How can you tell?"

"'Cause you're my girl. Now, what is it?"

Patrice cut a glance at Alex, who was still seated in the dining room, scraping the last bit of vanilla frozen yogurt from his bowl. He appeared absorbed in his dessert, but Patrice could tell that both his ears were tuned to their conversation.

"Don't you have any homework tonight?" Patrice asked.

Alex craned to peer through the door, his pleased smile rimmed by a pale film of vanilla yogurt. "I did it before we played basketball."

"All of it?"

"Almost all."

"That's not good enough, and you know it. C'mon, if you get busy now, you'll have some time to watch TV before bed."

"Okay," the little boy grumbled. He licked his spoon before reluctantly scooting back his chair.

Patrice waited until Alex had deposited his dessert dish in the sink and then trooped out of the kitchen before resuming her conversation in a low voice. "Anne-Marie has done a little background work on her own before coming to me. In the process, I think she may have stumbled onto a nut."

Tony Lafon shrugged lightly. "That isn't very hard to do these days. You think it's someone related to her?"

Patrice frowned. "It's too early to tell. But right after she made an inquiry about her birth certificate, she received a voodoo doll in the mail."

"I hope she didn't take it seriously."

"She was pretty shaken," Patrice conceded. "Not only did it have a pin stuck in the general vicinity of some fairly vital organs, but there was a threatening note with it, too."

Tony Lafon's laugh was short and unamused. "That sounds like standard voodoo fare to me."

"Probably." Patrice hesitated. "All the same, would you mind taking a look at it?"

"You have it with you?"

Patrice pressed a finger against her lips. She nodded pointedly toward the dining room, where Alex was now bent over an arithmetic workbook. "It's upstairs in my briefcase."

Tony Lafon pushed away from the counter and followed Patrice up the stairs. He watched while she swung the briefcase onto the bed and then unlocked it. For a few seconds, they both stared in silence at the grotesque doll nestled among the papers.

"What do you think?" Patrice at last ventured.

"That some crank sent it to Anne-Marie, trying to scare her for whatever reason. Beyond that, I wouldn't worry."

"What about the note?" Patrice persisted.

Her father's mouth pulled to one side. "It's not exactly a Hallmark greeting, but a lot of chain letters make more direct threats."

Patrice sighed, looking back at the ugly doll. "I suppose you're right, but..." She broke off when she caught sight of Alex standing in the doorway.

Her son instantly interpreted her disapproving look. "I'm having trouble with fractions," he pleaded in an exceptionally innocent voice, but his eyes had already settled on the open briefcase. "Wow! A voodoo doll!"

Although Patrice normally kept strict boundaries between her investigations and her home life, she realized that, at this point, slamming the briefcase shut would only whet Alex's curiosity. Best to let him have a look at the hideous thing and then lock it up in her office safe tomorrow morning.

Bracing one knee on the edge of the bed, Alex gingerly touched the pin protruding from the doll's chest. "Is this supposed to kill somebody?"

An involuntary shiver quivered up Patrice's arms, raising the hair in its path. "No, that's only in the movies. It's just meant to look scary," she told him with more conviction than she felt.

Alex wrinkled his nose skeptically. "I don't think it's very scary. It just looks like a dumb doll to me."

Patrice smiled at the little boy's frank pronouncement. As she closed the briefcase, she only hoped her investigation would prove him right.

THE TOWN OF PORT LATANIER was less than a two-hour drive from New Orleans, a fast stretch west on I-10 followed by a brief but circuitous route that penetrated deep into the Atchafalaya Basin. Patrice was too familiar with the bayou country, however, to be misled by the town's close proximity to the teeming Crescent City. The bayou belonged to another world, with its own traditions that stubbornly resisted the pressures of time.

Gradually the motel chains and chemical plants dotting the basin's main thoroughfare disappeared, yielding to faded white houses and little tin-roofed stores with a single gas pump out front. Occasionally a grand house, the legacy of a sugar baron or local politico, would loom from behind the screening Spanish moss. Just as abruptly, it would recede, ebbing back into the shadowy, fertile bayou as Patrice's car sped past.

When she spotted a sign designating the Port Latanier town limits, Patrice slowed her car. In a small town, outsiders generally stood out like sore thumbs, and she could see no point in attracting any extra attention by blazing down Main Street as if it were New Orleans's Ponchartrain Expressway.

Patrice drove the length of the town's business district, twelve-block span that it was, sizing up the assortment of small businesses and shops before pulling in at a service station. She filled the Accord's tank, making small talk about the weather with a portly man dismantling a carburetor inside the open garage bay.

"You just passin' through?" The mechanic eyed her curiously, wiping his hands on a greasy rag before accepting the twenty-dollar bill Patrice handed him.

"Uh-huh. Although since I have some time to kill, I wouldn't mind having a look around. This is such a picturesque town with so many pretty old houses." She flashed the mechanic the sort of nice-Southern-girl smile guaranteed to make him melt. "You wouldn't happen to have a map of the town or anything like that, would you?"

The man gave his blackened hands an extra swipe before fishing a single-fold pamphlet from the stack next to the cash register. "This here's from the chamber of commerce," he told Patrice. "It'll help you get 'round pretty good."

Patrice glanced at the computer-generated sheet that boasted a small map in addition to a brief history of Port Latanier. "Thanks a lot."

"You bet, now."

Outside the gas station office, Patrice headed for the pay phone mounted between the two rest rooms. The directory was less than a half inch thick, its meager bulk reduced even further by the numerous pages that had been ripped out. She quickly located Dr. Alphonse Hamilton's listing. After noting his home address on the tourist pamphlet, she flipped to the yellow-page section at the back of the directory. As luck would have it, Port Latanier boasted a single medical clinic, aptly called the Port Latanier Clinic. Patrice jotted down its address and phone number and then returned to her car.

Given Dr. Hamilton's age, his grandson's story about multiple heart attacks seemed plausible enough. Patrice nevertheless decided to cruise the Hamilton house, on the outside chance she might find the old gentleman hale and hearty, pruning shrubs in his garden. She was disappointed but not surprised when the only sign of life at the imposing Victorian house was a white-uniformed woman watering geraniums on the front porch.

At the end of the heavily shaded lane, Patrice turned her car and then headed back into town. Cutting one eye to the pamphlet map she had clipped to her dashboard notepad, she ticked off various local landmarks: an elementary school encircled by yellow buses; the courthouse with the inevitable equestrian statue of some local hero gracing its lawn; Madge and Jimmie's Café; and, at last, the Port Latanier Clinic. Patrice pulled into the parking lot behind the rectangular brick medical building.

A plaque mounted beside the front door listed the clinic's hours, as well as the names of the physicians practicing there. Patrice studied the names, taking a few seconds to collect her wits before pushing through the door. The waiting room was decorated in generic doctor's-office fashion, rust-and-green tweed sofas, a few molded plastic chairs, potted rubber plants, and well-thumbed copies of *Ladies' Home Journal, Newsweek* and *Highlights for Children* scattered across the lamp tables. Patrice excused herself as she sidestepped the outstretched swollen ankles of a pregnant woman and then tapped the bell inside the reception window. A slim, redheaded woman dressed in a blue tunic and slacks pushed away from a computer terminal in response to the ring.

"How are you today?" she asked cheerfully. Not waiting for a reply, she slid a clipboard across the counter to Patrice. "If I can just get you to sign in, please. Who do you have an appointment with?"

"I don't have an appointment, actually, but I'd like to make one."

The receptionist nodded accommodatingly and reached for a spiral-bound register. "And that would be with...?"

"Dr. Alphonse Hamilton."

The woman stopped, pen poised in midair, her brisk efficiency suddenly derailed by Patrice's request. "I'm sorry, ma'am, but Dr. Hamilton has been retired for almost twenty years. Let's see. Dr. Morris has had a cancellation, and he could see you at two."

"I really need to talk with Dr. Hamilton."

The receptionist shook her head. "I'm afraid that's simply not possible. Perhaps if you could describe your condition, I could recommend one of our doctors."

Patrice lowered her voice and leaned closer to the window. "Well, you might be able to help me. You see, I need to get a copy of some medical records. You have kept Dr. Hamilton's records, haven't you?"

"That depends," she hedged. "When were you last treated by Dr. Hamilton?"

"Actually, my mother was Dr. Hamilton's patient."

The receptionist closed the register firmly. "Medical records are strictly confidential. We couldn't possibly release information without the expressed permission of the patient."

Patrice frowned. "What if the patient is *dead?* What if I'm planning to have children and have no other way of finding out if some congenital illness runs in my family? Then what?"

The woman looked offended. "Of course, arrangements can be made in extraordinary cases. I suggest you have your personal physician contact the clinic."

Patrice ignored the suggestion. "I'd like to talk with one of the doctors."

The woman drew herself up. "The doctors in this clinic are very busy...."

"Why don't you put me down for Dr. Morris at two?"

The receptionist glared at Patrice for a moment before reluctantly opening the register. "What is your name, please?" she asked, tight-lipped.

"Patrice Ribeau. That's R-I-B-E-A-U." Patrice turned her head to one side, checking each letter as it was entered. Then she smiled sweetly. "Thanks. See you later."

Outside the clinic, Patrice let out a long breath. "Whew! And this is only the beginning!" she muttered to herself on her way back to the parking lot.

In truth, she had little hope of gleaning any more information from Dr. Morris than the receptionist had been willing to provide. With confidentiality laws protecting patients' privacy, it was easier to get a body exhumed than to find out if someone had gotten a flu shot. Still, Patrice knew of many instances where sympathetic medical personnel had dropped hints to help adopted children reconcile their past. With any luck, Dr. Morris might be willing to offer some aid without compromising medical ethics. Patrice entered the two-o'clock appointment in her pocket calendar and then considered the best way to spend the next four hours.

She had just cranked the ignition when she noticed someone waving frantically in the rearview mirror. Turning, Patrice recognized the medical receptionist jogging across the parking lot toward her. As the woman approached, Patrice put down the window.

"Miss Ribeau, thank heaven, you're still here." The receptionist paused to catch her breath. "If you like, Dr. Lowndes can make time to see you before his next appointment."

Patrice blinked. This was certainly a switch, from persona non grata to preferred customer in less than ten minutes. Could this be an omen for a breakthrough? Patrice kept her fingers crossed as she followed the receptionist back to the clinic.

The woman ushered Patrice into a tiny paneled office and indicated a brown leather chair. "Dr. Lowndes will be right with you." Her voice had dropped to a reverential hush. Stepping into the hall, she silently closed the door behind her, as if she were tucking a child in for the night.

Patrice was pondering the giant stuffed panda propped incongruously next to a bookcase filled with medical tomes when the door swung open. Turning in her seat, she looked up at a tall man dressed in a white coat.

"I'm Dr. Alan Lowndes," he announced, offering her his hand.

Patrice returned the introduction and the handshake, using the opportunity to give Dr. Lowndes a quick appraisal. She judged him to be somewhere around her own age, in his early to mid-thirties. His face was lightly tanned, with even features and a strong jawline. With his warm brown eyes and sandy hair falling over his brow, Dr. Alan Lowndes was good-looking in a comfortable, cider-by-the-fire sort of way. Outdoor activity and laughter had added a few lines at the corners of his eyes and mouth, but they did nothing to detract from the overall impression of health and vitality. Here was a man who would age well. As Dr. Lowndes scooted behind his desk, Patrice abruptly interrupted her private study.

"I appreciate your taking the time to talk with me." She gave him a smile and was pleased to win one in return.

"Not at all. Although I don't know how much help I'll be to you. I'm a pediatrician, actually."

Patrice eyed the stuffed panda and grinned. "So that explains that guy."

"Don't laugh. He helps me out with a lot of my patients." Dr. Lowndes chuckled softly. "Small-town clinics like this one usually don't merit a specialist's services full-time, but they often work out an arrangement with someone like me to come in on a part-time basis. I spend three days a week at my New Orleans practice and two down here."

"The best of both worlds," Patrice remarked.

"You might say that." Dr. Lowndes flashed her another charming smile. "Miss Stover said you had some questions about your mother's medical records. Your mother was Dr. Hamilton's patient, I understand."

"My client's mother was," Patrice corrected. When one of Dr. Lowndes's brows rose, she went on smoothly. "I must not have made myself clear to Miss Stover."

"Are you an attorney?" When Dr. Lowndes folded his arms across his chest and looked right at her, the golden brown eyes suddenly did not look all that warm.

"A private investigator." Patrice slipped a business card out of her bag's side pocket and placed it on the desk blotter in front of Dr. Lowndes.

The chair creaked as he leaned forward to examine the card. He picked it up, tapping the crisp edge with one immaculate fingernail. "I'm sure you understand that we're not free to divulge information about patients."

Patrice shook her head impatiently to ward off yet another lecture on confidentiality. "What about a patient's name? That's all she wants, Dr. Lowndes, just her mother's name."

"She's adopted?"

"Yes. According to her amended birth certificate, Dr. Hamilton delivered her twenty-six years ago." Patrice searched the lean, handsome face for a glimmer of encouragement.

"These cases are so tough, balancing the rights of the parent with those of the child. And you know, after twenty-six years, even the records might be hard to find." Dr. Lowndes drummed his fingers against the blotter, frowning.

"If you could help me put her in touch with Dr. Hamilton..." Patrice broke off as the young doctor began to shake his head.

"If that were possible, believe me, I'd be more than happy to oblige. But from what I hear, his doctors have ordered strict rest for the foreseeable future." Dr. Lowndes shrugged and smiled apologetically. "I wish I could be more helpful."

"So do I." Patrice looked into the honey brown eyes, trying to get a sounding on what was going on behind them.

"May I keep this?" Dr. Lowndes gestured with her business card.

"Sure." Patrice reached for her bag, accepting his signal that the interview was over.

Dr. Lowndes skirted the desk to escort her into the hall. When they reached the waiting room, he held the front door for her. "I'm sorry I couldn't offer you concrete information, but I'll be in touch if I think of anything that might be useful."

"Thank you, Dr. Lowndes."

He offered his hand again. When they shook this time, Patrice felt like a boxer being asked to touch gloves with his opponent. For all his sympathetic smiles and affability, there was something calculating about Dr. Lowndes, as if he was gauging his every move to match hers.

As she drove back down Main Street, Patrice tried to assess the investigation so far. The word *zero* kept coming to mind, but she stubbornly refused to write the morning off as an entire waste. She had managed to confirm a few hunches, albeit only discouraging ones. Dr. Hamilton was indeed an invalid. Medical records were off-limits without a legal battle. There was more than met the eye with Dr. Alan Lowndes. Perhaps this last suspicion had not been verified beyond a doubt, but Patrice could not shake the feeling that Lowndes had been sounding her out during their conversation. Then again, maybe she had misread him. Maybe she was too rusty where attractive men were concerned to have the vaguest notion what one might be thinking.

Patrice shrugged, turning her attention to squeezing the Accord into a tight parking space. She checked her watch before crossing the street and entering the storefront office of the *Port Latanier Gazette*. The front office was furnished with a solid oak desk and an old-fashioned swivel chair. One wall was devoted entirely to framed front pages spanning the paper's ninety-three years of publication. Patrice craned for a look into the back room and was rewarded with the appearance of a freckled elfin face.

"Be with you in just a minute," the young man called. "You want to buy an ad?"

"No, I need to look at some back issues."

The elf beckoned through the open door. "Well, then, come on back."

As Patrice sidled past the big desk, she noticed an ancient manual typewriter parked on the desk's return, and her heart sank. Poring over newspapers was tedious business at best, but if this office still depended on 1945 Smith Coronas to pound out copy, chances were one in a thousand that the paper's back issues were microfilmed. *Wrong again,* Patrice thought, this time with relief, when the young man rolled a sagging chair up to a microfilm reader and gestured for her to have a seat. After showing Patrice the cabinets where the film was stored, he retreated to his office.

Patrice located the drawer containing the 1967 files and selected a few rolls of film. Squinting into the reader's vaporous blue screen, she scanned the records of engagements, church suppers, and Little League baseball games. As in most small towns, very little hard news seemed to break in Port Latanier. Save for the murder of a prominent attorney's daughter in late July, that summer's *Gazette* devoted itself to recording the quiet rhythms of everyday life.

The birth announcements shared a page with the obituaries and public notices. Patrice remained at the machine, patiently loading and unloading film, until she had noted the names of every baby girl born within eight weeks of the date shown on Anne-Marie's birth certificate. By the time she had flicked off the reader's lamp and thanked the young man for his help, it was almost two o'clock. If she hurried and the traffic cooperated, she could get back to New Orleans before Alex finished his after-school basketball practice.

Walking back to her car, Patrice glanced over the list of names. Any one of them could provide a clue to Anne-Marie's identity. But which one? Tomorrow Patrice hoped to come one step closer to answering that question.

Chapter Three

"You're not hungry?" Alan frowned at his grandfather's plate, taking stock of the scarcely touched food.

Dr. Hamilton continued to stare at the cut-glass bowl of tulips gracing the center of the table. When he at last glanced up, he looked startled, as if he had forgotten that he was not alone.

"Forgive me if I'm not very good company this evening, Alan, but I'm terribly tired," Dr. Hamilton apologized. When his explanation failed to banish the concern mirrored on his grandson's face, he reached for his fork and speared a tiny bite of asparagus. "I fear I sat up reading too late last night."

Alan nodded, but the light conversational tone his grandfather had adopted, like the smile he offered as he nibbled at his food, was too forced to be convincing.

"So how was your day at the clinic?" Dr. Hamilton blotted his mouth with the napkin and then lifted the goblet of ice water, gamely going through the motions of eating.

"As busy as you'd expect it to be with chicken pox going around." Alan studied the bread basket's contents for a moment. "Remember that woman who phoned the other evening? The one who was interested in a birth certificate you had signed?"

"Yes. What about her?" Dr. Hamilton asked almost gruffly.

"She came by the office today. It turns out she's a private investigator, trying to track down the birth mother of a client who's adopted." Alan buttered a roll carefully, not looking up at his grandfather. "She wanted to know if the clinic might still have the woman's record on file."

"Surely she realizes that medical records are confidential."

"I pointed that out, of course." Alan propped the knife on the edge of the plate and then leaned back in his chair. "All the same, you can't help but sympathize with someone who's trying to find out where she came from." He paused, gauging the effect of his words on the elderly man seated across from him.

"Sympathy is no reason to compromise one's integrity, Alan," his grandfather reminded him in an unusually grave tone. When their eyes met, a trace of uncertainty—or was it fear?—flickered across Dr. Hamilton's gaunt face. "What does this woman expect us to do? Violate the trust of a patient to satisfy her client's curiosity?" Dr. Hamilton was beginning to sound indignant, a faint flush creeping up his thin neck.

Alan hastened to calm his grandfather. "I really discouraged her, so I doubt if we'll hear from her again." He was not at all certain that he had seen the last of Patrice Ribeau, but right now his main concern was reassuring his grandfather. "How about some dessert? Lucille made your favorite, banana pudding."

Dr. Hamilton shook his head briefly. "Not for me, thank you, but please help yourself. If you don't mind, I think I'm going to turn in early and try to make up for the hours I squandered last night on that silly detective novel."

Alan rose to lend an unobtrusive hand as his grandfather pushed away from the table and then tottered to his feet with the help of the walker. Alan took his time collecting the dishes, keeping an ear trained on the hall until Dr. Hamilton's shuffling steps had disappeared into the ground-floor bedroom.

Something about his grandfather was bothering him. Of course, fluctuations in appetite and energy were to be expected for an eighty-year-old man recovering from a serious operation. Yet it was more than the uneaten food and fatigue that had put Alan on alert. His grandfather simply did not seem himself.

He thought about the man's reaction to Patrice Ribeau's inquiry at the clinic. While Alan had not expected him to advocate exposing a patient's records to public scrutiny, his grandfather's lack of sympathy for the adopted woman had surprised him. Hadn't Granddad always maintained that a physician was no mere mechanic of the human body, but a healer of the *whole person?* That axiom had been the guiding principle of his grandfather's medical practice, and one he had instilled in Alan at an early age. For his grandfather, sharing an all-night vigil with a worried family or occasionally overlooking the bill of a patient fallen on hard times was as much a part of medicine as suturing wounds and setting bones. That he would now dismiss an adoptee's painful search as mere "curiosity" was completely out of character.

Alan leaned against the counter, trying to make sense of his grandfather's altered mood. Although his own practice was confined to children, he knew that depression could be a deadly problem for an elderly patient. And in the past week for some reason, his grandfather had become progressively more withdrawn, shrinking away from the world he had once embraced with such zest. Perhaps he should give Granddad's personal physician a call and ask his opinion.

Pushing away from the counter, Alan took stock of the kitchen. All that remained was to take out the trash, and then he could head back to New Orleans. He removed the waste bin's lid and shook the plastic liner, jiggling the assortment of junk mail, paper towels and plastic wrappers into a compact pile. Alan was preparing to tie the plastic bag closed when he noticed a lumpy brown shape half-hidden by a discarded cereal box.

Surely Lucille, in one of her periodic cleaning frenzies, would not have discarded Benjamin Bear. Still, Alan was unwilling to take chances with the beloved teddy bear that had been handed down through three generations of Hamiltons. Gingerly lifting the cereal box by one corner, Alan reached into the bin to rescue the stuffed toy. He started when he got a better look at the ugly figure that he had mistaken for Benjamin.

Frowning, Alan turned the doll over in his hands, studying its misshapen form. Far from being a child's plaything, this was a voodoo doll. He swallowed hard, sobered by the sight of the stickpin skewering a scrap of paper to its middle. Alan loosened the pin as cautiously as if it were contaminated with hazardous medical waste and removed the tattered paper.

Everyone must pay for his sins—if not in this life, then in the next.

For a moment, Alan could only stare at the crudely lettered message, too stunned to react. What sort of warped idiot made voodoo dolls and pinned ominous warnings to their chests? More disturbing still, how on earth had this vile thing found its way into his grandfather's kitchen waste bin?

Angrily tossing the note onto the counter beside the doll, Alan began to paw through the rubbish. When he found a crumpled ball of brown paper, he pulled it out of the trash and spread it open on the counter. Whoever had printed his grandfather's name and address on the paper with a felt-tip marker had tried to disguise his handwriting, if the irregular, clumsily shaped letters were any indication. Not surprisingly, there was no return address. Alan examined the New Orleans postmark in a vain search for a clue as to who might have sent the hideous doll.

Alan had little patience with malicious pranks, even when they harmed only the ego or the pride of the recipient. Mailing an elderly heart patient a voodoo doll with a threatening note attached to it, however, was no joke. Even a person who gave no credence to curses and potions—and Alphonse Hamilton was such a person— would be unsettled by the unmistakably vicious intent of the anonymous sender. No wonder his grandfather had seemed so preoccupied and depressed during dinner. But why had he said nothing about the wretched doll to Alan?

Much as he dreaded upsetting his grandfather further, Alan was convinced that to ignore the voodoo doll and return it to the rubbish bin would be an even greater mistake. Suppressing his revulsion, he picked up the doll and walked out of the kitchen. At the end of the hall, a narrow band of light still shone beneath the closed bedroom door. Alan tapped on the doorframe before quietly opening the door.

Dr. Hamilton was seated in the overstuffed chair beside the window, gazing solemnly out at the garden. He turned his head slowly to look up at Alan. "I thought you would have gone home by..." Catching sight of the stuffed figure clasped in Alan's hands, he broke off.

"I found this in the trash," Alan began.

"And that's precisely where you ought to have left it!"

Alan blinked, startled by the harsh edge to his grandfather's voice. "Do you have any idea who might have mailed it to you?"

The wrinkles draped about his grandfather's hazy blue eyes seemed to deepen. "What difference does it make?"

"Granddad, what's going on? You don't have to put up with this kind of nonsense. Who's threatening you, and why?"

"No one is threatening me," Dr. Hamilton insisted, but a detectable quaver cast doubt on his assurance. "Good Lord, Alan, you talk as if someone were trying to blackmail me."

Alan looked uncertainly from his grandfather's blanched face to the misshapen voodoo figure. "At the very least, this is an invasion of your privacy, Granddad. I'd like to call the police and see what they think."

"I'll not hear of it, Alan. The police have better things to do than chase after some young fool who can't wait for Halloween." Dr. Hamilton loosened his grip on the chair arm and waved his hand in shaky dismissal. "For heaven's sake, throw the thing away and be done with it!" He sank back into the chair, his meager reserve of strength spent from the effort.

"All right, Granddad," Alan quickly conceded. "I guess I'm just overreacting to a stupid prank. I'm sorry I bothered you. Sleep well tonight. And no late-night reading, doctor's orders," he added with a smile.

"Good night, my boy." Dr. Hamilton managed a smile of his own, but the haunted expression lingered in his dim eyes as they followed Alan out the door.

On his way down the hall, Alan heard the faint murmur of a television program emanating from the sitting room, a sure sign that Mrs. Bates, the practical nurse who looked after his grandfather in the evening, had arrived. He paused to peek through the half-open door and greet the plump, middle-aged woman busily crocheting an afghan in front of the TV.

"Now don't you worry one bit about your granddaddy, Dr. Lowndes." The nurse's cheerful voice carried after Alan as he let himself out the sun room door.

"I know he's in good hands, Mrs. Bates," Alan assured her over his shoulder.

As he walked to his car, Alan wished that he could genuinely take the nurse's admonition to heart. Not that he ever doubted Dorothy Bates's competence or dedication, but the shadowy malaise now menacing his grandfather's fragile health was not one that her solicitous care could banish.

He looked down at the repulsive doll he had carried out of the house. Granddad had been so upset by their discussion of the voodoo doll that Alan had agreed with him out of desperation. The elderly man's agitated reaction, however, had only strengthened Alan's suspicion that the doll's creator had chosen Dr. Hamilton not at random, but with a specific purpose in mind.

Blackmail. Granddad had used that term in his effort to discredit Alan's concerns. Had the word popped into his head without forethought, or had his grandfather inadvertently allowed a secret misgiving to slip? On the surface, the notion that someone would try to blackmail his kindly, unassuming grandfather seemed patently absurd. As absurd as mailing him a voodoo doll, Alan reflected soberly. Even allowing for the farfetched possibility of blackmail, what could be the motive? In Port Latanier, Dr. Hamilton was practically revered as a saint, a man with no enemies. Then again, the doll was mailed from New Orleans. Who in that city...?

The sudden jolt to his memory caused Alan to search his pockets. When he located the business card, he pulled it out and cupped it in his palm. "Patrice L. Ribeau." The name sat squarely in the middle of the card. Below it, the same clean, no-frills type declared *Private Investigator.* The lower third of the card listed a phone number and an office address in New Orleans.

Alan frowned at the card, mulling over the possibility of a connection. Certainly any private eye interested in keeping her license would think twice before mailing out a voodoo threat. Then, too, Patrice Ribeau hadn't impressed him as the kind of person who would resort to such tricks to shake information out of people. In fact, she had seemed like a nice woman, a little tough on the surface, perhaps, but anyone who came across as a cream puff wouldn't last a New York minute in her business.

He wished he had found out more about her client, although he imagined Patrice would guard confidential information as zealously as any physician. As it was, he could only speculate about the significance of the birth certificate that his grandfather had signed, but the connection was rife with possibilities. Any number of people could be desperate enough to try blackmailing Dr. Hamilton into sharing his knowledge or keeping his secret: a wounded child bent on punishing the parent who had disavowed him; a frightened woman frantic to conceal her past; a prominent man struggling to preserve his reputation.

Alan glanced back along the driveway. Evening was sinking over the house, enveloping its gables and cupolas in a nebulous dark shroud. Turning his back on the shadowy house, Alan unlocked the trunk of the car and stuffed the voodoo doll into the toolbox. Somehow he was going to find out who had sent Granddad that doll and why, even if it meant beating Patrice Ribeau at her own game.

THE STUDY WAS DARK, the heavy drapes choking what little light still threatened to penetrate its windows. Not bothering to switch on the lamp, Julia Broussard let her fingers trace the edge of the massive walnut desk. She sank into the high-backed chair and closed her eyes for a moment, shutting her senses to everything but the smell of leather accented with the faintest trace of expensive tobacco. When she opened her eyes, they fell as if beckoned on the framed portrait standing on the corner of the desk. Her father had been in his prime when he had sat for that photograph, a man who not only possessed wealth and influence but also knew how to wield them. Tonight, however, his direct, confident gaze only seemed to mock her.

Julia stared across the room at the wall of books and tried to bring some order to her chaotic thoughts. Daddy had always placed such faith in Alphonse, but Hamilton was a sick old man now, useless to everyone including himself. When he had phoned tonight, babbling about the voodoo doll, he had revealed the timid weakling that Julia had always sensed hiding behind the courtly doctor's facade. Let him stew over his worries, she thought, her lips tightening in contempt. His fears were nothing compared to those menacing her own life.

She had to do something, Julia realized. To hope that the girl and now this detective would simply give up and leave them in peace was as futile as Alphonse's self-indulgent brooding.

When Julia reached for the phone, the instrument felt heavy in her hand, as if it were weighted with lead. She hesitated, struggling with her own pride and hatred, before dialing the number that would connect her with Alonzo Finch.

SAINT VINCENT DE PAUL Catholic Church stood within walking distance of Port Latanier's shopping district, a dignified gray stone structure rising over a grove of ancient magnolias. In contrast to the church's Gothic architecture, the rectory was a late-fifties brick bunker with a flat roof and jalousie windows. No wonder they tucked it behind the church, out of sight, Patrice mused as she pressed the buzzer mounted beside the rectory's mailbox.

"Can I help you?" A small woman with a round face answered the door.

"I hope so. My name's Patrice Ribeau, and I'm looking for the record of a little girl who might have been baptized here about twenty-six years ago."

"Oh, dear! That was some time ago, wasn't it?" The little woman frowned, rolling her eyes up to the ceiling as if she was trying to recall the event in question.

"Doesn't the church keep records?" Patrice prompted.

The woman nodded. "Yes, of course. But I'm afraid Father Doyle isn't in this morning. He's visiting at the hospital."

Patrice overlooked the non sequitur. "Oh, I wouldn't want to take up his time anyway. If I could just have a look at the records, I'm sure I could find my cousin's name without any trouble." She didn't like to tell lies, especially not on church property, but Patrice sensed that this lady would respond more warmly to a family relationship than to a private eye's license flashed in her face. She was heartened when the woman unlatched the storm door to admit her to the foyer.

Patrice followed the church secretary down a linoleum-tiled hall to a small room crammed with folding chairs and cardboard storage boxes. The woman blew dust from the top of a gray metal file cabinet before yanking open the bottom drawer.

"The 1960s are all here—baptisms, first communions, confirmations *and* weddings," she announced, brushing the files stuffed into the drawer.

Patrice smiled as she pushed up her sleeves. "Thank you so much. I'll put everything back where I found it."

She waited until the little woman had left her alone before digging into the files. Patrice opened one of the folding chairs to serve as a makeshift desk and then began to leaf through the baptismal records for the summer of 1967. One by one, she ticked off the names of the infant girls that she had obtained from the newspaper yesterday. When she discovered a baptismal certificate with a name that had not appeared in the *Port Latanier Gazette*'s birth announcements, she pulled it out for closer examination.

The baby had been baptized Helene Louise Guidry on July 23, 1967. Patrice's eye raced down the certificate to the lines reserved for the names of the parents. Cassandra Guidry was listed as the mother of little Helene. The space designated for the father, however, had been left blank. She felt her pulse quicken when she spotted the godparents' signatures: Dr. Alphonse Hamilton and Bernice Lacourier. Patrice was too seasoned a detective to jump wildly to conclusions, but under the circumstances she doubted that the doctor's sponsorship of Helene Guidry was merely coincidental. To be on the safe side, however, she examined the baptismal records through to the end of October 1967. She permitted herself a modestly triumphant smile when her search failed to uncover another child not accounted for in the *Gazette*'s birth announcements.

Leaning back against the file cabinet, Patrice considered the evidence at hand. Godparents were almost always relatives or close and trusted friends of the child's family. It stood to reason that the Guidrys must have enjoyed some standing in the community to have had a man of Dr. Hamilton's prominence sponsor their daughter. Why then had the local paper failed to note the little girl's birth? Barring an unlikely editorial oversight, Patrice could think of only one logical reason: Helene Guidry was illegitimate. Dr. Hamilton had delivered the baby and then acted as her godfather prior to her adoption.

Patrice drew a long breath as she returned the folder to the cabinet and shoved the drawer closed. Promising as the scenario she had just constructed might be, she had a long way to go proving it. At least she had some more names to work with. Since Dr. Hamilton's illness had rendered him off-limits for the foreseeable future, she needed to concentrate on tracking down Guidrys and Lacouriers to further her investigation.

After stopping by the church office to thank the secretary, Patrice returned to her car and then drove back through town. During her reconnaissance of Port Latanier's business district the previous day, she had noticed a sign posted outside the city offices, listing the days and times at which driver's-license exams were administered. If licenses were issued locally, then the office must maintain drivers' records. With any luck, Patrice hoped to turn up a few Lacouriers or Guidrys among them.

She glanced at her watch and was surprised to find that the morning had already slipped away. She ought to phone her office and retrieve any messages from the answering machine. Then, too, it wouldn't be a bad idea to fortify herself with a sandwich and some coffee before tackling the municipal office and its inevitable cadre of small-town bureaucrats. Madge and Jimmie's Café looked like a suitable place to accomplish both goals. Patrice turned into the side street flanking the restaurant and squeezed her car between a vintage Cadillac and a pickup with tires the size of a road grader's.

Inside Madge and Jimmie's, lunch service was in full swing. The customers jamming the booths and tables seemed to represent the full spectrum of Port Latanier's society. Professionals in suits hunched over their gumbo alongside farmers dressed in overalls and boots, with a policeman and a couple of women wearing generic white uniforms thrown in for good measure. An unflappable-looking woman glided between the lunch counter and the kitchen pass-through, dishing out wisecracks and plates of crawfish *étouffée,* the day's apparent blue-plate special. Patrice was relieved to find the pay phone a respectable distance from the jukebox blaring Cajun music.

Fortunately, none of the messages recorded on her office answering machine demanded immediate attention. After making a note to phone the insurance company for which she was currently completing a job, Patrice reached for the Port Latanier phone book. She was disheartened when she failed to find a single Lacourier in it. The directory more than compensated for its dearth of Lacouriers, however, with an abundance of Guidrys. Patrice fished out a supply of quarters and started to dial.

No, the woman on the line had never heard of Cassandra. Was she any kin to Eveline up in Baton Rouge? The next gentleman sounded as if Patrice had roused him from a nap, smacking his lips sleepily over the unfamiliar name. She continued down the line, apologizing for the intrusion and repeating the same question, until she had exhausted the directory's supply of Guidrys without finding a single Cassandra among them.

Patrice hung up the receiver and resigned herself to scouring the driver's-license records as soon as she had gulped down some lunch. All of the counter stools were occupied, but the waitress noticed her standing by the cash register before Patrice had finished scanning the menu. After ordering a BLT and a large coffee to go, Patrice pretended to look over the day's newspaper while she eavesdropped for useful gossip among the diners.

"Hey there, Doc! How you doin' t'day?"

At the word "doc," Patrice instantly perked up her ears.

"Not bad, Charlie. How about you?"

The vaguely familiar voice that replied caused Patrice to cut an eye cautiously in the direction of the exchange. Dr. Alan Lowndes's back was turned to her as he chatted briefly with four men seated at one of the window booths. Patrice watched him as he sidled between the crowded tables, smiling and trading greetings with the café's patrons. When he glanced her way, she turned her full attention to the paper, but not quickly enough. Realizing he had caught her red-handed staring at him, Patrice smiled over the edge of the paper. She was pleased when he grinned in return and began to work his way to the lunch counter. Without the white coat to mask his lean, athletic build, he looked as if he would be as at home on the deck of a sailboat as he was in a medical office.

"So you're back in town today?" The golden brown eyes were friendly but could not entirely conceal the subtle appraisal Patrice had marked during their first encounter.

"Yep, I sure am." An obvious question deserved an obvious answer.

"How's your investigation going?" Alan shifted to examine the daily specials chalked on a small blackboard posted over the coffee warmers.

"It's...going."

Alan turned back to her, looking a little surprised.

"You could make it go a lot better by giving me a lead." Patrice was still smiling, but she could tell he knew she was serious.

Alan chuckled and turned his hands palms up. "Sorry, but I don't have any to give. The best I can do today is to recommend the red beans and rice." A wave of sun-streaked brown hair fell over his brow as he inclined his head toward the menu.

Patrice shook her head, matching his laugh. "Thanks, but I've already ordered." Seeing the waitress approaching with a paper sack, she dug her wallet out of her shoulder bag.

Resting one hand on her hip, the waitress rapidly jabbed several keys of the cash register. "That comes to $3.45, hon'." Without pausing for breath, she turned to Alan. "How you doin', darlin'? What's it gonna be t'day?"

"I'll have the red beans and rice, Madge, and unsweetened iced tea, please." When Patrice reached for the paper bag, Alan startled her by intercepting it. "Why don't you join me?"

Patrice was so surprised by his move, her normally quick reflexes failed her momentarily. "Well, actually I was planning to do some research at the municipal offices, and I was just going to wolf this stuff down."

When Alan wrinkled his nose, his face took on an irresistibly boyish appeal. "That doesn't sound like much fun."

"Which? Working in the municipal offices or wolfing lunch?"

"Both." Alan's smile widened, as pleasantly slow and easy as his low-pitched voice. "Besides, I've *never* in my life had lunch with a private eye."

That sort of comment normally made Patrice want to roll her eyes and run in the opposite direction. The teasing spark in his honey brown eyes, however, suggested that he was gently poking fun at himself. Anyone—especially a *man*—who didn't take himself seriously all the time deserved a concession, Patrice reminded herself. Not that having lunch with a man as personable and good-looking as Alan Lowndes would be any great chore. Besides, who knew what sort of helpful tidbits she might pick up? People who were tight-lipped and resistant in an interview often opened up in a more relaxed situation.

"Here's your big chance, then," Patrice told him. Reclaiming the bagged sandwich and coffee, she followed Alan through the labyrinth of tables to a vacant one in the corner.

Although Alan kept a decorous distance as he pulled out a chair for her, Patrice was keenly aware of their height differential. If she looked directly at him, her eyes connected with the midpoint of his chest, right where the well-developed pectoral muscles began to swell above the tight rib cage. That observation aroused an unexpected sensation that she quickly squelched.

By the time Patrice had unwrapped the sandwich and doctored her coffee with sugar and cream, Madge arrived with Alan's order. After checking the status of Patrice's coffee, the café's proprietress hurried off to wait on her other customers.

A deprecating expression spread over Alan's face as he squeezed a wedge of lemon into the iced tea. "I know people probably ask you this all the time, and you probably get tired of coming up with an answer, but..."

"How did I get into this business in the first place," Patrice supplied wearily, but she could feel the unfailing Lafon dimples undercutting her jaded tone.

The humorous glint that added such appeal to Alan Lowndes's eyes flared. "Yeah."

Patrice's shoulders lifted in a good-natured shrug. "When I was working as a paralegal, I started doing some extra research for the attorneys, mostly background checks on people, you know, looking up criminal records, talking with their neighbors and co-workers, that kind of thing. Pretty soon, I realized I enjoyed snooping more than delivering briefs to the courthouse. I got my license and opened my own business four years ago."

"So now you're a licensed professional snoop."

"That's one way of putting it." Patrice eyed him pointedly. "You know, for someone who calls me a snoop, you sure do ask an awful lot of questions yourself."

Alan swallowed before replying. "Let's just say I'm nosy, too." He took a sip of the tea. "I suppose that's a virtue in your business?"

Patrice surveyed the nibbled edge of her sandwich, poking an escaping frill of lettuce back into place. "Actually, patience is probably the most valuable skill a detective can develop. Despite the brilliant insights that help Travis McGee solve his cases, real-life investigators spend an enormous amount of time simply plodding through official records and asking the same questions over and over again.''

''You must get some exciting cases every now and then, something with human interest.''

''Oh, sure.''

''I'll bet you run into some really weird stuff, too.''

''Occasionally.'' Patrice regarded him carefully over the edge of her coffee cup. Was it her imagination, or was this conversation leading somewhere she didn't particularly want it to go? ''I guess you do, too, though, don't you?'' She looked into the enigmatic brown eyes and smiled innocently. ''I mean unusual diseases, things that are hard to diagnose.''

''Now and then.'' Alan's unblinking gaze contrasted with the offhand tone he fostered. ''Whatever the case, I never get bored with my work.''

''Neither do I.'' Patrice popped the remaining fragment of toast into her mouth.

Alan gave her a sly look. ''Not even when it takes you to the municipal offices?''

''Um,'' Patrice hedged. ''Let's just say some aspects of investigation are more stimulating than others. On that note, I'd better get going if I hope to accomplish anything this afternoon.'' She pushed her chair back, signaling her intentions.

''Thanks for the good company.'' Alan's tawny eyes followed Patrice as she stood and hiked the shoulder-bag strap up her arm. ''And good luck with your investigation.''

"Thanks. Luck is one thing I can always use." On her way to the door, Patrice paused to wave over her shoulder. "'Bye."

Alan was leaning back in his chair, finishing off the last of his iced tea. "See you around," he called after her.

Now what the hell did *that* mean? Unless Alan Lowndes was planning on springing some valuable information on her within the next few days, what reason would they have to see each other? Of course, limited as Port Latanier's dining resources were, there was a good chance they would run into each other again in the café. Who knew? Maybe he had actually enjoyed having lunch with her. He had said as much. But maybe he was just trying to be polite.

Patrice caught herself and frowned. With a tough investigation on her hands, she could ill afford to waste valuable brain circuits pondering Alan Lowndes's intentions. Was she so socially deprived that a handsome, charming man could distract her that easily? As she crossed the plaza with its flamboyant equestrian statue, Patrice decided to leave that last question unanswered for the time being.

The building housing Port Latanier's government offices was a plain two-story affair crouched in the shadow of the stately old courthouse. At one end of the lobby, someone had posted a sign with the words *Motor Vehicles* hand-lettered over a big black arrow. Patrice followed the arrow's direction down a corridor and through a similarly labeled door. A scarred wooden counter separated the official side of the room from the waiting area. Small signs were arranged along the counter like a row of miniature pup tents, indicating the correct line for paying traffic tickets, taking driver's tests and renewing licenses. Patrice chose the space labeled "Other" and waited for one of the uniformed clerks to note her presence. When she cleared her throat, a stocky young woman looked up from the papers she was sorting and ambled over to the counter.

"Ma'am?"

"I need to see if you have a driver's license on record." Over the years, Patrice had tried various techniques for making requests likely to meet opposition. She had found that the simplest, most direct statement usually garnered the best results.

The clerk eyed her warily, hinting at obstacles to come. "Is this your license?"

"No." Seeing the dubious frown growing on the clerk's plump face, Patrice knew she needed to think fast. "Look, I know you probably don't get this kind of request every day, but I'm in sort of a bind. I run a day-care center in New Orleans, and I'm trying to hire someone who's good with kids and can drive the van, too." She gestured with the notepad. "Both these applicants seemed really nice, but I want to be sure they're licensed before I commit. You can't be too careful where little children are concerned," she added sternly.

The clerk nodded as if she couldn't agree more completely. She took the sheet of paper that Patrice had ripped out of the pad and read the names aloud before retreating to a computer terminal on the far side of the office. Patrice watched the clerk cursor up and down the screen for several minutes. As she walked back to the counter, she was already shaking her head.

"I don't have anything on file on either of them."

"Is there a chance the licenses could have expired?" Patrice asked.

"If they had, it would have shown up on the computer. It looks like you did the right thing to check on these ladies."

Patrice clucked under her breath. "Who would have thought? They both seemed so honest. Well, thanks for your help."

Another day, another dead end. As Patrice trudged down the municipal building's steps, she tried to think of a fresh gambit to pursue. She could always try the scattergun approach, wander around town and simply ask anyone who would listen if he or she had heard of Bernice Lacourier or Cassandra Guidry. Right now, however, the mere thought of slogging door-to-door made her tired. Best to head back to New Orleans, pick up Alex, have a quiet, restful evening and get an early start tomorrow.

Patrice was concentrating on the details of the quiet, restful evening as she turned into the side street where she had left her car. Unless her dad had gotten inspired to cook and invite them over, this was definitely a night to pick up pizza or Chinese. If Alex didn't have much homework, maybe she would make popcorn later and rent a movie, preferably one that didn't involve detectives.

Slinging her shoulder bag to one side, Patrice unlocked the car door. Only when she had swung the door open did she notice the dark red pool collecting in the driver's seat. Her stomach lurched at the sweet, metallic smell of blood permeating the car. Blood was everywhere. Livid stains streaked the upholstery and dribbled onto the floor while a mass of gory pulp oozed onto the console. But it was the single word, finger-painted in red on the dash, that caused her heart to stop.

Death.

Chapter Four

"Oh, my God!" Patrice gasped under her breath, recoiling from the ominous graffiti smeared across the dashboard.

As she stepped back, her shoulder-bag strap caught on the door handle, and she yanked it free. Patrice slammed the car door in an effort to erect a barrier, however symbolic, between herself and the bloody mess. She scanned the street and tried to get her bearings. Another block away, she could see a woman hustling two preschoolers into a station wagon. Otherwise, the street was deserted. At least, it appeared to be. Usually vandals didn't hang around and risk getting caught, but a lunatic who wrote messages in blood was no ordinary vandal—and not someone she cared to meet face-to-face.

Throwing the shoulder bag over her back, Patrice jogged to the corner. The first order of business was to notify the police, something she could accomplish in Madge and Jimmie's Café. She had started across the street to the diner when she heard a car brake abruptly behind her. Not looking back, Patrice broke into a run.

"Hey, it's me! Are you hurt?"

Patrice glanced over her shoulder to see Alan Lowndes climbing out of a dark blue convertible. She sucked in a deep breath, trying to steady her thumping heart, as he loped across the street toward her.

"What on earth happened to you? Did you have an accident?"

Following Alan's concerned gaze, Patrice looked down at her hands. Until now, she had not noticed the brownish red smudges staining her fingers. Matching blotches marred the shoulder bag, as well as one leg of her gray linen slacks.

"No...no. I'm okay." Patrice jerked open the shoulder bag and began to search for a tissue.

"You sure don't look okay." Alan regarded her uncertainly. He reached for her free hand and gently examined the sticky palm. "This is blood, isn't it?"

"Yeah." Patrice dabbed futilely at the front of her slacks with the crumpled tissue. When she attempted to withdraw her hand from Alan's clasp, he held on to it for a moment, as if he did not quite trust her judgment. "Some nut broke into my car and plastered the front seat with blood. I must have touched some of it before I realized what had happened."

Alan's frown deepened. "Did you see who did it?"

Patrice shuddered in spite of herself. "No, and that's probably just as well." She nodded toward the café. "I was on my way to report the incident to the police when you stopped."

"We can call the sheriff on my car phone. Come on."

Alan's voice was low and calm, as reassuring as the light hand he placed against her back to guide her back to his car. For once, Patrice suppressed her deep-rooted inclination to handle everything herself and she let Alan summon the police.

"Sheriff Wade is on his way," Alan told her as he hung up the car phone. He gave her shoulder a brief squeeze. "He should be here in a wink."

As if to confirm his prediction, a black-and-white cruiser squealed to a halt beside Alan's Saab only minutes later. A fiftyish man with a weather-beaten face and reflective sunglasses right out of a Dirty Harry movie mumbled something into the radio and then climbed out of the police car. He adjusted his belt as he circled the cruiser to survey Alan's convertible.

"'Afternoon, Doc. Ma'am." The sheriff nodded to each of them in turn. Although Patrice could not see his eyes, she could tell he was sizing up her bedraggled condition. "This the vehicle?" He nodded toward the Saab.

"No," Patrice told him. "My car was vandalized. It's parked over there."

She led the way across the street. When they reached the Accord, Patrice gave Sheriff Wade a recap of the past half hour and then stood to one side while he inspected her car. The sheriff whistled softly as he peered through the driver's window at the blood-spattered interior. Swinging the door open, he rested one knee on the edge of the seat, grunting with the effort of wedging his burly shoulders through the relatively small opening.

"Do you have any idea what that stuff on the console might be?" Patrice ventured.

The sheriff was quiet for a few moments. "Looks like chicken guts," he announced at length.

Sheriff Wade took his time backing out of the car. Then he stalked to the other side of the Accord and briefly fiddled with the door. As he walked back to Patrice, he scribbled notes on his clipboard.

"Some joker busted the lock on the other side," the sheriff muttered. Without looking up from his report, he pointed to the red handprint stamped on the car door. "Yours?"

"Mine."

"And you say there was nothing missing?"

Patrice hesitated. "Not unless they broke into the trunk." She hastened to check the trunk and was relieved to find her briefcase exactly where she had left it. "No, everything seems to be here."

Sheriff Wade poked the bridge of his sunglasses into place with the tip of his pen. "Well, then, it looks like we got us a case of malicious vandalism. You want to sign here, ma'am?"

Patrice gingerly took the pen in her grubby fingers and signed on the line that Sheriff Wade had checked. The sheriff ripped off a copy of the report and handed it to her.

"I 'spect your insurance feller'll be happy to get this."

Patrice stuffed the police report into her shoulder bag. "What are the chances of catching the person who broke into my car?" Not good, she imagined, but she felt obligated to ask all the same.

Sheriff Wade snapped his ballpoint and tucked it into his breast pocket. "I'll drop by the high school and see if any of them young fools has showed up with bloodstains he can't account for."

"What about the death business?" Patrice persisted. "You think some teenager would have written that on the dash?"

Wade's mouth twisted to one side. "With this crazy, damned music they listen to nowadays—pardon my language—I wouldn't doubt it one bit. But I don't see any cause for you to worry, ma'am. Just call your insurance man and try to forget it all."

Patrice nodded and thanked the sheriff. In spite of his assurances, however, a gnawing uneasiness lingered with her. Never one to give in to irrational fears, she nonetheless would be relieved to get on the road back to New Orleans. Only when she turned to the car did she notice Alan Lowndes still standing on the curb.

Patrice tried to smile. "Got any secret doctor's remedies to remove bloodstains?"

"No, just the plain old soap-and-water routine."

When Alan joined her, he slipped an arm lightly around her shoulders. Although they had spent only a very short time together—and then under fairly adversarial circumstances—the gesture somehow seemed perfectly natural. Patrice did not like feeling as vulnerable as she did right now, and the comforting pressure of Alan's arm reminded her that she was not alone.

"You can get cleaned up at the clinic. Then we'll come back here and see what we can do for the car." Alan spoke matter-of-factly, as if he were suggesting where to hang a picture or which movie to see. Patrice guessed that he had honed his calm, soothing manner dealing with his young patients, but it was a talent she now greatly appreciated.

"Thanks. That's kind of you."

Alan shrugged off her gratitude as he escorted her back to his car. When they reached the clinic, he unlocked a rear door and led the way through a storage room stacked with cooler chests and cardboard boxes. After collecting a few towels from a linen closet, Alan flicked on the light inside a small bathroom.

"There's plenty of soap and stuff under the sink. Take your time. I need to check on a couple of things and then I'll drive you back to your car." Alan gave her one of those warm smiles that Patrice by now regarded as his signature characteristic before retreating down the corridor.

"God, what a mess!" Patrice grimaced at herself in the mirror.

As she filled the basin with warm water and began to lather her hands, Patrice avoided looking at her image. Worse than the stains spattering her clothes, the tension reflected on her face reminded her of the trouble she was having putting the vandalism behind her. On the face of it, Sheriff Wade's explanation seemed perfectly plausible, one that common sense argued she should be quick to accept. But what did common sense have to say about voodoo dolls and the people who sent them?

Patrice blotted her face with a thick terry towel and pondered the unsettling question. Okay, maybe she was making a big leap of faith to connect the doll Anne-Marie had received with the bloody message scrawled inside her car. Maybe she was overreacting to the occult overtones of both pranks. Maybe the voodoo doll and the vandalism had nothing at all to do with the case she was investigating. Patrice continued to play devil's advocate with her own intuition as she rolled down her sleeves and switched off the bathroom light.

The waiting room was empty, illuminated only by one table lamp and the dwindling sun streaming through the glass door. Patrice peered into the receptionist's deserted cubicle before taking a seat on one of the sofas. She was flipping through a dog-eared issue of *National Geographic* when Alan appeared in the doorway.

"Feel better?" He gave her an encouraging smile guaranteed to further that cause.

Patrice nodded, tossing the magazine onto the side table. "Much better, thanks. Is there a self-service car wash around here?'' she asked as she followed him down the corridor.

"You don't need to worry about your car," Alan told her over his shoulder. "I cleaned up the worst of the mess, at least enough for you to drive home this evening."

Patrice stopped in her tracks. "I didn't intend for you to do that."

"I know." Alan busied himself with the lock and then held open the door.

"I mean, I could have done it myself," Patrice felt bound to insist.

"I know," Alan repeated. When Patrice refused to budge, he gestured, a little impatiently, toward the parking lot. "Look, I wanted to do it, okay? It was no big deal. Besides," he added as she reluctantly accompanied him to the parked Saab, "I thought you'd had your fill of chicken guts for the day."

Patrice glanced up to find him grinning at her. "Apparently you hadn't," she remarked dryly.

Shaking her head and laughing, Patrice slid into the car next to Alan. More than the unpleasant task he had performed for her, however, she was grateful for that small bit of humor to lighten her tense mood. Independent by nature, Patrice had never been smitten with knight-in-shining-armor-type men. A too-elaborate display of chivalry had always seemed suspect to her, a cover for a hidden agenda that required her to play the damsel in distress. She sensed, however, that Alan Lowndes's solicitude wasn't part of an act. No, he seemed like a genuinely nice man, Patrice reflected, surreptitiously studying his handsome profile while he drove. She imagined him going about his daily routine, cajoling a smile from a frightened child, teasing and bantering to ease the

sting of a shot or a suture, dispensing comfort for body
and soul. Every now and then, adults could use that kind
of treatment, as well as kids. Even very adult women. An
unexpected twinge pricked her senses, and Patrice hast-
ily turned her attention to digging her keys out of her
bag.

"Well, thanks again," she repeated as she prepared to
climb out of the car.

"Sure." Alan shrugged, resting his wrists on the steering wheel. "I put some towels on the seats, so you really
can't tell any damage has been done. Try not to worry
about this," he added, his quiet voice suddenly earnest.
"Ninety-nine percent of the folks in Port Latanier are as
nice as you could ever hope to meet. I'm just sorry you
happened to run into the other one percent."

"In my business, I have a way of doing that." Patrice
gave him a wry grin through the open window. She took
a couple of steps backward in the direction of her car.
"Look, I'd better get going before my son's basketball
coach puts out a dragnet for me."

Alan nodded and returned her smile. Patrice pulled the
Accord away from the curb, but before she turned onto
Main Street, she glanced in the rearview mirror. For some
reason, the memory of Alan Lowndes's smile lingered in
her mind long after she had left Port Latanier behind.

THE SLOPE ASCENDING from the intersection was a killer,
one of the few hills in the Garden District worthy of the
name. Alan suppressed his usual tendency to take the last
mile of his run easy and pushed himself into a sprint. He
was panting when he reached the crest of the hill, his
heart pumping to deliver the oxygen his straining muscles demanded. Over the years, he had grown dependent
on running to siphon off the stress that was an inevitable

part of his profession, and tonight he had more than his usual share of tension to defuse.

For Patrice's sake, Alan had tried to play down the vicious act of vandalism. After finding her car splashed with blood, the last thing she needed was someone making ominous conjectures about the vandal's intent. Privately, however, the incident had disturbed him deeply. Alan was not given to drawing wild conclusions, but he could not slough off the suspicion that the gory vandalism was in some way connected with the voodoo doll his grandfather had received. It did not take a very active imagination to link the veiled curse accompanying the voodoo doll with the word *death* scrawled in blood on Patrice's dashboard.

At least he could eliminate Patrice Ribeau as a suspect in the voodoo-doll business. Although she had put on a good front, finding the front seat of her car doused with blood had obviously shaken her. The tension written in her big dark eyes had been too genuine to fake. Alan was surprised by how relieved he was to arrive at that conclusion. He supposed no man, even one who prided himself on being exceptionally levelheaded, liked to discover that an attractive woman was rotten on the inside. Then, too, there was more to Patrice than a pretty face and a knockout figure. She was smart, funny and resilient to a degree that demanded respect. In short, he found her very likable indeed.

But if Patrice and her client had nothing to do with sending the voodoo doll, then who did? Alan knew he would not rest easily until he had the answer.

SOMEWHERE PATRICE had read that the first thing you needed to do after falling off a horse was to get right back on again. Whether that dogged approach was for the benefit of the horse, the rider or both, she couldn't recall, but whatever the case, the principle seemed to apply to her investigation in Port Latanier. If someone had hoped to scare her off the case with that chicken-blood hocus-pocus, he was in for a big surprise, and she intended to advertise that fact by establishing her presence in town the very next day.

By the following morning, Patrice had managed to put the experience in perspective. On her way home the previous evening, she had stopped by an auto supply and bought a pair of cheap seat covers to conceal the ruined upholstery. A locksmith had done his best with the passenger door, and by the time she had picked Alex up from basketball practice, she half believed her own angry denunciation of dumb juvenile delinquents.

When she reached Port Latanier, Patrice drove down Main Street more slowly than the town's conservative speed limit required, giving shoppers, village idlers, and anyone else who might be watching a good chance to see that she was back. After parking squarely in front of the library, she spent the morning approaching store clerks and proprietors in search of leads on Bernice Lacourier and Cassandra Guidry. Patrice dutifully noted every recollection of someone bearing either surname, but by midafternoon, she was discouraged that her canvass had yielded no Bernices or Cassandras. Even Madge at the café only frowned and shook her head when Patrice presented her with the names.

After lunching on the café's electrifyingly hot chili, Patrice yielded to Madge's urging and indulged in a slice of pecan pie and coffee. The sugar and caffeine would help her get through a long and potentially frustrating afternoon, Patrice argued. Then, too, if she hung around the café long enough, Alan Lowndes might show up. Not that she still hoped to milk any information out of him, she was quick to remind herself. In the wake of yesterday's ugly vandalism, however, she had come to see Alan as an ally of sorts, someone who was steady and supportive when it mattered most.

Patrice polished off the pie and downed two cups of coffee without Alan Lowndes putting in an appearance at the café. After settling the check, she decided to drive by the clinic. She needed to drop off the sheets and towels that Alan had used to cover the front seat anyway, and she could use the opportunity to say hi and thank him again for his help. Patrice was disappointed when the receptionist informed her that Alan was working in his New Orleans office and would not be back in Port Latanier until next Tuesday.

"Strike two," Patrice mumbled to herself as she drove back to the town's business district.

Actually, if she was being a real stickler on points, Alan's absence was probably about the fiftieth strike in the current investigation. The way things were going, however, she could rationalize giving herself a break on the scoreboard. Gathering up her notepad and bag, Patrice administered a mental pep talk before setting out for the *Port Latanier Gazette*'s storefront office.

After exchanging pleasantries with the puckish-faced newspaper man, Patrice settled herself in front of the microfilm reader in preparation for a long siege. Ordinarily she limited her research to specific areas likely to yield the most promising leads. Given the paucity of information she had turned up in Port Latanier so far, however, she was willing to try a broader approach—even if it entailed reading through ten years of the *Port Latanier Gazette*. At least it was a slim paper, not much larger than a city newspaper's classified section, she consoled herself.

Patrice forced herself to skim carefully, scrolling the microfilm at a pace that permitted her to pick names out of the chronicles of weddings and garden club events. For a brief period, the sensational debutante murder crowded less newsworthy items to the back pages, but after the investigation of Melanie Reed's death was closed, the *Gazette* quickly returned to its familiar mainstays. By the time Patrice reached the spring of 1980, she was beginning to wish she had accepted another refill of Madge's strong coffee. She was about to rewind a spool of tape when a small entry on the society page caught her eye. Twisting the control, she frowned at the letters sinking into focus.

"Alan Lowndes." Patrice's lips traced the name.

Apparently the local paper had noted Alan's graduation from Tulane. Summa cum laude, no less, but then that wasn't surprising. He had impressed her as sharp and hardworking. The article went on to list Alan's various achievements during his college career, but it was the concluding line that leapt off the page with startling impact.

"Mr. Lowndes's parents, Dr. and Mrs. Richard E. Lowndes, reside in New Orleans. Mrs. Lowndes, the former Annette Hamilton, is the daughter of Dr. Alphonse Hamilton of Port Latanier."

Patrice read the last sentence twice, unable to believe the shocking revelation contained in it. Alan Lowndes was Alphonse Hamilton's grandson! *The* grandson she had spoken with the evening she had phoned Hamilton. Staring at the milky blue screen, Patrice recalled her meeting with Lowndes in his office. Never once had he alluded to the fact that he was related to the doctor who had signed Anne-Marie's birth certificate. His sympathetic comments, the chummy conversation over lunch, his helping hand the previous evening, all of it had been a sham.

"That sneaking bastard!" Patrice muttered, flicking off the microfilm reader with an angry snap.

Patrice continued to fuel her anger with conjectures about Lowndes long after she had returned to her car and set off for New Orleans. When she reached Loyola Avenue, she had to pinch herself mentally and concentrate on the traffic. No sense in having a wreck on account of a miserable, lying jerk like Alan Lowndes, she told herself as she pulled into the school parking lot to wait for her son.

Fortunately, Alex was bubbling over with the details of his class's outing to Audubon Park. As Patrice drove them home, she inhaled deeply, relishing the innocent scent of fresh air and concession popcorn that Alex had carried into the car. By the time she pulled into the driveway, his account of a spirited volleyball game and the zoo sea lions' antics had helped to crowd Alan Lowndes's duplicity to the back of her mind.

"What's for dinner?" Alex asked as soon as he bailed out of the front seat.

Patrice shook her head as she retrieved her briefcase from the Accord's trunk. "Good heaven, Alex. From the sound of things, you've eaten all day. You can't be hungry already." She steadied the briefcase between her ankles, tossing her keys to her son before pulling the day's mail from the box at the end of the driveway.

"But I am," the little boy insisted.

Patrice paused at the bottom of the front steps, shuffling through the mail. "Okay. Let me change clothes, and then we'll go out for a pizza. How does that sound?"

"Great! Hey, you got something!"

Patrice looked up to see Alex grab a package wedged inside the storm door. A sudden pang grabbed at the pit of her stomach as she followed him into the house.

"Wait a minute, Alex!" she called after him.

In typical ten-year-old fashion, Alex had already ripped away the package's brown-paper wrapping, but he obediently surrendered the box to Patrice. Her hands felt unsteady, almost numb, as she opened the lid of the nondescript cardboard box. As if an electric current had passed through her nervous system, Patrice shuddered at the sight of the voodoo doll, its eyes gouged by two long pins. With shaking fingers, she removed the scrap of brown paper anchored between the pins. An acrid taste flooded her mouth, the flavor of raw fear, as she read the message.

A spirit aroused from the grave will not return alone.

Chapter Five

"Who's going to help me finish off the last piece?" Patrice's father tilted the flabby box to display the solitary wedge of pepperoni pizza.

"I will!" Alex rose in his chair and braced both hands on the edge of the table.

As Tony Lafon scooped up the slice of pizza, he eyed Patrice, who was seated across from him, frowning into her tumbler of cola. "Just one taker? It's an awfully big piece."

Patrice looked up and shook her head. "No, thanks, Dad. I'm full. You guys have it."

"Okay, but I don't want to hear anything about starvation halfway through the movie," Tony warned.

Patrice gave her father a smile. Since arriving at their house a couple of hours ago, he had focused all his energy on counteracting the voodoo doll's menacing effect. As if he could read her mind, Tony had immediately herded Alex into his car and set out to pick up dinner. By the time the two of them had returned with pizza and a rented videocassette of *E.T.*, Patrice had locked the voodoo doll and its wrapping into her briefcase and gotten the house—if not her unsettled thoughts—in order. The nasty surprise had rattled her more than she wanted to admit, and she was determined not to communicate her uneasiness to her son. Thank goodness Alex seemed to be taking the voodoo doll in his usual unflappable stride, regarding it more as a curiosity than an ill-intentioned threat.

"Are you gonna find out who sent us the voodoo doll, Mom?" Alex asked, coiling a gooey string of mozzarella into his mouth.

"You bet your boots I am," Patrice assured him. "And when I get through with him, he'll be looking for another hobby besides doll making."

Alex giggled as he polished off the last bit of crust. "What are you gonna do to him?"

Patrice was trying to think of a suitably amusing answer—not an easy task, given her dark mood—when the telephone conveniently rang. "Would you get that please, Alex? And if it's someone from school who wants me to bake cookies or volunteer for a committee, I can't this time, okay?"

As soon as Alex had pelted out to the kitchen, Tony leaned across the table. "What *are* you going to do?"

"Bake cookies and volunteer next time."

Patrice's father gently nudged his daughter's arm. "Very funny. Come on, sweetheart, you know what I'm talking about. Do you have any idea who's responsible for that doll?"

"I have a hunch." When Patrice nodded, she was surprised at how heavy her head felt. Like it was weighted down with miserable thoughts. For more disturbing even than the voodoo doll itself was her suspicion about its most likely source: Alan Lowndes.

Now that Patrice had connected him with Dr. Hamilton, an unpleasant pattern had begun to emerge in her mind. For some reason, Lowndes had sought to conceal his relationship to the doctor from her. He would have known about Anne-Marie's phone call to Hamilton, just as he had intercepted Patrice's call two weeks later. He had sent the voodoo doll to Anne-Marie in hopes of scaring her into reconsidering her search and had resorted to the same tactic to discourage Patrice. For all she knew, Lowndes might even have vandalized her car. He had shown up on the scene pretty promptly, hadn't he?

Patrice winced inwardly at the repugnant conclusions, shrinking from the duplicitous character it imposed on Alan Lowndes. How could she have misjudged him so badly? A fresh wave of anger surged through her at the thought that she had allowed herself to be duped. Well, everyone made a bad call now and then, even tough-minded private investigators. Try as she might, however, Patrice could not dispel the big queasy knot of disappointment lodged solidly in her stomach. For whatever reason, she wished that in this particular instance her usually reliable judgment had not failed her.

When Alex bounced back into the dining room, Patrice managed to put on a cheerful face for his benefit. "That wasn't a big cookie-and-volunteer conversation, I hope?"

Alex shook his head, clasping the back of her chair. "No, just something about the basketball tournament on Saturday." He jostled the chair slightly. "Can we watch the movie now?"

Patrice reached to pat one small hand curled around the chair rung. "I don't see why not. Why don't you and Grandpa cue up the tape while I dump this stuff into the trash?"

With the menfolk dispatched to the den, Patrice carried the empty pizza box and soda cans into the kitchen. She stuck a bag of popcorn into the microwave and dug a can of lemonade concentrate out of the freezer. Even if no one was hungry, lemonade and popcorn added a modestly festive touch, and in her present frame of mind, she needed all the distractions she could muster.

As she joined her father and son in front of the television set, however, Patrice found her mind stubbornly dwelling on the voodoo doll and Alan Lowndes. She had indicted Lowndes in her mind, but it served little purpose if he was allowed to continue his dirty tricks. Anne-Marie's case was proving difficult enough without Dr. Hamilton's grandson working in the wings against her. No, Lowndes needed to be stopped before he could do any permanent damage to her investigation.

With this thought in mind, Patrice consulted the telephone directory the following morning while Alex assembled his books and gym clothes. As soon as she had dropped her son at school, she drove directly to the central business district. Rush-hour traffic, coupled with the frustration of jockeying for a space in the parking tower, did little to improve her already foul mood. At least all that vitriol wouldn't go to waste today, Patrice reflected as she waited for the elevator in the lobby of the Medical Arts Building.

Unlike the bland trading-stamp decor of the Port Latanier Clinic, the waiting room of Alan Lowndes's New Orleans practice was designed to delight anyone between the ages of six months and twelve years. Plump floor cushions and scaled-down tables and chairs mixed with adult-proportioned sofas, all in natural woods and tastefully muted fabrics. A plush gorilla wearing a striped engineer's cap and a red kerchief sat astride a rocking horse in one corner, his shiny-prune eyes fixed on the aquarium filled with tropical fish. Patrice stepped around a toddler fitting plastic doughnuts onto a fat peg and approached the shuttered window cut in the rear wall.

The receptionist was sorting invoices at her desk. When she looked up and smiled, she reminded Patrice of those gently rounded, motherly women who read bedtime stories on children's television programs.

"Is Dr. Lowndes in this morning?" Patrice flashed a cheerful smile of her own to conceal the anger brewing inside her.

"Yes, he is."

"Wonderful. Could you please tell him that Patrice Ribeau is here? If he could just give me a few minutes before his next appointment, I promise not to take up too much of his time."

Patrice waited at the window while the receptionist disappeared into the inner recesses of the office. When she reappeared, her genial expression told Patrice that her request had been granted.

"Dr. Lowndes will be right with you," the receptionist assured Patrice as she escorted her down the corridor and into a private office.

Patrice surveyed the selection of chairs and then seated herself in the least cushy-looking one. Given the purpose of her visit, she didn't want to make herself too comfortable on Lowndes's turf. True to the receptionist's prediction, Patrice had waited only a few minutes when Alan Lowndes hurried into the office, white coat furling open behind him.

"Patrice! What a pleasant surprise to see you here!" The dazzling white smile dimmed slightly when Lowndes caught sight of his visitor's formidable expression. "You look upset. Don't tell me something else has happened...."

Patrice nipped the phony well-wishing in the bud. "I'm fine. I just dropped by to return something."

Rounding his desk, Alan shook his head. "You could have just junked those sheets and towels. We have hundreds more at the clinic."

Patrice hoisted the briefcase onto her lap and snapped the locks open. "Do you have hundreds of these, too?" Swinging open the briefcase lid, she pulled out the voodoo doll and dropped it in the middle of Alan Lowndes's desk.

For a moment, Lowndes only gaped incredulously at the crude figure. It was more than enough time, however, for Patrice to read the umistakable glimmer of recognition in his dark eyes. Despite her outrage, a sick feeling washed over her, as if she had just witnessed a gruesome accident. In her business, Patrice often discovered a seamy side to people who gave the outward appearance of being decent and well-meaning. Never before, however, had she recoiled with such distaste from the unpleasant truth.

"Where the hell did you get this?" A sandpaper hoarseness roughened Lowndes's voice.

"I should be the one posing that question, don't you think?" Patrice shot back.

Alan looked from the doll to Patrice, frowning as if he was unsure which disturbed him the most. "What do you mean?"

Patrice's short, derisive laugh sounded more like a hiccup. "I know you're Dr. Hamilton's grandson, Alan, so please spare me the innocent bit. It's one act I've never been able to stomach."

Bracing the knuckles of one hand against the desk, Alan leaned toward Patrice. Agitation had heightened the color of his suntanned face, giving it a warmth she could almost feel across the narrow distance separating them. "Patrice, I'm going to ask you once more. Where did you get this doll?"

Patrice locked eyes with Alan Lowndes. She had run into some tenacious liars before, but he was about to set a record. "Give it up, Alan. It's written all over your face. You've seen this doll before."

Alan drew back as if she had slapped him. "One like it, yes, but..." He broke off and looked down at the voodoo doll.

It was the admission for which Patrice had been angling, yet she felt none of her usual triumph in confirming a suspicion, just a dull sickness. "You know, my ten-year-old son was there when I opened the package you sent. That mumbo jumbo about spirits in the note made quite an impression on him. As if it weren't enough that some nut was mailing his mother voodoo dolls!"

Alan looked up suddenly, his handsome face contorted in disbelief. "You think I sent you this voodoo doll?" he gasped, almost choking on the words.

Patrice wanted to roll her eyes in despair. "Well, at least you're starting to catch on."

"This is insane!" Alan glanced helplessly around the office. "I swear, I had nothing to do with—" his hand grazed the outstretched voodoo doll "—with this whole absurd mess."

Patrice reached to retrieve the doll and then returned it to her briefcase. "Just in case I need evidence," she said tersely.

Shaking his head like someone who had just awakened from a bad dream, Alan clasped the back of his neck with one hand. "Evidence?"

Patrice tried to ignore Alan's pathetic charade as she secured the briefcase. Straightening herself, she looked him in the eye. "Listen to me, Alan," she began in a studiously low, calm voice. "I don't know yet what you're trying to hide, but I want you to understand one thing—stay out of my way."

Snatching up the briefcase, Patrice turned on her heel and marched out of Alan Lowndes's office.

WHY WERE THE excruciatingly boring cases often the most time-consuming? Patrice pondered that conundrum while she sifted through the photographs of crumpled fenders, smashed taillights and other assorted bashed-in automobile components, matching them with body-shop invoices. She must have photographed over a hundred cars in the past two months, documenting the sad results of various fender benders. It was uninspiring work, but when a body shop was in the habit of exaggerating damages, netting itself and the claimant a tidy profit, the insurer had a right to get upset. Then, too, she was eager to wrap up the insurance-fraud case so that she could devote all of next week to Anne-Marie's investigation.

Patrice stared blankly at the pictures of mutilated automobiles. Heaven knows, Alan Lowndes wasn't the first joker who had ever tried to put one over on her. Fortunately, she had caught on to his game early, and if his flustered reaction this morning was any indication, he would think twice before trying to sabotage her investigation further. There was simply no practical reason for her now to feel so unsettled about the whole affair.

That's your reward for letting yourself get interested in a guy you meet on a case. Patrice winced at the stinging reminder of her own human frailty. If Alan had merely posed as a good-looking charmer, his deceit would have been less reprehensible. He had violated her trust on a much deeper level, however, by convincing her that he was a decent, caring man. Never one to lament life's givens, she nonetheless could not help but wish that Alan Lowndes had not *seemed* so thoughtful and sensitive and likeable.

By four o'clock, Patrice had substantiated enough wrongdoing to make the insurance company's lawyers chortle with glee. She was bundling the evidence into heavy manila envelopes when the door buzzer sounded. Shoving a wayward curl off her forehead, she hurried into the vestibule and unlocked the front door. She started in spite of herself when she found Alan Lowndes standing in the corridor.

"What do you want?" Patrice demanded.

"To talk with you." Alan took a step forward, but Patrice braced the door with her knee, blocking his progress. He halted, swallowing audibly. "May I come in?" When Patrice said nothing, he heaved an impatient sigh. "Look, when you dropped in on me unannounced this morning, I agreed to see you. You owe me at least as much."

"I don't owe you anything, Alan." Patrice could feel her anger festering, roused no doubt by the complex feelings his sudden appearance had elicited. The sooner she got rid of him, the better.

"Damn it, Patrice! You burst into my office and dump a voodoo doll onto my desk, hurl crazy accusations at me and then tear off without even giving me a chance to explain myself. If you're so sure you're right, then why are you afraid to hear me out?" Anger had chalked a thin white line around Alan's grimly set mouth, and his eyes had darkened to a forbidding shade.

Patrice glanced down the corridor to see one of the orthodontists who occupied the corner suite peep out the door. She had always taken pains to counter any misgivings her fellow tenants might have about sharing space with a private eye, and she was not about to let a noisy row with Alan Lowndes undermine four years of good PR.

"All right. Five minutes." Patrice stepped back stiffly to hold the door open for Alan.

"Thank you." Alan's small victory had banished none of the tension in his voice.

"Hold it. What's in the bag?" Patrice nodded toward the shopping bag Alan carried awkwardly at his side.

He dropped the bag and lifted both arms in the classic gesture of defenselessness. "I'm unarmed, if that's what you're worried about," he informed her sarcastically.

Patrice pursed her lips, hinting at the retort she was holding back. She folded her arms across her chest and watched as Alan dug beneath the crumpled newspaper crammed in the shopping bag. Her face tightened, betraying her revulsion, when he unwrapped a voodoo doll.

Patrice shook her head when he held the grotesque figure out for her inspection. "Thanks, but I already have one."

"My grandfather received this voodoo doll in the mail last Monday." Alan loosened the pin stuck in the doll's middle and removed the piece of paper attached to it. "Here's the note that came with it."

Patrice warily eyed the scrap of wrinkled brown paper Alan offered her, hesitating a moment before taking it.

"Everyone must pay for his sins—if not in this life, then in the next," Patrice slowly read aloud. Frowning, she looked up at Alan.

"Now you see why I was so dumbfounded when you threw that doll in front of me today. Yes, it did look familiar, but not because I sent it to you."

Patrice regarded the ugly figure Alan clasped in his hand, trying to make sense of the wild card he had suddenly dealt her. "How do I know you didn't make both voodoo dolls? You could be spinning this story just to clear yourself."

"I know you have to say that, Patrice, but you and I both know it isn't true," Alan said quietly.

"Your track record in the honesty department isn't very good, Alan," Patrice hedged, buying herself some time to evaluate the matter. "Why didn't you tell me you were Dr. Hamilton's grandson?"

"If you had been in my place, what would you have done?" Alan countered.

Patrice drew a deep breath. "Probably the same thing," she admitted at length.

To his credit, Alan did not look in the least triumphant, only relieved. "I don't have any idea who sent my grandfather the voodoo doll, but I can't believe it's just a coincidence that you got one, too. There has to be a connection between the two." He hesitated. "What about this client whose birth mother you're trying to find? Could there be something shady about her?"

Patrice shook her head adamantly. "No." The single syllable and the tone in which it was delivered left no room for questions or arguments.

Alan stared in silence at the voodoo doll for a few moments. When he looked up at her, his handsome face was solemn. "My grandfather is eighty years old and not in the best of health, Patrice. I'm not going to stand by while someone tries to frighten or threaten him. I need to find out who sent him this awful thing and why."

Patrice studied him, trying to read his intent. Regardless of her earlier suspicions about him, there was no mistaking the inflexible determination written on his lean face. She imagined that Alan Lowndes would no sooner consider abandoning his purpose than she would hers. "Maybe if you could help me find out a little more about the birth certificate your grandfather signed, I could piece together some leads that might help us both."

Now it was Alan's turn to look wary. "That sounds a little too one-sided to suit me. You want information from me, but you're not willing to part with any of your own."

Patrice sighed in exasperation. "I have a comtract with my client, Alan, and confidentiality is a big part of it. I work for *her*."

"Then work for me." Catching Patrice's uncomprehending frown, Alan went on. "Take my case."

Patrice cleared her throat, still having trouble coming to terms with this wholly unexpected twist. "You want to hire me to find out who sent your grandfather that doll?"

A faint smile relieved the tense lines of Alan's face. "As someone recently remarked to me, 'At least you're starting to catch on.'"

Patrice raised an eyebrow. "You'd have to be straight with me."

"I'll be as honest as I expect you to be," Alan returned evenly. "So do we have a deal?"

"We're working on it. Let's go into my office, and I'll draw up a contract."

Patrice ushered Alan into her private office and gestured for him to have a seat. While she rummaged through her desk for a contract form and cleared a space among the smashed-car photographs, Alan sat on the love seat, taking in his surroundings. Her cramped, messy little room with its permanent scent of burned coffee must have seemed a far cry from his own bright decorator-stamped office, but then few of her clients were in the mood for giant pandas or butterfly mobiles.

Patrice handed Alan the contract to examine while she explained her fee structure. His amber eyes traveled from the legal form to her face, regarding both with equal interest.

"Do you have any questions?" Patrice asked in conclusion.

"Where do I sign?"

Patrice smiled in spite of herself. "We'll get to that in a minute. First, I need some more information from you."

As Patrice moved through the contract, Alan provided the bare-bones documentation of his personal life: address, telephone number, birth date, Social Security number and the various other cryptic details that tabulated a late-twentieth-century American's identity.

"Marital status?" Patrice glanced up from the form. "I need to ask clients, you know, in case there's a vengeful ex-spouse who might play into the picture." She had never before apologized for the question, but for some reason, she felt as if she was prying into Alan's personal business.

"I'm divorced, but Melissa isn't the vengeful type."

Patrice's smile felt awkward. "That's good." She checked the appropriate box before proceeding to the next blank. When she had completed filling out the contract, Patrice leaned back in her chair.

"Do you have any idea who might have sent Dr. Hamilton the voodoo doll? Even the vaguest notion?"

Alan heaved a rough sigh. "I honestly don't have a clue. I know it sounds corny, but he really is a man with no enemies. Everyone who knows him likes him. The package was mailed from New Orleans," he added hopefully.

"Mine was, too, but the person who sent it could live anywhere. Think about it. If you were serious about throwing someone off your trail, you'd probably find it worthwhile to drive a few hours to mail your little present from another town. It's a good bet whoever dreamed up these notes and voodoo dolls *doesn't* live in New Orleans."

"At least that clears me, once and for all," Alan remarked dryly.

Patrice swung the chair slowly on its axis. "What about someone connected with the birth certificate that your grandfather signed back in 1967?"

"That's a possibility, but I know as little about that certificate and the people involved as you do." Alan's gaze was so forthright, Patrice had no doubt that he was telling the truth.

"You might learn something useful if you were to discuss the certificate with your grandfather," Patrice suggested, but Alan was already shaking his head.

"Granddad didn't even want me to notify the police about the voodoo doll. He told me in no uncertain terms to throw it away, so I'm really working behind his back. I sense that he's scared for some reason."

"Sounds like it," Patrice agreed. She hesitated for a second, weighing the possible consequences of her next question. "Does the name Cassandra Guidry ring any bells? What about Bernice Lacourier?"

"No, I'm afraid not."

Patrice tipped the chair forward and folded her hands on the contract. "You've got to give me something to start with, Alan, or I'm not going to have much of an investigation. I'm not asking you to go against your principles, but it would be extremely helpful to know if your grandfather ever had either of those women for a patient.''

Alan studied his hands spread on his knees. "I'll see what I can do."

Patrice could tell that Alan was making a major concession, one that not only might render a major breakthrough in both investigations but also represented a new degree of trust between them. The latter thought was reassuring to Patrice—on more levels than she dared consider at the moment. Unlikely as the prospect would have seemed only a few hours ago, Alan Lowndes and she had become partners.

Chapter Six

"Hurry up, Alex. The basketball-tournament express leaves the station in exactly five minutes." Patrice leaned on the banister to call up the stairs. She listened to the thump of sneakered feet overhead, a reliable indicator that her warning had not gone unheeded.

With rusty brown hair still wet from the shower, Alex peered over the rail from the landing. "I'm coming, Mom. I just need to get my stuff together."

Shaking her head, Patrice decided against delivering her standard lecture on the value of assembling school materials and sports equipment the previous night. It was Saturday, after all, and ordinarily she would have been in no great hurry to tackle her weekend errands. With Alex's junior basketball league scheduled to play into the early evening, however, Patrice had planned to dispatch the shopping as quickly as possible and then spend the afternoon working on her two pending cases.

When the phone rang, Patrice cursed under her breath for not having turned on the answering machine sooner. The last thing she wanted to hear right now was a tele-marketing sales pitch or a plea to lend a hand at the school bazaar. "Hello?"

"Patrice? Hi, it's Alan Lowndes. I hope you don't mind my calling you at home, but I tried your office and got the machine." He spoke more quickly than usual, as if he was eager to get to more important issues.

"No, no, that's okay. What's up?" Patrice tried to subdue the anticipation in her voice.

"I checked on those names you gave me. I couldn't find a thing in the clinic's records on either woman. Here's the kicker, though." Alan's voice was so low, Patrice could imagine him cupping his hand around his mouth. "I spent last night digging through Granddad's old office calendars. As luck would have it, most of his stuff is still collecting dust in the clinic's storage room. There's no record of any delivery on July 6, 1967, or for that matter, during that entire week. It's beginning to look as if the birth certificate your client gave you is bogus."

Patrice frowned. "Or that your grandfather deliberately omitted recording the baby's delivery to keep the whole affair as hushed as possible."

"I'm ready!" Alex whooped as he charged down the stairs, dribbling a basketball in front of him.

"Excuse me, please." Patrice covered the mouthpiece with her hand. "I'll be just a minute, Alex. Why don't you go outside and shoot a few warm-up baskets?" She waited until the little boy had bounded out the front door before resuming the phone conversation. "Look, I'd like to talk with you about this, but I have to drop my son off at a basketball tournament right now."

"Can I meet you afterward?"

Patrice hesitated, caught off guard by Alan's request. "Uh, actually I had planned to do some investigative work."

"On my case?"

"Well, as a matter of fact, yes."

"What exactly? I'm curious."

"I was going to get a voodoo practitioner's opinion on those dolls." Patrice tried not to sound testy. As a client, Alan Lowndes certainly had a right to monitor the progress of her investigation on his behalf. She had simply not expected him to be such a demanding consumer.

"A voodoo practitioner?" Alan whistled under his breath. "I'd like to come along. That is, if you don't mind."

Oh, but I do. Patrice bit her tongue before the instinctive parry leapt out. Over the years, she had developed her own way of doing things, and the mere thought of another person tagging along raised unwelcome specters of meddling and interference. At the same time, Alan Lowndes was no ordinary client. She had taken his case with the hopes of learning at least as much from him as he would from her. Perhaps having him join her this afternoon would yield more benefits than she could foresee at this point.

"Okay, but you've got to understand that I'm conducting the investigation."

"That's what I'm paying you to do," Alan remarked dryly. "But I see your point. It's much the same in my profession. I try to explain a procedure or a diagnosis as thoroughly as I can to a child's parents. Then I expect them to trust me."

Alan had an extraordinary knack for sounding reasonable, a technique she would do well to master, Patrice noted with grudging admiration.

"Where and when shall we meet?"

Patrice checked her watch before replying. "How about in front of Saint Louis Cathedral at three?"

"It's a date. I'll see you later."

Some date, Patrice mused as she drove Alex to the neighborhood community center hosting the kids' basketball tournament. Even allowing for bizarre tastes, paying a call on a voodoo priestess hardly fit the mold of the all-American social outing. Of course, Alan had not used the word *date* in the classic male-female sense, and she certainly wasn't thinking of their joint excursion in that way. So why was she wasting time mulling over semantics? Patrice frowned in the rearview mirror and then brightened when she glanced over at her son.

"What time should I pick you up?" Patrice reached over the seat back to scoot Alex's gym bag within his reach as he clambered out of the car.

The little boy shrugged, his attention now firmly focused on the youngsters shoving and clowning outside the community-center door. "I don't know. It all depends on when we'll be through playing."

"I'll call to check later. How about that?"

"Okay. 'Bye, Mom!" Alex shouted over his shoulder as he dashed off to join his friends.

" 'Bye, Alex," Patrice called after him, although she had little hope of being heard over the children's din. She waited long enough to spot a couple of adults who appeared to be in control before setting off for the French Quarter.

To avoid the congestion that inevitably plagued one of New Orleans's premier attractions, Patrice parked her car near the riverfront and then walked the short distance to Jackson Square. As on any Saturday, the plaza was thronged with camera-toting tourists, street vendors, roving mime troupes, amateur musicians, and artists recording the whole melee on canvas. Using her briefcase as a gentle battering ram, Patrice pushed through the crowd gathered at the foot of Andrew Jackson's heroic statue and made her way to the white-spired cathedral. She spotted Alan almost immediately. When he saw her, his tanned face broke into a big grin, and he threw up his hand.

He was dressed in casual tan slacks and a coral-colored polo shirt that accented both his athletic physique and healthy complexion. The breeze had tousled his thick tawny hair, and the bright sunlight coupled with his smile had intensified the pleasant tracery of lines fanning out from the corners of his eyes. Although less than twenty-four hours had elapsed since Patrice had last seen him, she didn't recall Alan as having looked *this* good. Then again, maybe her frame of mind was affecting her memory.

"Have you waited long?" Patrice said by way of greeting.

"I just got here." Alan's eyes drifted from her face down the length of her, making a brief but thorough reconnaissance of their own. He straightened himself, as if he needed a reminder to get back to the business at hand. "So where are we going?"

Patrice dug into her shoulder bag in search of her notepad, welcoming the chance to concentrate on something besides Alan's matinee-idol eyes. "Last night I phoned a friend who's a detective with Homicide. She gave me the name and address of the voodoo practitioner she consults whenever anything with wacko-occult overtones crops up. According to Odette, Madame Voisin is the real thing."

"I guess we'll see what that means." Alan grimaced as he fell in step beside Patrice.

Following her scribbled directions, Patrice led the way past Saint Louis Cathedral and then down Royal Street. Only when they cut into a narrow alley did the bustle of

the lively square fade in the distance, supplanted by a
damped stillness. Here the buildings hovered close to the
street, their peeling pastel facades broken at irregular in-
tervals by cast-iron galleries and louvered cypress doors.
Occasionally, music or a snatch of conversation drifted
from one of the open courtyards, remote and elusive like
the voices of spirits. Patrice unconsciously quickened her
pace, not pausing as she referred to the directions.

"It should be one of these storefronts." Still clutching
the notepad, Patrice surveyed the row of shabby buildings.

Alan consulted the notepad over Patrice's shoulder.
"This is it." He indicated a narrow arched door bearing
rusty iron numbers that matched the address.

Cupping her hands on either side of her eyes, Patrice
peered into the single dirty window, straining to penetrate the gloom. A shadowy movement inside the room
caused her to pull back in haste. "Shall we?" She smiled
grimly, gesturing toward the door.

"After you." Alan shoved the weathered cypress door
open and held it for Patrice.

Once inside the shop, Patrice hesitated for a moment,
taking time to size up the place. The walls were lined with
an assortment of homemade shelves and flea-market
bookcases crammed with glass jars, plastic bags, wooden
crocks and an astonishing variety of candles. At first
glance, the place could have passed for one of those alternative health-food stores, the kind specializing in bulk
spices and grains, with a few scented candles thrown in.
Only when the visitor noticed the jar labeled "snake-
root" or the gummy black candle shaped like a skull did
he begin to suspect that this might not be the place to buy
organic brown rice. Patrice guessed that business was
conducted at the wooden table situated a few feet in front

of the rear wall, a sort of checkout counter for the occult consumer.

"Not exactly F. A. O. Schwarz, is it?" Alan whispered hoarsely. "I wonder if we need to ring for service."

As if conjured by his remark, a woman suddenly parted the print bedspread tacked over the door behind the counter. The second Patrice saw her, she knew that this was Madame Voisin. She was not very tall, and the long purple robe she wore gave her body a round, shapeless quality, like a human-size lump of clay that could reform itself at will. Her face reminded Patrice of a crumpled piece of silk, wrinkled but possessing a fine sheen. A turban in a violent shade of red covered her head, save for a few snarled wires of white hair. Most startling of all were her milky blue eyes, opaque, unblinking and bottomless. Patrice realized with a jolt that Madame Voisin was blind.

"Yes?" She turned directly toward Patrice and Alan.

"I'm looking for Madame Voisin," Patrice began. She already knew she was looking at her, but she needed to start somewhere.

"I am Madame Voisin." Her voice rose and fell in a rhythmic Creole accent. "You seek help, no? For what you want gris-gris?"

"I don't need any gris-gris," Patrice told her. Thanks to her recent conversation with Odette, she recognized the voodoo term for a magic charm.

"What *you* want?" Madame Voisin demanded as she thrust her arm out to point at Alan, as if she could see him.

"Nothing in particular. I'm with her." Alan sounded as uncomfortable as Patrice felt.

Patrice cleared her throat, trying her best to keep an already shaky situation from slipping farther away from reality. "Lieutenant Odette LeBlanc with Homicide suggested I get in touch with you."

"Ah, Mademoiselle Odette!" When Madame Voisin interrupted to nod knowingly, Patrice was struck by her uncanny ability to give the impression that she was aware of far more than appeared on the surface.

"Lieutenant LeBlanc thought you might be able to tell me more about something I've run across in my work." Patrice cut an uncertain glance at her briefcase, wondering how on earth Odette had expected a blind woman to identify a voodoo doll.

"What you have?" Madame Voisin smiled, crinkled lips pulling away from toothless gums.

"Voodoo dolls." Patrice slid her briefcase onto the counter and opened it. She started when Madame Voisin's gnarled hand began to paw its contents. The bony fingers closed over the doll Anne-Marie had received like a bird of prey grasping its hapless victim.

Patrice watched Madame Voisin turn the voodoo doll over in her hands. A disquieting sensation filled her, tempered by an almost hypnotic fascination, as her eyes followed the long fingers plying the voodoo doll. Like a bizarre parody of a child opening Christmas gifts, Madame Voisin examined each of the dolls in turn.

"Do you recognize any of them?" Patrice prompted.

Madame Voisin stared straight ahead as if in a trance, her opaque eyes fixed on a point known only to her. "Bad *gris-gris*." She shook her head. "Very bad."

"Does that mean they're authentic?" Patrice fished for more information.

"I feel hatred. Much hatred." Madam Voisin's eyes rolled back in her head, and a tremor seized her shapeless body. "A killing hatred!"

"You mean the doll is evil?" Alan's low voice was tense, betraying the impact that Madame Voisin's unsettling pronouncements had on him.

"Doll no evil. Doll only rag and dust. *Person* evil." A cackle shuddered through Madame Voisin's body, as brittle as dry leaves swept along an empty street.

"The person who made them, you mean?" Patrice interposed.

"Full of evil!"

Madame Voisin flung the doll she held back into the briefcase so suddenly Patrice jumped in spite of herself. She felt Alan flinch behind her. She swallowed hard, trying to keep a handle on her nerves. Although she was accustomed to thinking on her feet, her normal presence of mind had deserted her for the moment. Call it irrational, superstitious, whatever you please, more than anything Patrice simply wanted to get out of Madame Voisin's eerie shop.

"Thank you, Madame Voisin." Patrice reached to lock the briefcase, fighting the slight tremor that threatened to undermine her fingers' efficiency. "You've been quite helpful." Sliding the briefcase off the counter, she glanced at Alan and then turned for the door as quickly as her pride would permit.

Madame Voisin followed them to the front of the shop. "You come back!" Madame Voisin called after them. Patrice was left to guess if her parting comment was an invitation or a prediction.

"Where the hell did you get a third voodoo doll?" Alan demanded the moment they were outside Madame Voisin's shop.

Not looking at Alan, Patrice forged down the narrow street at double time. "Someone sent it to my other client," she told him through tight lips.

Alan balked in his tracks. "I don't believe this! In the entire time we talked about the dolls yesterday, you never said a word about your client getting one, too!"

Patrice halted to face Alan. "I told you I don't discuss my clients' business."

"I'm a client, too, remember?" Irritation had ignited a hot spark in Alan's dark eyes. "And I happen to think that this other voodoo doll very likely has a direct bearing on my case."

"Take it easy, okay?" Patrice glanced down the street, evading Alan's annoyed glare. "We can talk all this through, but I'd prefer to find a more suitable spot."

A frown still clouding his handsome face, Alan reluctantly yielded to Patrice's suggestion. As they approached Jackson Square, he tapped her elbow and nodded toward a small sidewalk café. "How's this?"

"Fine."

Patrice followed Alan through the maze of round white tables. He pulled out a chair for her, sternly holding the curving wrought-iron back until she had seated herself. Patrice busied herself tucking the briefcase under the table while Alan ordered coffee and éclairs. As soon as the waiter had been dispatched to the kitchen, Alan swiveled in his chair to face her.

Patrice decided to test the old saw about a good offense being the best defense and speak up before Alan had a chance. "I'm not playing coy games with you, Alan. I didn't mention the voodoo doll my other client received for the same reason I haven't told her about the one your grandfather got. I'm simply not in the habit of discussing evidence until I'm sure what it means. And

I'm still far from certain what's going on with these dolls,'' she added, her eye inadvertently shifting to the briefcase resting beside her feet.

She was pleased when Alan's taut face relaxed slightly. "That makes two of us. I guess I was being unrealistic to assume Madame Voisin would give us the make, model and reorder number for the voodoo dolls, but somehow I expected something more enlightening than 'bad gris-gris.'''

Patrice frowned, not liking the conclusion forming in her head. "It was almost as if she could feel the evil will of the dolls' creator still clinging to them." She chafed her arms lightly to counteract the ticklish sensation creeping beneath her skin. "I'd better watch it before all this black-magic business gets to me."

"I'm sure that's exactly what the person who sent those dolls wanted to achieve." Alan fell silent as the waiter arrived with their order, waiting until the young man had departed before resuming the conversation. "What are you going to try next?"

Patrice stirred her coffee thoughtfully. "I'll go back to Port Latanier and continue looking for Bernice Lacourier and Cassandra Guidry. Someone somewhere is going to remember those women." She took a bite of the éclair and then checked her watch. "Gee, where has the afternoon gone? I should probably be picking up Alex pretty soon."

"Alex is your son?" An affable smile had displaced the tension that had hovered on Alan's face for the past hour.

Patrice grinned as she nodded. "The best in the world, too."

"How old is he?" Arms folded on the table, Alan looked as if he was truly interested.

"Ten, but he's a really mature little guy. Which I suppose is another way of saying that he's very tolerant of his mother's goofy career," Patrice added ruefully. "Actually, I get to spend more time with Alex than I would if I had a conventional job. It doesn't matter when I do a lot of my work, just as long as I do it."

"How long have you been divorced?" Alan posed the question casually, not looking at Patrice as he refilled her cup from the small carafe.

"I'm not divorced. My husband was killed in an automobile accident four years ago."

"Oh, Patrice, I'm sorry." A look of such genuine pain passed across Alan's face that Patrice felt compelled to reassure him.

"That's all right. You had no way of knowing. And it doesn't hurt to talk about it now the way it used to." Patrice sighed, fingering the edge of her saucer. "When you lose someone so suddenly, the shock insulates you for a while. Then you go through all the stages of loss—denial, anger, just plain feeling scared and alone. It takes some time to work through." She broke off, feeling a little embarrassed by the intensely personal revelations she had just shared with Alan.

"You're doing all right now?" Alan's hand lightly brushed the back of hers.

Patrice nodded, still focusing on the coffee. "I think so." When she looked up at Alan, she was startled by the tender expression in his dark eyes. She managed a smile that felt surprisingly untrustworthy. Scooting her chair away from the table, she unhooked the shoulder-bag strap looped over the back of the chair. "I'd better make that phone call, or Alex is going to wonder what's happened to me."

What has happened to me? As Patrice wove between the tables to the café's tiny dining room, she tried to recover her normal self-possession. She rarely talked with anyone about losing Gerry, let alone with a client she scarcely knew. Yet something in Alan's quiet manner had encouraged her to open up, tacitly assuring her that he would understand all the complicated, contradictory feelings she had carried around inside her for so long.

All the same, she needed to bear in mind that he was a client. Spilling her personal life in a weak moment did little to reinforce his confidence in her as a professional. There had to be loads of other compelling reasons not to get too comfortable with Alan Lowndes, all of which would occur to her when she had a chance to think more clearly.

Juggling the receiver on her shoulder, she located the community-center phone number in her address book. The waiter was steaming milk for café au lait behind the bar. Patrice waited until the noisy espresso machine had subsided before depositing her coin and dialing.

"River Street Community Center," a reedy voice piped on the line.

"Hi, this is Patrice Ribeau. My son plays with the Tornadoes, and I was calling to see how much longer the tournament is going to last." Seeing another waiter heading for the steamer, Patrice pressed one hand over her ear.

"Well, let's see. The Sidewinders-Red Hawks game is in progress right now, and we've still got the Rebound Demons-Cruisers coming up."

Patrice chewed her lip. Alex was such a die-hard basketball enthusiast, he might well want to hang around until the bitter end. Then again, depending on how the Tornadoes had fared, he could be ready to call it a day.

"Can you have my son come to the phone, please? His name is Alex Ribeau."

"Sure. Hang on."

Patrice braced her elbow with her free hand and waited for the young man to accomplish his mission. When the receiver rattled on the other end, she said, "Alex?"

"No, ma'am. This is Jack again. It looks like your son's already gone."

Patrice frowned. "That's impossible. He was expecting me to pick him up. Did you try the rest room? What about the concession area?"

"All I know is what the assistant coach told me."

"Let me talk with him, then." Patrice shifted the phone to her other ear in annoyance. Like any ten-year-old, Alex was certainly capable of mischief, but he knew where he could push her and where she would draw the line. For safety's sake, she had always been strict about knowing his plans, and Alex had never before violated that ground rule.

"Hello, this is Ron Champion. Jack says you're calling for Alex Ribeau."

"That's right. I'm his mother, and I'd like to speak with him."

"He hasn't gotten to the garage yet?"

"What garage?" Patrice demanded.

A puzzled silence followed. "You're Mrs. Ribeau, right?"

"Patrice L. Ribeau, mother of Alex A. Ribeau," Patrice snapped. "Now would you please find my son, or put someone on the line who can."

"Alex has gone to meet you."

"That's ridiculous! He doesn't even know where I am!"

Champion swallowed audibly, hinting that he recognized a problem. "He told me that the woman from the tow company gave him directions."

"What woman? What tow company?" Patrice was shouting loudly enough to attract the waiters' attention, but she was too upset to care. "Damn it, I want to know where my son is!"

"Okay, Mrs. Ribeau, just calm down. About an hour ago, a lady from the towing service called and said you'd had a wreck. She explained that you wanted Alex to take the streetcar to meet you at the garage. We called him to the phone, and she gave him directions. He left, oh, say, forty-five minutes ago."

"Do you..." Patrice's mouth was so dry, it hurt to swallow. "Do you know where he was headed?"

The few intervening seconds seemed to last an eternity.

"No, ma'am. I'm afraid I don't."

Chapter Seven

Patrice flung the receiver onto the hook and dashed out of the café dining room. In her haste, she bumped against one of the vacant sidewalk tables, upsetting the silver bud vase. Not bothering to retrieve the metal cylinder clattering across the floor, she rushed to the corner table. Before she reached him, Alan was on his feet.

"What's wrong?"

"Something's happened to Alex." Patrice felt as if she would choke on the awful words.

Alan was at her side immediately. "Is he hurt?"

Patrice shook her head. "I don't know. My God, I don't even know where he is. A woman phoned the community center with a trumped-up story about my having had a wreck. She said she was with a towing service and told Alex he was supposed to take the streetcar to meet me at some garage. No one at the center knows where he's gone." Her voice almost broke, and she swallowed hard in an effort to get a grip on her nerves.

Alan placed a steadying hand on her arm. "We need to notify the police."

"I'll call my Dad. He's a retired cop, and he'll be able to get things moving fast."

Patrice forced a deep breath as she reached for her change purse. If ever she needed to be calm, it was now. Alex's very life might depend on it. She focused on the mechanical motions of walking back to the pay phone and calling her father, refusing to let her mind stray from the immediate task at hand. Her voice sounded lifeless, disembodied, as she recapped her conversation with the basketball coach for Tony Lafon.

"What was Alex wearing today?" Her father's voice was uncharacteristically terse.

"Acid-washed jeans. A Michael Jordan T-shirt, the one with long sleeves. The red baseball cap you gave him." Patrice closed her eyes, overcome by the image of her son.

"Okay, that's all I need. I'll get them to put out an APB on him. Then I'll meet you at the house." Tony's breath rasping over the line sounded ragged. "Hang on, sweetheart. We're gonna find that boy."

"Thanks, Dad." After Patrice hung up the phone, she held on to the receiver for a moment, uncertain what to do next. She turned when Alan touched her shoulder.

"Why don't we drive to the community center?" he suggested. "Alex could still be wandering around trying to find the right streetcar. I'll drive, and you can look for him."

"Let's go," Patrice agreed without hesitation. Although she realized the chances of finding Alex near the community center were remote, she needed to do something, anything to counter her paralyzing sense of helplessness.

Alan's car was parked only a couple of blocks from the café. Patrice hovered close to the window, scanning the passing landscape in hopes of a miracle, while Alan sped to the community center. He drove with a sureness that she appreciated, following her clipped directions and smoothly evading traffic. Only his rigid profile, outlined in the dusky light, betrayed his own tension.

The area surrounding the community center was clogged with the cars of parents picking up their children. Alan slowed the Saab to a crawl as they cruised the vicinity. At the streetcar stop, he double-parked while Patrice climbed out and questioned the clerks at a nearby drugstore. None of them recalled seeing a child matching Alex's description. Patrice combed the block, repeating her son's description in a half-dozen businesses, all to no avail.

"No one's seen him." Patrice pressed her lips together, fighting their trembling, as she climbed back into Alan's car.

Alan clasped her shoulder with a firm hand. "It was a long shot that we'd intercept him around here anyway. Let's head for your house. He may have realized he'd been led on a wild-goose chase and simply gone home."

"Alex isn't used to riding public transportation, not by himself," Patrice murmured dubiously.

"Maybe not, but from what you've told me, he's a resourceful kid. I bet he wouldn't be shy about asking someone which bus to take home." Alan's voice was low and even, calculated to instill confidence and subdue fear. "What's the best way to get to your house?"

"Turn right at the corner." Patrice pointed and then clenched her hand into a fist, fighting the unsteadiness that betrayed the fear running rampant inside her. All logic to the contrary, she strained to scan the pedestrians dotting the sidewalks, silently praying that Alex's small freckled face would appear among them.

When Alan reached to shift, he gave her hand a supportive squeeze. "It's going to be all right, Patrice," he assured her softly. "Either he's going to find us, or we're going to find him."

When they turned into the subdivision, Patrice could see the revolving lights flashing in front of her gray-shingled bungalow a block away. Two squad cars filled the driveway while another idled at the end of the walk. Tony Lafon was standing on the lawn, talking with a uniformed officer. Before Alan had cut the motor, Patrice lunged out of the car and ran to her father.

"Any word on him?" she asked breathlessly.

"Not yet, baby." Her father's big, callused hand closed around hers.

Patrice covered her mouth with her free hand, stifling the anguished cry straining for release. She jumped when a policeman shouted across the lawn from one of the squad cars.

"Sergeant! We've just got a report from the Transit Authority. A driver's spotted a boy resembling the subject near Saint Louis Cemetery."

Patrice dashed to the police car, followed by her father, Alan and the police sergeant. "Has a car picked him up?"

"Not yet, ma'am, but we've got three units on the way."

"Let's go!" Retirement had not robbed Tony Lafon's voice of its authority. Without waiting for an invitation, he ushered Alan and Patrice into the back of the squad car and then climbed in behind them.

As the squad car raced through the city streets, painting the night air with its shrill siren, Patrice held her breath, daring to permit only one thought: someone had seen Alex. When a voice crackled something about a "possible kidnapping" over the police radio, her heart lurched. She felt Alan's hand close tightly around hers, and she laced her fingers through his, welcoming the comforting pressure of his grasp.

In the dank fog rising from the old cemetery, the mausoleums resembled phantom ships cast adrift on a misty sea. The police cruisers' undulating lights cut through the gloom, casting shadows among the moss-encrusted statuary. As the sirens died, Patrice shoved the door open and ran to the circle of squad cars.

"Mom!"

Alex dashed past the officers to meet her. Patrice dropped to her knees and opened her arms, sweeping the little boy into her embrace.

"Oh, God, I'm so glad to see you!" Patrice gently rocked her son, hugging him to her. Then she loosened her hold to clasp his face with both hands. "You're okay?"

The small face bobbed in her hands, nodding affirmation. "Uh-huh, but it was kinda spooky around here. I couldn't figure out how to get home. Where were you?"

Patrice smoothed the damp auburn hair protruding beneath the bill of Alex's baseball cap and smiled shakily. "That's what I was wondering about you. Someone played a mean trick on us, Alex."

"You mean you weren't in a wreck?"

Patrice shook her head. "No, that was just a big lie." She glanced up at the policewoman hovering behind Alex. "I guess you'd like to question him?"

The officer, a trim young woman with sympathetic gray eyes, nodded. "We've already got the basic story, but I need to complete the report. If you like, I'll drive back to your house first. Something tells me this young fellow is pretty eager to get home."

As Alex slipped his hand inside hers, Patrice rose and followed the young officer back to the clutch of squad cars. As she guided her son into the back seat of the cruiser, she felt a warm hand press her back. Patrice turned to see her father smiling over her shoulder, with Alan close behind him.

"You're doin' okay, sport?" Tony Lafon leaned to give the bill of his grandson's baseball cap a playful tug.

"Yeah, Grandpa."

When Alex grinned, Patrice felt a fresh surge of anger at the malicious person who would use an innocent child as a pawn in his evil game. She held Alex close during the ride back to their home, reassuring both of them that their little family had been safely reunited.

When they reached the house, the policewoman unlatched the rear doors for them before collecting her clipboard and quickly glancing over the report. She looked up from the form to wave as another police car pulled into the driveway and then turned back to Alex and Patrice.

"Okay, Alex. I just have a few things I'd like to go over again, and then we'll be all done. Why don't you tell me one more time about the phone call you got at the community center?"

"Coach Champion told me someone was calling with a message from my mom, so I went to the phone." Alex looked from the policewoman to Patrice. "This lady said you'd been in a wreck and that you wanted me to take the streetcar to the place where they'd hauled our car."

"Did she give you the name of that place, Alex?" the officer asked.

Alex nodded. "Uh-huh. Smith's Garage. She told me how to get there, but it was kind of confusing. I'm pretty sure I got off at the right stop, but there was nothing there except some ratty old buildings. Then I just started walking, trying to find it." He wrinkled his upturned nose. "All I found was the cemetery, though."

Patrice had never considered herself a violent person, but she could easily have strangled the miscreant who had played the frightening and potentially dangerous trick on Alex. "Do you remember this woman's voice on the phone? Did she sound young or old?" Patrice prompted gently.

Alex thought for a moment. "She sounded a lot like the lady who called about the tournament." When Patrice looked puzzled, he went on. "It was the day you got that stupid doll in the mail, remember? Anyway, she said she was calling from school and wanted to know what I was doing Saturday. When I told her about the tournament, she said, oh, yeah, she'd almost forgotten. Then she asked me where it was and everything so she could tell her class about it." Catching the dismay written on Patrice's face, Alex asked, "Did I do something wrong?"

Patrice gave him a firm hug. "No, Alex, not at all."

"You've been a big help, Alex," the police officer concurred. She turned to Patrice, took her telephone number and then gave her the report to sign.

Patrice pocketed her copy of the police report and then laid a hand on the back of Alex's neck, guiding him up the walk to the house. From the porch, she noticed Alan standing to one side, talking quietly with her father. In her single-minded concern for Alex, she had neglected the usual social niceties, but apparently her father and Alan had managed introductions on their own. It was hard to imagine two men more different in appearance, the one tall and muscular, the other short and comfortably settled in middle age. Yet an indefinable quality seemed to unite them: they had both been there for her when she had needed them. Patrice had always known she could rely on her father, but the idea of another man willingly assuming that role had not entered her mind in a long time.

"All squared away with the cops?" Tony asked from the bottom step.

Patrice nodded. "I hope so. Right now, I think I have just enough energy left to make a sandwich for this young man and then get him settled in for the night." As she inserted the key in the lock, she winced. "Oh, Lord, I'd forgotten all about my car. It's still parked down by Moon Walk."

Her father reached to intercept the keys. "I'll pick it up for you. The sergeant can drop me off on his way back to headquarters." He gave her shoulder a fatherly pat. "Go on, honey, and don't worry about a thing. Your car will be waiting in the garage when you get up in the morning."

"Which is going to be *late*, if I have any say in the matter," Patrice assured him. She paused in the doorway. "Thanks so much, Dad. For everything."

Her father shrugged off her gratitude with a smile. "That's what family's for."

As Tony Lafon hurried down the walk to the parked squad car, Patrice turned to Alan. "I owe you a big thank-you, too."

The vaporous porch light had smoothed the lean angles of Alan's face, easing the tense lines that had been so prominent only a short while ago. "No, you don't," he countered, almost diffidently.

"Can we eat soon, Mom?" Alex's wheedling voice interrupted from behind the two adults.

Patrice stifled a groan. "My feet are moving toward the kitchen." She hesitated, looking back at Alan. "Can

I offer you a bite? It won't be anything fancy, but you're welcome to join us.''

"Only if you'll let me lend a hand."

"I won't argue with that!" Turning, Patrice followed Alex down the hall to the kitchen.

When she switched on the light, she glanced around at the tidy oak-paneled cabinets for a moment. The evening's disturbing events had left her feeling off balance, disoriented even in the cozy, familiar surroundings of her own kitchen.

Alan clutched her elbow gently and guided her to the breakfast bar. "Why don't you have a seat while Alex and I rustle up some chow? We promise not to make a mess, don't we, Alex?"

"Uh-huh." When the little boy grinned, Patrice was heartened by that outward sign of resilience.

In fact, Alex seemed more concerned with the Tornadoes' narrow loss to the Wildcats than with the harrowing experience that had followed. From her vantage point on the bar stool, Patrice listened to the cheerful banter passing between Alan and her son while they toasted rolls and filled them with ham, cheese, alfalfa sprouts and tomato.

"Alan is a pediatrician like Dr. Baird," Patrice informed Alex as he presented her with her plate.

"You give shots?" Alex regarded their male companion with a newfound hint of caution.

Alan's mouth quivered slightly as he opened a chilled bottle of tomato juice. "Sometimes, but only when I have to."

Alex appeared satisfied enough with the answer to climb onto the stool next to Alan and resume their discussion of the upcoming NBA play-offs. When they were finished eating, he helped clear the breakfast bar and carry dishes to the sink.

Patrice glanced at the wall clock and then slid off the bar stool. "It's past your bedtime, pardner," she announced. Seeing her son's small face knotting into a frown, she went on. "Why don't you brush your teeth and wash your face? Then you can watch TV for a half hour or so." After the ordeal Alex had been through, he deserved a little concession tonight.

"Okay." Alex trooped toward the hall. In the door, he paused. "G'night, Alan."

Leaning against the counter, Alan smiled. "Good night, Alex. The Lakers are gonna win. You heard it here first."

"Uh-uh! The Chicago Bulls are!" Alex countered. "You just wait and see!" His giggle preceded him as he raced up the stairs.

Patrice followed her son at a more sedate pace. While Alex busied himself at the bathroom sink, she prepared his room for the night. Countless times, she had performed the tasks of drawing blinds, plumping pillows and adjusting the nightstand lamp. Yet tonight the ritual took on a deeper significance, a sobering reminder of how precious life's daily rhythms are. When Alex hugged her prior to scrambling into bed, Patrice held him a little longer than usual, reassuring herself that the warm, vibrant child in her arms was truly safe.

"Half an hour only, okay?" Patrice cautioned with a smile as she pointed to his TV. Never before would she have imagined how comforting the music to a monster movie could sound, wafting from behind the partially closed door.

Downstairs, Patrice found Alan standing in front of the den wall unit, inspecting her CD collection. When she entered the room, he turned. "Got him into bed withou a hitch?"

"With some help from *Godzilla Meets the Smo Monster.*"

Alan laughed softly. "Can I get you anything before head for home? A shot of brandy, maybe?"

Patrice shook her head. "I'm afraid the strongest thing I have on hand is diet Coke, but don't worry. I don' think I'll have any trouble sleeping tonight."

Clutching both arms, Patrice followed Alan into the hall. At the door, he turned to face her. "Are you sur you're going to be all right tonight?" His dark eyes swep her face in the low light.

Patrice felt almost too spent to nod. A bone-deep weariness had descended on her, draining her of the strength even to hold her emotions in check. Withou warning, warm rivulets began to course down her cheeks She closed her eyes, pawing at her face. "Oh, God, wha am I doing? I'm...I'm sorry." She tried to smile through the tears that had surfaced without warning.

Patrice felt Alan's arms close around her shoulders "Shh," he whispered into her hair. "There's nothing wrong with crying. You've been through so much, you need to let it out."

"It's just when I think what might have happened, tha I could have lost him..." Patrice broke off, gulping back a sob.

A shudder quavered through her. Without opening her eyes, she fastened her arms around Alan's waist, holding on to him as if he were the only mooring holding her back from the abyss. His hand stroked her shoulder, soothing her with its gentle, sure touch.

"Alex is fine, and that's all that matters right now," Alan murmured, his lips moving against her brow.

Patrice drew a deep breath, trying to regain her composure. This was not like her at all, making a spectacle of her emotions. Straightening herself, she gently loosened her hold on Alan. When she looked up into his eyes, however, her resolve faltered. She held her breath as he reached to touch her face, his finger lightly brushing away the moisture still clinging to her cheek. He hesitated for a moment before letting his hand fall to his side.

"I'll be in touch." Alan's voice sounded husky in the dark foyer. "Good night, Patrice." He stepped back onto the porch.

"Good night, Alan," Patrice called softly. As he retreated down the walk, she pressed her hand against her damp, throbbing eyes. She opened them again to see the bright taillights of Alan's car recede into the night.

A HEAVY CLOAK OF DEW clung to the lawn, shimmering in the sunlight filtering through the trees. Coffee mug cradled in his hands, Alan leaned against the deck rail and watched the robins harvesting their breakfast from the rich soil. Normally he counted on Sunday mornings to catch up on the sleep deficit he always managed to accrue during the week. He had been up before dawn today, however, unable to escape his restless thoughts for more than a few hours.

He hoped that Patrice had enjoyed a more peaceful night. Slim chance of that, Alan reminded himself grimly as he trekked back to the kitchen to refill his mug for the third time. His anger still rose to a boil when he recalled the terror-stricken look in her eyes the previous evening. Even Patrice's cool self-possession had not been able to withstand the fear of an unknown threat to her son.

Up until last night, Alan had glimpsed only small chinks in the tough, strong-willed side of Patrice. He had never imagined that she could look so vulnerable, fighting back her tears in the dark hallway. Even more surprising had been his own reaction to her plight. Since his divorce, caution had been Alan's watchword regarding his dealings with women. Taking Patrice into his arms, however, had happened as naturally as if they had known each other much longer than a scant week. He had been on the verge of kissing her, Alan reflected soberly, had been a second away from irrevocably overstepping the bounds of their professional relationship. Thank God, he had caught himself before he had gone too far. With the forces conspiring against his grandfather becoming more sinister by the day, the last thing he wanted was to alienate the woman he had hired to unravel the mystery.

Alan took a sip of the fragrant coffee, frowning at his unshaven reflection in the window as he considered the latest attempt to intimidate Patrice. What kind of monster would use an innocent child as a pawn in his vicious game? The answers that came to Alan's mind raised chilling implications about the opponent that he and Patrice faced. More unsettling still was the pattern of steady escalation in the threats. Beginning with the psychological terror of voodoo dolls, the fiend had progressed from vandalizing property to jeopardizing Alex Ribeau's safety. What would be the next step?

If only they could uncover a real lead in the case, a solid clue that they could sink their teeth into! Until a breakthrough occurred, however, they could only guess what form their opponent's next attack might take. Of course, there was one person who might be able to enlighten them.

Pushing away from the counter, Alan glanced at the microwave's clock and then drew a slow, deep breath. Granddad would be up by now, reading his newspaper while he nibbled at the sticky buns Lucille always dropped off on her way to church. His grandfather cherished Sunday, for it was the one day when he was allowed to live for a few hours independent of caretakers. Much as Alan hated to disturb the elderly man's quiet morning, however, he knew he could not put off the conversation that had been taking shape in his mind all night.

Alan walked to the cordless phone anchored next to the pantry and dialed his grandfather's home in Port Latanier. With Lucille off for the day, Granddad would take a bit of time getting to the phone. Alan waited patiently, counting eleven rings before his grandfather picked up.

"Hello?"

"Good morning, Granddad. I hope I'm not bothering you."

Dr. Hamilton chuckled. "What nonsense! Of course you're not! I was just putting the rest of Lucille's sweet rolls in the kitchen. The dear soul brought me a dozen, as if I still had the appetite of a twenty-year-old. If you like, I'll ask her to freeze them, and you can have them when you get back from that convention this week."

"That would be nice, Granddad." Alan hesitated, hating the artificially chatty tone he had adopted. He cleared his throat. "I'd like to drive out this afternoon if you don't mind."

"Of course I don't mind, although you really don't have to check on me. Mrs. Bates will be here at four."

"Actually, I need to talk with you, Granddad. About that birth certificate you signed in July of 1967."

"For heaven's sake, Alan, I'm an old man! I do well to remember what I had for dinner last night." Dr. Hamilton's voice rose in agitation. "And you're asking me to recall a single infant among the hundreds of babies I must have delivered over the years!"

"I'd like for you to try, Granddad, because this is very important." Despite the urgency of his request, Alan spoke quietly in an effort to spare the convalescent man unnecessary stress. "The detective who approached us last week received a voodoo doll in the mail, and her car was vandalized. Last night, someone lured her ten-year-old son to Saint Louis Cemetery on a false emergency." He paused, giving his grandfather the chance to absorb the full impact of his revelations. "Whoever is doing this needs to be stopped before someone gets hurt."

"I don't . . . I don't know who's behind all these awful things, Alan."

"But you might be able to help us discover who is," Alan countered. "Please, Granddad. You've got to trust me."

"Why can't people simply let the past be?" Dr. Hamilton murmured. When he sighed, the quavering, protracted breath was laden with despair. "Very well, Alan. We can talk this afternoon."

Alan closed his eyes in silent thanks. "I'll plan to drive out around twelve-thirty, if that's okay with you." When only an empty silence followed, he went on. "You won't be sorry, Granddad. I swear you won't."

"No, perhaps not."

Alan winced at the despondent resignation in his grandfather's voice. When the phone clicked in his ear, he stared at the receiver for a moment. No, he had done the right thing. He need only recall Alex Ribeau's trusting little face to convince himself that the dangerous game engulfing them must not be allowed to continue. As for his grandfather's misgivings, he would simply have to shield him as much as possible from any unsavory developments in Patrice's investigation.

It probably wouldn't be a bad idea to consult Patrice prior to talking with his grandfather. Cordless phone in hand, Alan walked down the hall to his bedroom and dug her business card out of his jacket pocket. Seated on the side of the bed, he dialed her home number that he had noted on the back of the card.

"Hello?" Alex's cheerful voice gave no inkling of the previous evening's ordeal.

"Hi, Alex. This is Alan Lowndes. How's it going today?"

"Great! Grandpa's going to take us on a picnic later. You want to come?"

Alan felt uncommonly flattered by the little boy's invitation. "I'd love to, but I've already planned to visit my own grandfather this afternoon. If your mom isn't busy, could I talk with her for a few minutes?"

"Sure." The phone clattered against a hard surface as Alex's rubber-treaded feet thumped into the distance.

"Alan?" Patrice sounded a little uncertain when she picked up the phone, but then, who wouldn't after the weirdness she had experienced in the past week?

"How are you doing?" Alan posed the question gently, as if he were broaching a far more delicate issue.

"Okay." Patrice blew out a long breath. "I have to confess the night was short on sweet dreams. By the time I got up to cook breakfast, though, I was past feeling scared and helpless. Now I just want to get even."

Alan chuckled. "'Atta girl! That's one of the reasons I called, actually."

"You have a master plan for revenge?"

Alan settled back against the pillow, relishing the sound of Patrice's laughter. "I've persuaded my grandfather to talk about the birth certificate."

Patrice was instantly serious. "That's wonderful! How on earth did you manage to change his mind?"

"I told him about what happened last night. Granddad is a stubborn man and loyal to a fault, but if he has to choose between a child's safety and protecting the reputation of some pillar of the community, the child is going to win hands down. We're going to talk this afternoon. I'll need some background information so I'll know what I'm fishing for."

Patrice was quiet, and Alan could tell that she was thinking carefully. "I suppose I could give you a copy of the amended birth certificate," she began slowly.

"Better yet, why don't you come with me?" The thought had not occurred to Alan until then, but it made perfect sense. Why risk overlooking a crucial clue that would be immediately apparent to Patrice? "I hate to ask you to pass on the picnic, though."

Patrice brushed off his reservations. "Believe me, we do that sort of thing with Dad almost every weekend. He and Alex won't even miss me. What time did you say you were driving to Port Latanier?"

"Granddad is expecting me around twelve-thirty." Alan shook back the sleeve of his sweatshirt to consult his watch. "I could pick you up in an hour, if that's enough time."

"More than enough." Patrice sounded a trifle impatient, anxious to get any information she could.

"See you shortly, then." Alan clicked the disconnect button and tossed the phone onto the rumpled comforter.

He shaved and showered in record time, driven by a heightened nervous energy. When he pulled into the driveway of Patrice's pleasant little bungalow, Alan realized that he had overshot his projected arrival time by a good fifteen minutes. True to her word, however, Patrice appeared in the door before he could kill the motor. She was dressed in a green-and-white striped rugby shirt and white denim jeans that did nothing to camouflage her distracting curves. Alan reached to unlatch the door, trying to keep his eyes trained somewhere to the north of the formfitting jeans.

"Were Alex and your dad disappointed?" he asked as he took her briefcase and shoved it into the back seat.

"Not as much as I would have liked," Patrice joked. "I rarely renege when Alex and I have planned something, so when I do, he knows it's important. I explained that this was business."

Was he imagining it, or was Patrice's tone more brisk than usual? From the corner of his eye, Alan watched her adjust the shoulder harness, her pretty heart-shaped face a study in concentration. Small wonder if she was trying to establish some distance after his performance the previous evening. Having a client within a heartbeat of kissing her was not a situation that someone as professional as Patrice would probably welcome, regardless of the circumstances. Fixing his eyes on the road, Alan resolved not to permit any further emotional lapses to jeopardize their working relationship.

They passed the drive to Port Latanier discussing the research Patrice had done to date for her adoptee client. When Alan turned into the peaceful street leading to his grandfather's house, Patrice unsnapped the shoulder harness to retrieve her briefcase from the back seat. After he had pulled into the driveway, however, she hesitated.

"I'm going to let you do most of the talking. Your grandfather has been so reluctant to discuss the birth certificate even with you, the last thing I want to do is upset him."

Alan nodded in agreement. "I think he's convinced this isn't a frivolous inquiry, but he needs reassurance." He rounded the car to open the door for Patrice, but she had already scrambled out and was waiting for him, briefcase in hand. Patrice followed Alan up the walk to the veranda, hanging back while he tapped briefly on the front door.

"Granddad is by himself right now, and he takes some time getting to the door," Alan explained over his shoulder. "His housekeeper has weekends off, but he refuses to have round-the-clock nurses for both days."

Alan inclined his head toward the door's beveled-glass window, listening for the familiar shuffle of his grandfather's footsteps. Then he rapped on the wooden doorframe again, this time with more force.

"Do you think he might have fallen asleep?" Patrice asked when Alan's knock failed to rouse any response.

"That's entirely possible, but don't worry. I have my own key to the house." Alan fished his key chain out of his pocket and then tried the lock. "Granddad?" he called softly as he pushed the door open. Getting no answer, he repeated himself a little more loudly. "Granddad, it's Alan."

The stillness pervading the house was so thick Alan could almost feel it engulf him like a suffocating vapor. He started down the hall, taking action to dispel the irrational uneasiness that had suddenly gripped him. Alan could hear Patrice's quick, light steps behind him. He glanced through the open bedroom door before heading for the living room.

One of the French doors opening onto the sun room was ajar, revealing a folded newspaper and a silver coffeepot on the wicker lamp table. Only when Alan reached the door did he notice the shattered remains of a porcelain cup strewn across the sun room floor. The blood drained from Alan's face as his eyes followed the pool of spilled coffee, finally coming to rest on his grandfather's outstretched body.

Chapter Eight

"Oh, my God!" The briefcase slipped from Patrice's hand to clatter against the quarry-tile floor.

"Call an ambulance!" Alan ordered. In a flash, he was bent over the elderly man, checking his vital signs. "You're going to be all right, Granddad. I'm here now. Hang on for me, okay?" He murmured reassurances as he ripped one leg of Dr. Hamilton's pajamas up to the knee to expose the swollen, discolored calf.

As Alan examined the distended leg, Patrice ran toward the door. When something rustled beneath a section of the newspaper lying on the floor, she drew up short. Patrice lifted the edge of the paper with her toe and then sucked in her breath. A black snake lay coiled beneath the discarded paper. The reptile lifted its heavy wedge-shaped head, its darting tongue testing the air in preparation for a strike.

"Look out, Alan! There's a water moccasin under the paper!" Patrice shouted.

In desperation, she shoved the potted ficus tree onto its side and pulled the terra-cotta planter free of the root ball. Just as the snake attempted to wriggle beneath the wicker rocker, Patrice clamped the planter over it.

Her breath was still coming in short, constricted gulps when she reached the phone mounted on the kitchen wall. Patrice punched out 911, weaving impatiently from one foot to the other while the emergency operator took her call. As soon as the dispatcher hung up, she rushed back to the sun room.

"A rescue unit is on the way," Patrice told Alan. She bit her lip, stifling the awful question lodged in her throat.

As if he could read her mind, Alan glanced over his shoulder. "He's breathing, but just barely. I found a snakebite on his ankle, two fang marks. That's why he's gone into shock. His pulse is so weak I could barely feel it." His voice was even and empty of expression, and Patrice could tell that Alan had, of necessity, blanked out his emotions, relying on the medical skills that were by now second nature to him.

The whine of a siren in the distance sent Patrice dashing out the door to the driveway. When the emergency vehicle turned onto the gravel driveway, she ran to direct the crew to the sun room. She hung back as the medics strapped Dr. Hamilton onto a gurney and rushed him into the back of the vehicle. To an uninitiated observer, Alan could have passed for any doctor going about his lifesaving vocation as he climbed into the vehicle with the rescue team. Only the unnatural pallor of his lean face betrayed the emotional maelstrom raging within him.

After the emergency van had sped away, Patrice hesitated only a moment before returning to the house. She found Alan's keys still dangling from the front door lock. Forcing herself to think calmly, she took time to secure the doors and collect her briefcase before running to Alan's Saab and backing into the street. The rescue unit's siren was now only a distant warble, too far away for

Patrice to follow its sound. When she spotted a woman walking a Yorkie at the end of the block, she pulled over to ask directions to the hospital. Driving as fast as safety would permit, Patrice pulled into the emergency room parking lot to find the rescue van still parked in front of the entrance.

The emergency room waiting area was a characterless vault of a room, furnished with molded plastic chairs bolted together in twos and threes. Like so many hospitals Patrice had visited, Colley Parish Memorial had chosen a pale green paint for the plaster walls. It was a shade calculated to soothe, she imagined, but the color always made her feel clammy and stiff, as if she had been temporarily placed on ice. A nurse was monitoring a desk positioned like a sentry's station beside swinging double doors.

"Can you tell me how Dr. Hamilton is doing?" Patrice asked at the desk. "I'm a friend of the family."

"He was just admitted, but I don't have any information on his condition," the nurse informed her. She gave Patrice a kind smile. "You're welcome to wait a bit, if you'd like."

Patrice thanked the nurse and retreated to the nearest bank of chairs. Closing her eyes, she massaged her temples, trying to quell the kaleidoscope of grotesque impressions spinning through her mind. How had a water moccasin managed to invade Dr. Hamilton's sun room on the very afternoon the elderly physician had agreed to discuss Anne-Marie's birth certificate with Alan? Patrice was trying to formulate a plausible answer for that question when Alan emerged through the swinging doors.

Patrice jumped to her feet and hurried to meet him. "How is he?"

"He's in serious condition. They've administered antivenin and have him on a respirator now. All we can do is wait and see." In the merciless fluorescent light, Alan's face looked haggard, its lean contours taut with anxiety.

On impulse, Patrice took his hand in hers and held it tight for a moment. "From what you've told me, he's a fighter, Alan. If anyone can make it, he can."

Alan's cool fingers laced through hers. "I hope you're right." He forced a deep breath. "I'll get you to New Orleans before dark, but I'd like to go back to the house right now and call the sheriff. That snake didn't just wander into Granddad's house on its own."

"That's exactly what I've been thinking."

Patrice fell in step with Alan as they left the emergency room and walked to his car. They rode in silence back to the big white antebellum mansion. While Patrice quickly examined the house's doors and windows for signs of forced entry, Alan phoned the sheriff's office. When she heard a car door slam, Patrice hurried to the front veranda.

"'Afternoon, Doc." Sheriff Wade nicked the brim of his Stetson as he climbed the steps to the veranda. "Now what'd you say you've got goin' on out here? Somethin' about a rattler on the porch?" When he noticed Patrice standing in the doorway, he looked startled, as if he thought he had seen the last of her the previous week.

Patrice took the sheriff's surprise in stride. "Good afternoon, Sheriff Wade. It was a water moccasin, actually. It bit Dr. Hamilton."

The sheriff frowned, looking from Patrice to Alan. "Most likely, the thing bit him out in the yard. Alphonse thinks he's hoodwinked everyone, but I've caught him puttering around those roses of his when Lucille's gone to the store."

Alan shook his head. "No, this snake was inside the house."

"Do you want to have a look at it?" Patrice interposed.

Sheriff Wade looked a tad uncertain. "I 'spect so." He followed Alan and Patrice back to the sun room, sweeping his hat off and smoothing the hair back from his brow.

"It's under that pot." Patrice pointed to the upturned planter.

Sheriff Wade gave her a dubious glance before gingerly tipping the planter to one side. One glimpse beneath the pot and he quickly clamped it back to the floor. "Whew! That's a big sucker, all right."

"Too big to squeeze under the door or any of the window screens," Alan concluded grimly. "I think someone deliberately brought the snake into the house. When we got here around twelve-thirty, we found Granddad lying unconscious on the floor. The snake was coiled up underneath some newspaper behind the rocker."

"Any idea how long your granddaddy'd been like that?" Sheriff Wade asked.

"We'll talk with the physician attending him at Memorial, but I don't think it could have been even a half hour, considering Granddad's age and the state of his health. He was on the brink of circulatory collapse when the medics arrived."

Sheriff Wade's eyes narrowed as they swept the glass-enclosed porch. "Did y'all notice any signs of forced entry?"

"I checked the doors and windows," Patrice told him. "Unfortunately, anyone who wanted to get in could have done so easily. The kitchen and downstairs bathroom windows were open, and the sun room's exterior door was unlocked when we arrived."

"Granddad has always been pretty lax about locking doors, but in a town like Port Latanier, I don't suppose he saw the need to make an issue of security," Alan explained.

Sheriff Wade shook his head. "Tell you what, Doc. I don't know who'd want to pull a fool trick like this on your granddaddy, but I'm going to have a look around the house and see what I can come up with."

"I'd appreciate that," Alan told the sheriff. "I'll be staying down here while Granddad is in intensive care, but I need to drive Ms. Ribeau back to New Orleans right now. You can conduct the investigation without me, I suppose?"

Sheriff Wade nodded, settling his hat onto his head as he followed Alan and Patrice out of the house. "I'll drop by the hospital later and see how your granddaddy's doin'. I 'spect it's going to take somethin' ornerier than a water moccasin to get the best of him, though." His robust face broke into a reassuring smile, obviously gauged for Alan's benefit.

"Thanks, Sheriff." Alan managed to return the smile, but all semblance of cheer vanished from his face as he slid behind the wheel of the Saab.

Arms folded across her chest, Patrice huddled in the passenger seat as they drove back to New Orleans. For once, she found it impossible to focus on her case, to think of anything but the frail, white-haired man lying on the brink of death. Alan looked so stricken, his handsome face set like a waxen statue's as he piloted the car along the interstate. Patrice longed to say something that would alleviate the pain written on his features. Any consolation that skirted the brutal possibilities, however, would only have sounded like a stale platitude. After a few feeble stabs at conversation, Alan flicked on the radio and selected a subdued classical station, mercifully relieving them of any pressure to talk.

When Alan pulled up in front of Patrice's house, he left the motor idling. "I really need to get back to Port Latanier. I couldn't reach Granddad's nurse, and she's going to fall to pieces when she gets to the house and finds him missing."

Patrice nodded her understanding. As she moved to slide out of the car, she was surprised to feel Alan's hand close on her shoulder. When she turned, he glanced down for a moment, as if he was trying to collect his thoughts.

"Thanks, Patrice." Alan's earnest eyes conveyed the depth of his gratitude.

"Don't thank me, Alan." Patrice shrugged, suddenly feeling self-conscious. "I didn't do anything. I just happened to be there."

Alan's hand tightened on her shoulder. "That was what I needed most, you simply to be there." He loosened his clasp with noticeable reluctance before turning abruptly to the wheel. "I'll let you know if Sheriff Wade's investigation turns up anything interesting."

"Please do." Patrice stepped out of the car, slammed the door and then turned to peer through the window. "And keep me posted on your grandfather's condition."

Alan only nodded as he shifted into gear. Watching the car slowly pull away from the curb, Patrice felt more desolate than she had in four long years.

UNDER NORMAL circumstances, Patrice would have considered lying in wait to collar a client a ploy beneath contempt. With Dr. Hamilton's bizarre accident looking more like an attempted homicide to her with every passing hour, however, the present circumstances seemed anything but normal.

After Alan dropped her at her house, Patrice had continued to mull over the chain of increasingly dangerous events that had unfolded since she had launched her search for Anne-Marie's birth mother. Patrice had phoned Anne-Marie, only to get the answering machine, and she had hung up without leaving a message. What she had to discuss with Anne-Marie needed to be said in person. Patrice next called the hospital where Anne-Marie worked and confirmed her suspicion that the young nurse was on duty. When she learned that Anne-Marie's shift ended at seven that evening, Patrice tarried only long enough to scribble a note to Alex and her father and then make a beeline for her car. She was hanging around the hospital lobby, feeling like a character in a spy-thriller B film, when Anne-Marie emerged from one of the elevators.

"Anne-Marie!" Patrice hailed the young woman in a loud whisper.

Anne-Marie wheeled in surprise. "Patrice! I wasn't expecting to see you here." An eager hush cloaked her voice. "Has something happened with the investigation?"

"Yes, a lot." Patrice gently slid her arm through Anne-Marie's. "Can we sit down and talk for a few minutes?"

"Of course." Anne-Marie's wide-set eyes grew anxious as they searched Patrice's face. She sank onto one of the overstuffed chairs tucked in a grove of potted palms and knotted her hands on her lap.

"Someone is really serious about keeping your past a secret," Patrice began. As she recounted the events of the past week, she watched Anne-Marie's expression progress from dismay to horror.

"You think someone intended to kill Dr. Hamilton?" Anne-Marie grimaced as if the words had left a foul taste in her mouth.

"I've racked my brain for another explanation of the water moccasin showing up in his house, but the only plausible conclusion I've come up with is that someone planted the snake. It wasn't merely a scare tactic, either. A harmless garden snake would have done just as well if that had been the case. Whoever planted that water moccasin didn't care if someone died as a result."

Anne-Marie looked down at the tightly balled fist clenched on her knees. "I want you to drop my case, Patrice. It isn't worth endangering people's lives."

"I'll do whatever you wish, but I'm not willing to let the person behind this mess get off scot-free. Voodoo threats and vandalism are one thing, but attempted murder..." Patrice broke off, shaking her head. "I need your help, Anne-Marie."

The young woman looked up in surprise. "What do you mean?"

"I'd like to talk with your parents about your adoption."

Anne-Marie's eyes darted around the lobby, giving her the look of a panic-stricken doe about to take flight. "They would never agree, Patrice."

"Not even if you told them that bringing a homicidal criminal to justice might depend on it?"

"They would be crushed if they found out I had hired you," Anne-Marie murmured, more to herself than to Patrice.

Patrice reached to clasp the young woman's wrist. "Please, Anne-Marie. If...if Dr. Hamilton doesn't pull out of this, your parents are our only hope."

Anne-Marie stood up. "I'll see what I can do," she said. Tearing her hand free from Patrice's grasp, she turned and dashed out of the hospital lobby.

"I'M SORRY FOR calling you so late last night." As Anne-Marie braked at the stoplight, she glanced over at Patrice. "But once I talked with Mother and Daddy, I wanted to get you all together before they had a chance to change their minds."

"Please don't apologize. I wasn't doing such a good job of sleeping anyway," Patrice assured her.

Since her midnight conversation with Anne-Marie, Patrice, too, had worried that the Bergiers might have a change of heart at the last minute. When Anne-Marie pulled up in front of the attractive suburban split-level, Patrice was heartened to see two parked cars through the garage door windows. She took her time collecting her briefcase, giving Anne-Marie ample opportunity to summon her parents to the front door. When she reached the porch, a robustly built man with luxuriant iron gray hair was unlatching the storm door.

"Patrice, I'd like you to meet my father, Paul Bergier. Daddy, this is my friend, Patrice Ribeau." Anne-Marie's normally soft voice had dropped to a near whisper as she handled introductions.

Patrice quickly offered her hand to Mr. Bergier, prolonging the exchange to allow for some reassuring eye contact. She followed father and daughter into the living room, where a slim woman waited anxiously in front of the empty fireplace. After being introduced to Anne-Marie's mother, Patrice took a seat on the sectional.

As she adjusted the hem of the navy linen suit she had chosen for the occasion, she glanced around the room. A movie-set designer trying to create an atmosphere of harmonious family life could not have improved on the Bergiers' living room decor. From the cluster of framed family photographs arranged on the mantel to the cheerleading trophies proudly displayed in the bookcases, every corner of the room offered evidence of Paul and Margot Bergier's love for each other and for their daughter. Although her work often required Patrice to rock the boat, she nonetheless felt like a clumsy intruder in this erstwhile happy home.

To judge from the Bergiers' pained and bewildered expressions, Anne-Marie had already briefed them with background information. "Patrice needs to ask you some questions," Anne-Marie murmured. Perched on the edge of the sectional like a high-strung bird, she seemed relieved to surrender the floor to Patrice.

"I know this must be very difficult for you." Patrice looked slowly from Margot Bergier to her husband, trying to convey her sympathy with their dilemma. "That's why I want to assure you that anything you tell me today will be handled with the strictest confidence. I'll take every precaution to protect your privacy." She paused, giving the couple time to consider her pledge, before going on. "How much did you know about Anne-Marie's background when you adopted her?"

Paul Bergier licked his lips as if he was about to speak and then glanced at his wife. She took his hand, cradling it in both of hers, and nodded. He began hesitantly. "Nothing, really. A lawyer handled everything for us. After we realized that we couldn't have children, we went to several adoption agencies. We had been waiting for an infant for over two years when an attorney who had

andled some legal work for my company offered to help.
At first, it seemed like a miracle. We had wanted a child
or so long." He hesitated, struggling to regain control of
is quivering lips. "We fell in love with Anne-Marie the
moment we saw her. After caring for her for six months,
iving her up was unthinkable—even when we learned
hat her mother had never legally relinquished custody.
Can you understand what I'm talking about, Ms. Ri-
eau?"

"I have a son," Patrice told him quietly. "I can sym-
athize."

Paul Bergier's mouth twisted into a bitter smile. "For
ears, we lived in fear that a strange woman would
omeday appear to claim Anne-Marie. We even talked
about what we would do, discussed going to Mexico,
anything to avoid losing our little girl. Over time, the fear
diminished. After Anne-Marie was grown, we thought
our nightmare had ended." He sighed heavily. "I guess
we were wrong."

Patrice felt Anne-Marie wince on the sectional next to
her. When she looked over at her, tears were streaming
down the young woman's face. "No one can come between us, Daddy. No one can make me love you and
Mother any less. You've both got to believe me." She
choked on her plea.

"I know that, sweetheart," Paul Bergier confessed in
a voice thick with emotion. "Your mother and I both do.
It's just that after so many years of feeling as if... as if
we'd *stolen* you from someone else..." He broke off.

"There's no reason for you to feel like a criminal,"
Patrice told the stricken man. "You acted in good faith
in what you were led to believe was a legal adoption.
Hard as talking about this has been for you, I'm convinced that it was a necessary step to at last putting your

fears to rest." She paused when Anne-Marie rose to join her parents on the other portion of the sectional.

Patrice cleared her throat, bridling the emotions evoked by the little family embracing in silent support. Now that they had faced the specter that had overshadowed their lives for so many years, the Bergiers needed time alone to reconfirm the love and trust binding them.

"I have only a couple of questions, and then I'll leave you in peace," Patrice promised. "Who was the lawyer who arranged the adoption?"

Paul Bergier took a deep breath before answering. "His name was Kenyon. Ben Kenyon."

"He practices in New Orleans?"

Anne-Marie's father nodded slowly. "Up until three years ago. That's when he had his last heart attack." Paul Bergier's sad, dark eyes connected with Patrice over the distance separating them. "Ben Kenyon is dead, Ms. Ribeau. Anything he knew about Annie's past, he took to the grave with him."

THE GAUNT FIGURE LOOMED in the headlights' beam, plucked out of the darkness as suddenly as an apparition. Julia Broussard reached to cut the lights, not taking her eyes off Alonzo as he rounded the car. An involuntary shudder skittered down her spine when he stooped to peer through the passenger window. Her head jerked in a nod, signaling her permission for him to enter the car.

"Good evenin', Julia." Alonzo's purplish lips curved into a smile as he slid onto the seat beside her.

Julia stared through the windshield, refusing to look at the hideous man sitting next to her. "He might die." She lifted her chin slightly in an attempt to relieve her constricted vocal cords. "What if he dies?" Her voice rose as she suddenly turned toward Alonzo.

"Then I guess you won't have to worry about him talkin' no more." Alonzo sank back into the seat, drawing his bony knees up as if he was settling in for a good, long stay.

Julia's lip curled in revulsion. "How you can live with yourself?" she spat at him through clenched teeth.

Alonzo shifted to regard her with lazy yellow eyes. A smile spread across his face as slowly as a knife cutting through flesh. "I ain't no different from you, Julia." He looked back out the window. "No different at all."

Chapter Nine

"Alan!"

Patrice thrust her head out the open car window and threw up her hand to wave. As Alan started across the lawn toward the graveled driveway, she grabbed her briefcase and shoulder bag and hurried to meet him.

"When I stopped by the clinic, they told me you wouldn't be in this week, so I figured I would find you here at your grandfather's house. I hope you don't mind my dropping in on you unannounced," Patrice apologized.

Alan shook his head. "Not at all. I could use some company. I had planned to fly up to Chicago for a medical convention this week, but of course, I've canceled the trip. I feel as if I spent most of yesterday on the phone, talking with all the well-wishers who called to ask about Granddad. Now I'm trying to find something to do with myself between visits to the hospital." His slight smile did nothing to relieve the fatigue imprinted on his face. He removed one hand from his pocket to gesture toward the garden. "I've been wandering around out here for the past hour or so, hoping it would clear my head."

"How is your grandfather doing?" Patrice asked, falling in step with Alan as he turned toward the house.

Alan's rangy shoulders rose in a helpless shrug. "They've taken him off the critical list, but his condition is still considered only fair. He's very weak, very disoriented. I ran into the sheriff at the hospital yesterday afternoon. He's eager to talk with Granddad, but needless to say, that's out of the question right now."

"Does Sheriff Wade have any leads?"

"If he does, he's not sharing them with me." Alan ran his hand through the tousled hair falling over his brow. "He said that no one in the neighborhood recalled any activity around Granddad's house on Sunday, but that's not really surprising. These houses aren't very close together, and in any case, the shrubbery is thick enough to block the driveway and sun room from view. Chances are no one would have noticed a prowler unless he just happened to walk or drive past the house at the exact time the intruder was slipping inside the house. So tell me how you've been." He sounded eager to change the subject. "Any news?"

"Sunday night after you dropped me off at home, I got in touch with my other client and asked her to try to persuade her parents to talk with me. When I told her about everything that's happened, she was really upset, and apparently, her parents were sufficiently alarmed to agree to a meeting yesterday morning. As I had suspected, my client was a gray-market baby whose adoption was arranged on the sly by a lawyer. By the time her adoptive parents became aware of any irregularities, they were too attached to her even to think of giving her up."

"Would they identify the lawyer?" Alan held open the sun room door.

Patrice nodded wearily. "Yes, but unfortunately, he's now deceased. I did a little background work, checked his legal credentials and Louisiana Bar Association affiliation. As far as I can tell, he was never involved in anything shady enough to jeopardize his career. My guess is that he fell into the role of adoption middleman as a favor to someone here in Port Latanier. Do you recall your grandfather ever mentioning a man named Ben Kenyon?''

"No, I'm afraid not." Alan shook his head as he paused to latch the door behind them. "In fact, I've never heard of any Kenyons around here."

"Your grandfather isn't the only possible connection, of course. It occurred to me that Kenyon could have mediated the adoption for a colleague in Port Latanier, so I spent yesterday afternoon setting traps for the lawyers here in town."

Alan chuckled. "That sounds interesting. Mind if I ask about the details, or would that involve your revealing trade secrets?"

"Not at all. It was actually very mundane business. Thank heaven, Port Latanier has only five practicing attorneys. I phoned each office and left a message for the lawyer to call me back. When they did, I simply introduced myself as someone for whom Ben Kenyon had done a special favor a few years back and asked if the same kind of arrangement would be possible now. My intuition isn't infallible, but I'm pretty good at gauging people's reactions. I'm almost certain that none of the lawyers I talked with had ever heard of Ben Kenyon."

"So it's back to square one?"

Patrice's face was chagrined. "Let's just say that I need some inspiration."

Alan gave her shoulder a sympathetic pat. "I don't have much to offer in that department, but I'll be glad to brew a fresh pot of coffee if you'll help me drink it."

"Sure. I'll even drink the burned stuff. It's what I'm used to in my office."

Patrice followed Alan to the kitchen. She posted herself in the doorway while he filled the coffeemaker well with fresh water and measured ground coffee into the basket. Simply watching him perform the homey task helped restore her sense of well-being, planted her feet more firmly on the ground, if only for a brief time. Alan was such a comfortable person to be around, it was a shame they had met under such crazy circumstances. Patrice abruptly checked her thoughts before they rambled too far into uncharted emotional territory.

Alan flipped the brew switch and then ushered Patrice into the breakfast nook. She seated herself at the small table while he selected two mugs from the china hutch. "You know, assuming Kenyon's contact in Port Latanier was a lawyer, there's always the possibility that he's retired or dead, too."

"I've thought of that," Patrice agreed glumly. "Do you have anyone in particular in mind?"

Alan placed the mugs on the table and then sank onto the chair opposite Patrice. "I know Granddad was friends with an attorney named Leon Reed."

"Reed. For some reason, that name sounds familiar." Patrice frowned, probing her cluttered mind for a moment. "Now I remember. I ran across the Reeds when I was poring over back issues of the newspaper. Wasn't Leon Reed's daughter murdered?"

"Now that you mention it, I do remember Granddad talking as if Leon had suffered some great tragedy in his life. Reed was a couple of years younger than Granddad, but they were childhood friends, even belonged to the same fraternity when they went to Tulane back in the thirties."

"Did Leon Reed have a partner or associate who might help us connect him with Kenyon?"

"I don't know," Alan confessed. "To be honest, Patrice, you probably know almost as much about folks in Port Latanier as I do. You see, I grew up in New Orleans. I saw Granddad regularly, of course, but I didn't really spend that much time down here until I was practically in my teens. After Dad died, Granddad did everything he could to fill the void. I used to stay with him almost the entire summer." Alan broke off abruptly, signaling that he had wandered into an emotional mine field he was ill-prepared to negotiate at the moment. "That coffee should be ready." Snatching up the mugs, he rose and hurried into the kitchen.

Patrice gazed out the window at the garden, now overgrown with ivy and periwinkle, and tried to imagine how it must have looked twenty years ago. She visualized Alan and his grandfather sharing Saturday afternoon chores in the yard, clipping shrubs and mowing the thick carpet of Bermuda grass. Alan had probably been tall for his age, with the natural grace of youth relieving his boyishly slender form of any awkwardness. Dr. Hamilton's hair would have shown only a little gray then, and age would not yet have robbed his movements of vigor and confidence.

Patrice had not realized until today that Dr. Hamilton had been a surrogate father to Alan, filling the same role that her father provided for Alex. Little wonder that Alan had been so adamant about shielding his grandfather from unwanted probing, was now devastated by the elderly man's precarious condition. Closing her eyes, Patrice offered a silent prayer that Dr. Hamilton would survive the vicious attempt on his life.

She looked up when Alan returned bearing the two steaming mugs. He slid one in front of Patrice before reclaiming his seat across from her.

"I have an idea," Alan announced.

"Great, because my mind has shut down—temporarily, I hope. Let's hear it."

Alan took a cautious sip of the scalding coffee. "I think we can be pretty sure that Ben Kenyon isn't a native of Port Latanier. What if Leon Reed and he met while they were students, either at Tulane or in law school? Most of my close friendships developed while I was in college. Maybe..." When Patrice continued to frown, he broke off and lifted his hand in a careless gesture. "Okay, I know it's probably a long shot, but why not give it a try? I'll even do the dirty work. Did you find out where Kenyon got his law degree?"

"Emory." Amusement played on Patrice's face as she watched Alan take a quick gulp of coffee and then push away from the table.

"That's all I need." Alan gave her a wry smile on his way to the kitchen. He returned before Patrice had finished her coffee.

"Bingo." Alan looked immensely pleased with himself as he slid onto the chair across from her. "The Emory University School of Law alumni office had never heard of Leon Reed, but..." His pause was obviously calculated for maximum effect. "Ben Kenyon was a member of Tulane University's class of '37, along with Leon Reed. We've found the connection."

"You found it," Patrice corrected, giving him an appreciative smile. "We're still missing a lot of pieces of the puzzle, but those we have are starting to fit together." She leaned back in her chair, trying to envision a likely scenario. "Your grandfather and Leon Reed were old friends, not just buddies but men who could trust each other when a scandal threatened someone close to one of them. Dr. Hamilton kept secret the infant's delivery. Afterward, Reed turned to his classmate, Ben Kenyon, to place the baby privately, without any embarrassing fanfare. Everything appeared to be going well, but then something happened. For some reason, they were unable to get the mother to surrender her claim to the child. Who was Cassandra Guidry and what made her ultimately balk at giving up the baby?"

Alan toyed with the handle of his empty mug. "If we could answer those last two questions, none of the others would matter."

"Do you know if Leon Reed has any survivors?"

Alan scooted down in the chair, stretching his long legs to one side of the table. "One daughter, Julia. I don't know her well, but she occasionally dropped by to visit Granddad when he was recovering from surgery. As I understand, she's widowed and pretty much keeps to herself."

"I wonder if Julia would remember Cassandra Guidry," Patrice mused aloud, dropping a shamelessly pointed hint.

Alan smiled. "I've inferred from Granddad that Julia Broussard places an awfully high premium on social standing. She sounds like the type who would clam up at the first whiff of scandal."

"All these nice, safe secrets." Patrice sighed, circling the coffee mug with both hands. "Two of the principals that we know of are dead, and none of the living is willing to talk."

Alan stared out the window at the pair of mockingbirds shuttling nest material into a thick holly bush. "Have you tried the cemetery?"

Patrice raised an eyebrow, regarding Alan with skeptical amusement. "Granted, I'm good at shaking information out of unwilling subjects, but don't you think that's going a bit far?"

"I wasn't joking," Alan explained patiently. "We've been operating on the assumption that Cassandra Guidry was a local woman, but think about it. All we really know is that Granddad delivered her baby. What if she lived in another town, but was related to someone here in Port Latanier? When she discovered the unwanted pregnancy, she might have turned to a sympathetic relative for help. Having the child here would also have minimized the risk of word getting around her own hometown. It might be a waste of time, but we could stroll through the cemetery and look for Guidrys who had married into local families."

Patrice waved aside Alan's disclaimer. "No, actually I think it's a good idea." As she collected the empty coffee mugs, she cut a sly glance at Alan. "You know, you just might have a knack for investigative work. Here I spend half a day playing phone games with lawyers, and in less than five minutes you manage to connect Ben Kenyon with a prominent attorney in Port Latanier."

"Amateur's luck," Alan scoffed. He rose and collected the coffee mugs, linking one finger through both handles.

"Where luck is concerned, I'm not one to quibble over the brand," Patrice remarked. She cut her eyes at the hand Alan had rested on her shoulder, wondering why she was so acutely aware of its warmth and pressure. *As if nothing stood between those strong, tapering fingers and her bare skin.* Patrice quickly checked her wayward imagination and stood up. "We need to get going." She offered the reminder to herself as much as to Alan.

Taking Patrice's cue, Alan quickly secured the windows, grabbed his keys from the kitchen counter and then led the way out of the house. After Patrice had locked her briefcase inside the trunk of her car, they climbed into Alan's Saab.

They followed the two-lane county road out of town. Gradually the tree-shaded frontiers between houses grew wider, the mailboxes mounted along the blacktop fewer. When Alan turned onto an unpaved road, the bayou seemed to close around them like a living curtain. Distant cries carried through the veil of Spanish moss, mysterious and unplaceable within the dense marsh. The cemetery appeared without warning, an island of marble and stone in the surrounding bayou. At first sight, the deserted graveyard reminded Patrice of an ancient city, its faded white remains laid bare by the archaeologist's spade.

Alan eased the convertible onto the side of the road and cut the engine. "This is actually the newest part of the cemetery near the road. We'll have to do some walking to get to the older family plots."

Patrice was already climbing out of the car. "Lead the way."

They scrambled up a gentle slope to the gate breaching the rusting wrought-iron fence. Although not apparent from the road, a network of narrow paths threaded through the cemetery. Patrice and Alan followed one of the wider lanes, scanning the headstones and monuments until they reached an imposing mausoleum with the name 'Reed' engraved on the lintel over its door.

Patrice peered through the window cut in the corroded iron door, squinting into the gloom while one hand searched her shoulder bag for the small flashlight she always carried. Snapping on the light, she slowly raked the beam across the rows of tombs.

Alan hovered behind her, one hand resting lightly on her shoulder. "Can you see?"

"Yeah, just fine. 'Matthews. Lescaux. Demarest. Johnson. Millau,'" she read aloud the maiden names of the Reed wives interred in the mausoleum. Patrice shook her head as she flicked off the flashlight. "If any Guidrys married into the Reed clan, they're buried somewhere else."

Shoving his hands into his pockets, Alan shrugged philosophically. "The Reeds are just one family. Let's keep looking, at least until we've checked the more influential families who would have been likely to turn to Leon for help."

"Don't worry. I'm nowhere near quitting," Patrice assured him with a determined smile.

As they continued their inspection of the mausoleums, Patrice was grateful to have Alan with her. With both of them examining markers, the rather morbid task went much faster. Then, too, the isolated cemetery was not a place she would have relished spending time alone. After the suspected murder attempt only two days earlier, Patrice had tempered her normally intrepid spirit with a good dose of caution.

Patrice was picking her way through a thicket of ground creeper when Alan called to her from the adjacent plot. "I've found the Hamilton plot."

"You've never seen it before?" Patrice asked as she joined him in the weed-choked yard surrounding the mausoleum.

"Oh, sure I have, but that must have been at least twenty years ago. I came out a couple of times with Granddad during those summers I spent with him as a kid. He liked to put flowers here on Grandma's birthday." A sad expression, elusive as a shadow, drifted across Alan's handsome face as he stared at the silent marble statue of an archangel guarding the tombs. He forced a brief smile. "I don't have any Guidry cousins that I know of, but it won't hurt to check while we're here."

Patrice placed a comforting hand against his back. "I'll take a look in the mausoleum with my flashlight. Then maybe we ought to head back to town." Patrice gestured toward the few moldering chunks of marble dotting the field before them. "None of those tombs looks recent enough to have any bearing on our case."

"You're probably right, but I'll have a quick look anyway," Alan volunteered. He eased through an opening in the iron picket fence encircling the Hamilton plot as Patrice turned to the mausoleum.

Patrice switched on the flashlight and began to scan the engraved plaques. Her lips shaped the names as the light traveled over each narrow rectangle. As she shifted the beam to the bottom tier of tombs, she started, almost dropping the flashlight.

"Cassandra Guidry Hamilton." Patrice repeated the name out loud to convince herself that her eyes had not deceived her. She stepped back from the mausoleum door to wave frantically to Alan. "Alan! Come here!"

Alan loped between the crumbling monuments and swung over the low fence. "What is it?" he demanded.

"I've found Cassandra Guidry!"

"In the Hamilton mausoleum?" Alan gaped in disbelief.

"Look!" Patrice channeled the flashlight beam through the window. "See? Right there, lower left corner."

The two of them crowded in front of the door to examine the marker more closely. "'Cassandra Guidry Hamilton.'" An excited hush damped Alan's voice. "'Born May 8, 1823. Died December 27, 1858. She will live forever in the hearts of her loved ones.'"

"My God, she died almost one hundred and fifty years ago!" Patrice gasped under her breath. She silently read the inscription again before flicking off the light and turning to Alan. "What was her name doing on the baptismal record of a child born in 1967?"

Arms folded across his chest, Alan frowned. "Maybe by some bizarre coincidence the mother had the same name as one of my ancestors, but more likely..."

"Your grandfather chose the name to conceal the mother's true identity," Patrice supplied.

Alan exhaled slowly. "I can't think of another explanation that comes even close to making sense. Who were they trying to protect?" His dark eyes connected with Patrice's gaze, adding their own puzzled query to the question.

"I want to talk with Julia Broussard, Alan." Seeing the dubious look in Alan's eyes, Patrice hastened to strengthen her point. "Look, I know you think she's not going to cooperate, but your grandfather and my other client's parents didn't want to talk at first, either. Maybe when Julia realizes what's at stake, she'll be willing to talk about her father. The alternative is to keep chasing phantoms."

Alan needed only a second to consider Patrice's argument. "Let's give it a shot, then."

They hurried back along the path to the cemetery gate. While Alan piloted the convertible over the rutted dirt road, Patrice mulled over the fragmented clues her investigation had so far netted. Little doubt now remained that Leon Reed and Dr. Hamilton had contrived to conceal the identity of Anne-Marie's mother. Patrice pondered the array of possible motives for their conspiracy.

Could Anne-Marie have been the result of a youthful indiscretion on Julia Broussard's part? Or perhaps a close friend or cousin of Julia was the mother? Then again, Anne-Marie's mother could have been a girl of little social standing whose clandestine affair with a prominent man threatened to become public. Patrice tried to imagine the anxious father-to-be appealing to his trusted friends, Leon and Alphonse, to protect his reputation and quietly place the infant who would never bear his name. Leon Reed himself could have been the father, for that matter. Or Dr. Alphonse Hamilton.

At the latter thought, Patrice glanced at the all-too-appealing man sitting next to her in the car, his handsome face set in concentration as he sped along the narrow county road. In her business, Patrice had never shrunk from facing the truth, regardless of how unpleasant it might be, and she would not allow the comfortable camaraderie developing between Alan and her to cloud her judgment. At the same time, she hoped with all her heart that her investigation would do nothing to diminish Alan's respect and admiration for his grandfather.

When they reached town, Alan slowed the Saab in accordance with Port Latanier's leisurely speed limit. "Should we call first?" he asked, gesturing toward the car phone.

Patrice shook her head. "Miss Manners might not approve, but I'd rather not give Julia a chance to evade us."

"You're the boss." Alan smiled slightly as he turned into a broad street shaded by ancient magnolia trees. He shifted down, leaning forward to survey the stately antebellum homes dotting the landscape like discarded chunks of wedding cake. As Alan braked in front of the last house on the block, he nodded toward a middle-aged black woman unloading shopping bags from the Mercedes parked in the driveway. "Looks like we're in luck."

Patrice and Alan were climbing out of the car when a tall woman appeared on the other side of the Mercedes sedan.

"Good afternoon, Julia," Alan called in greeting.

"Hello, Alan. What a pleasant surprise!" Julia's smile was stiff, in part, Patrice suspected, due to an overly generous application of makeup. "I heard about your grandfather's awful accident. I do hope he's improving," she went on, but her sharply defined dark eyes were trained straight on Patrice.

"Granddad is holding his own," Alan told her. "Julia, I'd like you to meet Patrice Ribeau. Patrice, this is Julia Broussard."

When Patrice offered her hand, Julia waited a brief but noticeable interval before shaking it, as if she were afraid Patrice might have a buzzer concealed in her palm. Her hand felt stiff as a mannequin's and not much warmer. In fact, from the severe line of her dark hair, swept back into a tight little knot, to the close-fitting tailored suit she wore like a coat of armor, everything about Julia Broussard seemed constrained.

"Patrice is an investigator I've hired to find out who planted a poisonous snake in Granddad's sun room," Alan went on.

"Oh, my God!" Julia's face contorted in horror, threatening to crack its alabaster mask. "You can't mean that someone deliberately tried to harm your grandfather!"

"I'm afraid it looks that way," Alan explained calmly.

"But who on earth would want to do such a dreadful thing?" Julia's hand clawed at the rope of pearls knotted on her breast.

"That's what I'm trying to find out," Patrice put in. "Maybe you can help us, Mrs. Broussard. Did your father ever mention helping someone place a child for adoption? This would have been in 1967."

Julia's flawlessly manicured fingers plied the tiny quilted-leather handbag hanging from her shoulder. "Oh, my goodness, that was a long time ago."

When Julia's eyes darted to the house, Patrice indulged in a little private gloating. She had seen that look too often to mistake its intent, the hallmark of a witness who desperately wishes to be somewhere else. For the first time in this frustrating investigation, Patrice was pleased to have the cards fall in her favor. She had Julia Broussard right where she wanted her, too far from her house to barricade herself in, not close enough to her car to flee.

"Try to think. It's very important." Patrice offered patient encouragement.

Julia drew a deep breath. "No, I don't recall his mentioning anything of the sort. But then, my father didn't often discuss his business with me."

"Does the name Cassandra Guidry mean anything to you?"

"No, nothing." When Julia shook her head, Patrice could almost imagine the taut sinews of her neck squeaking with the effort. "I'm afraid I'm not being much help."

No, you're not, lady, Patrice thought. She was still not sure how much Julia Broussard knew, but her reaction to

Patrice's questions had made one thing clear: she was being less than candid.

When a uniformed woman emerged on the side porch, Julia's eyes drifted to the house once more. "I hope you'll excuse me, but I'm rather busy this afternoon. Perhaps we can arrange to talk some other time. Although I'm not sure I'll be able to furnish any useful information, I'd certainly be willing to try," Julia offered in what had to be one of the most transparent lies Patrice had ever heard.

"Thank you, Mrs. Broussard. You'll be hearing from me," Patrice promised with a saccharine smile as phony as Julia's.

"Thanks, Julia," Alan chimed.

"Certainly. And please do let me know how your grandfather is doing." Before her visitors had even reached the curb, Julia turned on her heel and headed for the house.

"Shall I put the flat of begonias in the greenhouse or leave them on the porch?" the other woman called after her.

"I don't care where you put them, Bernice," Julia snapped without looking back.

Patrice halted in her tracks and pivoted. Jogging back up the driveway, she overtook the woman carrying the tray of plants. "Excuse me, but may I ask your name?" Catching the surprise registered in the woman's expressive dark eyes, she smiled. "Somehow I have the feeling I've met you before."

"Bernice Wood."

"Bernice!" Julia's voice carried from the enclosed porch. "Can you please lend me a hand?"

As Bernice Wood sidled toward the house, Patrice smiled once more. "Thanks."

She dashed back to the car and scrambled into the passenger seat. "Did you hear that? That woman who works for Julia is named Bernice!" Patrice smacked the dashboard in exultation.

"Bernice Lacourier?" Alan asked as he cranked the engine.

"No, Bernice Wood, but I'm guessing that's her married name. Unfortunately, Julia shooed her back into the house before I had a chance to ask. She looks to be in her fifties, so she was definitely an adult in 1967."

"It sounds like we need to talk with that lady again, when Julia's not around."

"My thoughts exactly." Patrice slumped comfortably down into the seat. "You know, Alan, I have this *feeling* that it's all starting to come together."

"I hope you're right."

When they reached Dr. Hamilton's house, Patrice checked her watch. For some reason, she felt none of her usual eagerness to return home once the day's investigative work was complete.

"Time to head back to New Orleans and pick up Alex?" Alan guessed with a smile.

"Actually, I was planning on stopping by the hospital to see how your grandfather is doing," Patrice admitted.

"Good, you can come with me."

As Alan reached for the ignition, Patrice intercepted his hand. Just as quickly, she released it. "*You* can come with *me,*" she corrected, climbing out of the car. "I'll drop you back by the house afterward. It's on my way out of town anyway."

While Alan locked his car, Patrice slid behind the wheel of the Accord. She drove fast but carefully, concentrating on the road to take her mind off the man sitting on the other side of the console. Why was she so damned conscious of every little brush with Alan? In this day and age, touching someone's hand was about as neutral as saying hello, certainly not something to release tingles in a thirty-two-year-old woman. *You're hopelessly attracted to him,* an exasperated voice inside her intoned. *With* hopeless *being the operative word.*

Patrice cut a surreptitious glance at Alan. His face wore a solemn expression that was probably far more indicative of his mood than the smiles and gentle ribbing he often fostered to lighten the moment. Dr. Hamilton was foremost in Alan's mind, and rightfully so. Patrice would never stoop so low as to begrudge the ailing man his grandson's attention. At the same time, she resisted a related and equally incontrovertible fact: Dr. Hamilton was the *only* basis for Alan's relationship with her. Regardless of how attractive Patrice found Alan, he was, in the final analysis, a client who had sought her out to do a job for him, and nothing more.

"A penny for your thoughts." Alan shifted slightly in his seat to look at her.

Patrice kept her eyes fixed on the white stripe racing past. "I was just thinking about the case," she hedged. "Oh!" She started as a squirrel darted directly into the path of the car.

Keeping a firm hold on the wheel, Patrice tapped the brake pedal lightly and attempted to circumvent the little animal. Her stomach lurched when the brakes failed to respond.

"Slow down, for God's sake!" Alan's voice registered alarm.

"I can't! The brakes are gone!"

Patrice shifted down and frantically pumped the brake pedal. A cold, sinking feeling washed over her when she spotted a tractor-trailor rig pulling into the road only a short distance ahead of them. Locking her fingers around the wheel in a death grip, Patrice swerved onto the shoulder.

A bone-deep jolt shuddered through her as the car crashed into a stand of trees. The sound of impact filled her ears, violent and sudden. Patrice's body was hurled forward, then back inside the shoulder harness like a rag puppet on a string. Pain exploded inside her head, followed by a clammy blackness that blotted out everything.

Chapter Ten

Alan grabbed a gulp of air, for a moment stunned by the silence that followed the violent impact. Twisting free of the shoulder harness, he turned to Patrice. She was slumped against the car door, a dazed expression lodged in her half-closed eyes. A thin trickle of blood oozed from a gash on her left temple.

"Patrice!" Alan released her seat belt and then checked her pulse. "Take it easy. You're going to be okay." He watched her try to focus, to fight the weight dragging her eyelids shut. "Come on, honey. Let's get you out of here."

Cradling her limp body against his chest, Alan tested the driver's door and found it jammed. He shoved the passenger door open and then lifted Patrice over the console as gently as possible, backing carefully out of the car. Leaking fuel was a threat in any serious automobile crash, and although Alan didn't smell gasoline, he was unwilling to take any chances. The sooner they put some distance between themselves and the wrecked car, the better.

Alan spied the truck driver running along the shoulder toward them. The husky fellow frowned when he caught sight of Patrice lying motionless in Alan's arms. "Is she hurt bad?"

"Call an ambulance and the police on the double."

The driver was already jogging backward toward his semi. "I got a CB in my truck."

Alan carefully laid her down on the grass. Patrice moaned softly. "What...oh..." Her hand faltered as it tried to paw the head wound. "Is that blood?"

"You got a nasty cut where you smacked the side of your head. That's why you passed out for a few minutes. That's all." Alan adopted the calm, reassuring voice that he often used to allay his young patients' apprehension.

"Actually, I don't feel too bad. I just need to get my bearings." As if to prove her point, Patrice made a feeble attempt to sit up. She blinked uncertainly and swayed to one side, signaling that she was about to faint again.

Alan caught her shoulders and eased her gently onto her back. Although he had not noticed any signs of fractured bones or spinal injury, he knew that Patrice had, at the very least, suffered a mild concussion. He needed to keep her quiet until the emergency team arrived. "Just lie still, honey. The ambulance is going to be here any minute now."

Patrice grimaced. "I don't want to go to the hospital."

"If you did, you'd be the first I've run into." Alan chuckled softly. He clasped her hand, stroking the back of it with his thumb. "I'm here with you, okay?"

Patrice's fingers curled inside his grasp. "I'm glad," she murmured. "Are you hurt?" She tried to lift her head, but Alan quickly placed a hand on her cheek, holding her steady.

"I don't have a scratch," he assured her.

"Lucky dog." Patrice attempted a grin. "Is that the ambulance?" Her dark eyes shifted in the direction of the wailing siren.

"It sure is. They're going to have you patched up in no time flat." Alan squeezed her hand, thinking how small and vulnerable it felt inside his own.

Only seconds after the emergency vehicle had pulled onto the shoulder, a team of medics sprang into action. For the second time in less than three days, Alan stood by while a rescue team performed a preliminary assessment of injuries and then immobilized the injured patient on a gurney. As the crew rushed Patrice to the waiting vehicle, Alan walked alongside the gurney, holding fast to her hand.

"I need you to do a couple of things for me, Alan." Patrice's hand twisted inside Alan's to clasp his wrist.

"Anything."

"Call Dad and ask him to look after Alex. Alex was going home with a friend after school to work on a science project. He's planning to have supper with Joey, but I'm supposed to pick him up around eight. Dad can find Joey's phone number and address on the magnetic pad I keep on the fridge." Patrice was beginning to sound like her old self, competently juggling the demands of her busy life. "Whatever you do, don't tell Dad about the brake failure. Just say I had an accident when I swerved to avoid hitting a truck."

"Don't worry. I won't alarm him." Without thinking, Alan reached to caress her brow, lightly brushing the loose curls away from the livid gash. When he bent over the gurney, a sudden and almost overpowering impulse to kiss the pale, damp cheek swept over him. "As soon as I fill the sheriff in on the accident, I'll come to the hospital," he promised.

"Wait! There's one other thing." Patrice clung to his wrist as two of the medics hoisted the gurney into the back of the van. "Get my briefcase out of the car's trunk and bring it to the hospital."

"I will." Alan felt the slim fingers reluctantly loosen their hold and then slide out of his grasp.

He watched a medic secure the van's rear door, sealing Patrice away from his view. The siren flared once more as the emergency van sped away.

"'Afternoon, Doc. You want to tell me what happened here?"

Alan wheeled to see Sheriff Wade ambling away from the wreck toward him. The sheriff removed his Stetson, adjusting the hat band as he listened to Alan's account of the accident.

"You say the brakes just gave out?" The sheriff's stubby fingers carefully shaped the Stetson's crown.

"Without any warning." Alan paused. "I think there's a chance someone tampered with them."

Sheriff Wade frowned, thoughtfully scratching behind one ear before settling his hat onto his head once more. "Tell you what," he said at length. "I'll have 'em tow the car to headquarters and then get one of our boys to look it over."

"Thanks, Sheriff."

"Don't thank me, Doc. If some heathen's fooled with those brakes, I'm going to do my damnedest to see his carcass rot in jail. Somebody could have gotten killed today." In the shadow of the hat's wide brim, Sheriff Wade's face was grim. "Come on, I'll give you a ride."

"Give me a second to fetch Patrice's handbag." Alan walked back to the mangled car.

A burly fellow with a mane of jet black hair was sizing up the battered car, trying to determine where best to attach the tow truck's hook. Alan nodded to him, wrenched open the passenger door and plucked Patrice's keys out of the ignition. He grabbed the shoulder bag lying on the floor and then hurried around the car. Fortunately, the rear of the Accord had not been damaged in the accident, and the trunk opened easily. Alan removed the cordovan leather briefcase before dashing back to Sheriff Wade's cruiser.

For most of the short drive to the county hospital, Sheriff Wade was occupied with the garbled dispatches coming from the police radio, leaving Alan to stare out the window at the blurred landscape racing past. *Somebody could have gotten killed.* The sheriff's sobering reminder echoed through Alan's mind. When he had ministered to Patrice on the roadside, Alan had relied on the calm, sure manner he had cultivated as a physician to reassure her. As he now considered the terrible possibility of what might have been, however, he felt none of his usual confidence in the face of a crisis, only a disquieting apprehension.

Sheriff Wade halted the cruiser in front of the emergency room entrance. "You tell Ms. Ribeau I want to talk with her when she's feelin' up to it." He nicked the brim of his hat in parting. "Take care now, Doc."

"Thanks, Sheriff." Alan managed a smile, but even the sheriff's harmless cliché had carried an ominous ring.

Eager as Alan was to check on Patrice's condition, he first headed for the pay phone mounted in the corridor outside the waiting room. Bracing the briefcase between his ankles, Alan called information and then dialed Tony Lafon's number in New Orleans. When the slightly gruff voice answered, Alan breathed a sigh of relief. He gave the retired police detective a brief account of the accident, taking care to omit any details that might cause alarm. After promising him that Patrice would phone later, Alan hung up and hurried to the waiting room. The nurse staffing the admission desk informed him that Patrice had been taken to Radiology and suggested he have a seat. Alan was trying to distract himself with an ancient issue of *Sports Illustrated* when Patrice pushed through the swinging doors over an hour later.

Tossing the magazine aside, Alan jumped to his feet. "How are you feeling?"

"A whole lot better now that I'm on my feet again. Let's get out of here."

Alan's gaze traveled uncertainly from the large gauze patch taped to her temple to the cervical collar encircling her neck. "Have you been discharged?"

"Yes, I have," Patrice told him with undisguised impatience. "Look, I've been arguing with doctors since I got here. Please don't make me wrangle with yet another one." Her frown loosened into a smile, and she gave his arm a gentle nudge. "They poked and prodded and x-rayed me, but except for a mild concussion and a few bruises, the verdict is that I'm none the worse for wear. Come on." She shoved through the door, leaving Alan no choice but to follow.

As they walked to the exit, Alan filled Patrice in on his activities while she had been hospitalized.

"Thanks for calling Dad." Patrice gave him a grateful smile.

"He's concerned, of course, but I gave him absolutely no indication of any foul play." Alan swallowed, not liking the taste of the sinister phrase.

Patrice sobered. "It was no accident that those brakes failed. My car is only two years old, and I've been religious about maintenance."

"I'm anxious to hear what the police find after they examine the car." Alan held the door for Patrice. "Wait here while I get a cab." As he turned toward the lone Chevrolet sedan parked near the loading zone, Patrice caught his elbow.

"Hold on a second. Let's talk about what we ought to do first."

Alan gave her a puzzled look. "We don't have much choice but to take a cab to Granddad's place. You can call your father from the house, let him know you're okay, and then I'll drive you back to New Orleans."

Patrice frowned. "I don't know if that's such a good idea, Alan. Maybe I'm getting paranoid, but after what happened today, I don't think you should drive your car until a reliable mechanic has given it a thorough inspection. The person who tampered with my brakes while it was parked at your grandfather's house could just as easily have sabotaged your car since we've been gone." The tense edge in Patrice's voice was thrown into relief against the still night air. "We don't know who this guy is, but he seems to be doing a pretty good job of keeping tabs on our activity."

"By that token, he could be just about anybody in Port Latanier," Alan commented with a mirthless chuckle. "In a small town, everyone makes it his business to know what you had for breakfast."

"Precisely why we ought to keep as low a profile as possible and minimize his chances of pulling any more surprises, at least for tonight."

"You've got a point," Alan agreed reluctantly. Knuckling under to intimidation went directly against his grain, but only a fool would ignore the seriousness of the threat recently aimed at them. "Any suggestions on what we should do in the meantime?"

Patrice took a deep breath and thought for a moment. "It's going to be obvious if we go to your grandfather's house. We've already ruled out driving your car, and even if we hadn't, we'd be sitting ducks on that long, lonely stretch of road back to the highway." Patrice motioned Alan toward the taxi stand. "I noticed a motel near the bypass exit when I followed you here Sunday. Unless we're dealing with a psychic, that's the last place anyone would expect us to hole up for the night. In the morning at least we'll have daylight on our side."

"Sounds fine with me. I've had enough surprises for one day," Alan remarked as he followed Patrice to the taxi.

The cabby folded the newspaper he had been reading and twisted in his seat to greet them. "Where to, folks?"

Alan braced one hand against the back of the seat. "The Blue Bird Inn. Do you know where it is?"

The cabby winked into the rearview mirror. "I sure 'nough do."

As the cab lurched away from the curb, Alan caught the faint smile playing on Patrice's lips, and he chuckled under his breath. If the grim situation in which they now found themselves afforded any humor, best to appreciate it while they could.

The motel's sign was easy to spot from the road, an obese neon bird with a stocking cap perched incongruously on its head. Thanks to some flaw in the electrical circuitry, spastic jerks afflicted its extended wings, and a portion of the tail feathers occasionally vanished into the dark sky. After turning into the driveway, the cabby cruised past the two-story block of rooms to brake in front of the office. Alan paid the driver while Patrice collected her briefcase and bag and then waited on the curb.

The office was deserted, but the sound of televised gunfire carried from a sitting room visible behind the desk. Patrice tapped the bell next to the register, and a stoop-shouldered man appeared in the doorway.

"Evenin'." The man pulled up his drooping suspenders as he ambled to the desk. "Can I help you?"

"We'd like to book a room." Alan caught himself and glanced at Patrice. "Actually, I guess we'd like two rooms, wouldn't we?"

The night clerk eyed them dubiously before turning to the row of hooks and selecting two keys. "Here you are. 12-A and 20-B."

Patrice frowned at the keys lying on the desk. "You don't have two that are adjacent?"

"No, ma'am. Y'see, what with that big fishin' tournament and the azalea festival..."

Patrice broke in. "We'll just take one room, then." Seizing the 12-A key, she turned to Alan. "Now don't you worry about my head, sweetheart. I'm sure the room has two beds. Doesn't it?" She looked back at the clerk.

"Yes'm. Two doubles. One of 'em will even shimmy if you put a quarter in it." The clerk patiently returned the extra key to its hook and then reached for the guest book.

Alan watched in respectful silence while Patrice registered Mr. and Mrs. Lawrence Scott of Baton Rouge, Louisiana. When she had completed the brief form, he took the cue to dig out his wallet and pay for the room with cash in advance.

"Y'all need any help with your luggage?" the night clerk asked as he thumbed through the bills Alan had handed him.

"Thank you, but we can manage just fine," Patrice assured him.

They hurried out of the office and across the parking
lot, not slowing their pace until they had reached the door
with 12-A emblazoned on it. The room smelled of chemical air freshener with a pronounced whiff of stale tobacco smoke. Alan drew the drapes before turning on the
lights.

"Ugh!" Patrice grimaced as she caught sight of herself in the dresser mirror. "No wonder that man at the
desk kept giving me weird looks."

"In this place, I'm sure he's seen worse than a head
bandage and a cervical collar," Alan remarked dryly.
"I'd say you don't look half-bad for someone who's just
come out of an emergency room."

Alan clasped her shoulders, lightly plying the tight
muscles with his fingers. When Patrice sighed, his hands
increased their pressure in response. His thumbs slid beneath her sweater's wide neckline, flirting for a moment
with the warm skin. A wave of heat, as intense as it was
sudden, rushed through Alan, a potent physical reminder of the intimate situation into which fate had
thrust them.

Patrice smiled self-consciously as she sank onto the
edge of one of the beds. "I guess I'd better get in touch
with my insurance agent and then call Dad."

"Good idea. If you don't mind, I'm going to take a
shower." *A cold one, if I know what's good for me,* Alan
added to himself.

"Save me a dry towel," Patrice called after him as she
reached for the phone.

Alan closed the bathroom door and then quickly
shucked his clothes. As he adjusted the shower's weak
spray, he mused over life's bizarre turns. Less than a week
ago, he had expected to pass this night in the Chicago
Hilton after a day of attending discussion panels on chil-

ren's health-care issues. Never in his wildest imaginings would he have guessed he would spend it in the Blue Bird Inn, registered under a phony name with Patrice Rideau.

When he cut the tap, Alan could hear Patrice talking through the cardboard-thin wall.

"Honestly, Dad, I'm just fine." Patrice paused. "It's a school night. If you drive down here to get me, that means Alex will be up way past his bedtime. Trust me, I can stand a motel room for one night. Besides, I still have a lot of work to do down here, and this will give me an early start tomorrow." Another brief interval, and she went on. "Okay, put Alex on again. Oh, and Dad, you know what Santa can bring me for Christmas this year." She laughed. "Well, a Mercedes would be nice. Hey, kiddo." Her voice softened, indicating that her son was on the line. "Just want to wish you good-night again. I love you, too."

When Alan realized that he was toweling his hair slowly in order to follow Patrice's side of the conversation, he felt both embarrassed and guilty. He had not intentionally eavesdropped on her. More than anything, he had simply been captivated by the shifting mood of her voice as she reassured her father and gave her son affection. Listening to her soft laughter and the palpable warmth in her voice, he had to remind himself that this woman was also a hard-nosed professional who could finesse a bogus motel registration and make Julia Broussard squirm in her Guccis.

Tenderness and strength were not mutually exclusive traits, of course, but Alan had never known anyone who demonstrated both in quite the way Patrice did. He wondered what her husband had been like, what sort of marriage they had. Alan abruptly pulled the curtain on that line of thought while he still could. It was going to be hard enough spending the night in the same room with her without egging on his imagination.

Alan toweled himself briskly and then dressed. When he returned to the room, he found Patrice lying propped on two pillows, arms stretched limply at her sides.

"How do you feel?" Resting one knee on the foot of the bed, Alan smiled down at her.

"Like I've gotten the worst of a confrontation with a steamroller. I didn't know the human body had so many muscles until all of mine started to ache. My eyes feel like boiled grapes, and this dumb collar is hot and scratchy. Since I haven't eaten since eight this morning, I'm famished. Other than that, I feel terrific."

Alan playfully wiggled her left foot. "Let's work on the hunger first. I could use something to eat, too." He glanced at the phone resting on the nightstand between the two beds. "I don't suppose this place has room service?"

Patrice chuckled. "'Fraid not. I did notice a soft-drink machine when we were looking for the room. Maybe there's a snack dispenser, too."

"I'll forage and see what I can find," Alan said. When Patrice started to sit up, he motioned her back. "Just lie there and quietly suffer until I get back."

Patrice sank back onto the bed, causing Alan to lose his balance for a moment. He caught himself with one knee on the edge of the bed, but not quickly enough to subvert the delicious image of his lying stretched beside her, his body sculpted to her alluring curves. Alan gazed down at Patrice. His shadow fell across her face, but her dark eyes shone with an inner fire that he had glimpsed only briefly in the past. When her full lips parted, he touched them with the tip of his finger, lightly tracing the soft, moist curve. A yearning throbbed inside him, so insistent he almost winced.

Patrice drew a deep, unsteady breath and turned her head to one side. She pushed up on her elbow and then somehow managed to climb out of the bed without touching him. "I'm going to take a shower. Don't forget to lock the door," she reminded him as she padded toward the bathroom.

Alan took a few moments to collect himself. He had come within a hairbreadth of yielding to impulse and covering Patrice Ribeau's pretty face with kisses. And for a split second, she had seemed not at all opposed to his following the urge. Still, he had learned all too well the folly of letting passion prematurely catapult two people into a relationship. He needed to watch himself tonight, or he stood a good chance of repeating a serious mistake.

Pulling the door closed behind him, Alan tested the lock and then pocketed the key. True to Patrice's prediction, two junk-food vending machines and an ice chest were tucked beneath the metal stairs leading to the second level. Alan surveyed the selection of snacks and canned drinks as he emptied his pockets of coins. He returned to the motel room with his arms laden with cans, bags and cellophane-wrapped packets. Patrice must have heard him juggling the load outside the door, for she unlocked it before he could locate the key.

"Looks like you had a successful raid." Patrice grinned as she relieved him of two bags of cheese squiggles and a package of marshmallow-filled cupcakes.

Alan dumped the remainder of his cache onto the bed. "Barbecued potato chips. Cola. Malted-milk balls. Peanut-butter crackers. It doesn't get any better than this, does it?"

"Alex would think so," Patrice commented as she popped open a can of cola. "With all the chemicals and preservatives in this stuff, we'll probably wake up mummified in the morning."

Despite their jokes, they devoured the snack food as if it were a five-course dinner at Antoine's. When they were finished, only one cupcake and a couple of cheese crackers remained. After they had cleared away the wreckage, Alan shook the crumbs from the bedspread and plumped Patrice's pillows.

"Back to bed, doctor's orders," he told her with mock severity. "I'm going to get some ice for you to put on those bruises."

With uncharacteristic docility, Patrice did as she was told. Alan located a waxed paperboard ice bucket in the bathroom alcove and then headed for the ice chest. When he returned with the ice, he found Patrice sitting cross-legged on the bed with the briefcase open in front of her. Only when he passed the bed did he notice the gun resting on her knee.

"What's that?" It was stupid question, but Alan was too startled at the moment to do any better.

"A Browning .22-caliber semiautomatic." Patrice continued loading bullets into a clip, not looking at him. When the clip was full, she carefully angled it into the slot on the bottom of the pistol's handle and gave it a firm cuff, seating it inside the slot with a dull metallic ring. "This is the main reason I wanted you to retrieve my briefcase before they towed the car."

When Patrice smiled briefly, Alan realized how stunned he must have looked. "I bought it right after I got my PI's license, and I have a permit to carry it," she explained. "Dad is a good shot, and he taught me to handle a gun. We still go to a shooting range every now and then for target practice. So far I've never had to use it to defend myself."

"You think . . . you think that's about to change?"

Patrice replaced the pistol in the briefcase and then looked up at Alan. "Someone tried to kill me today, Alan, and he wasn't overly concerned about taking you out along with me. I'm not going to take any more chances than I have to." She latched the briefcase and slid it onto the floor between the bed and the nightstand. Swinging her legs over the side of the bed, Patrice sat very still for a moment, staring at the dull green carpet.

"You know, even when I bought the gun, I never really thought about getting in this deep." Patrice's voice had dropped to a near whisper, as if she was thinking aloud. "Most of my cases are so tame, videotaping employee theft, documenting insurance fraud, catching spouses with the wrong person at the wrong time. I guess it was just a matter of time until I ran up against someone who meant business."

Without thinking, Alan sank onto the bed beside Patrice. He put his arm around her, gently rubbing her shoulder. "I don't know much about the guy who's trying to stop us, but I'm damned glad you're on my side and not his."

Patrice managed a faint smile as she reached to cover his hand on her shoulder. "You know, when I was riding in the ambulance today, I kept thinking about Alex, what it would be like for him if . . . if something happened to me. He's already lost his father." She broke off, pressing her lips together tightly.

Alan tightened his embrace, pulling her closer to him. When he felt a tremor run through her slender shoulders, he touched her cheek, guiding her face to rest against his chest. "We're going to win this one, Patrice.

I promise you we are.'' He was startled by the fervor in his voice, but as he held her in his arms, Alan realized he would risk anything to make good that vow.

His lips drifted across her hair, caressing the dark, tousled curls. When he felt her arms encircle his waist, he kissed her forehead, then her eyelids, each in turn. Patrice sighed as his mouth brushed her cheek, finally coming to rest on her soft lips. He kissed her lightly, then with more force, driven by an indescribable urge to taste and feel this marvelous woman he held in his arms. Excitement coursed through him with the intensity of an electric current when her lips parted slightly, responding to the pressure of his tongue.

Patrice abruptly drew in her breath. She lowered her chin, placing a hand against his chest to steady herself. Then she pulled back, drawing her arms slowly free of his embrace. For the first time since he had met her, Patrice Ribeau looked as if she hadn't a clue what to say.

"I didn't mean to fall apart on you like that. I guess my nerves just got the best of me." Patrice avoided his eyes as she walked to the alcove. "Thanks for getting the ice for me. My left arm is hurting like the dickens."

"Ice will help reduce the inflammation." The pedestrian textbook comment probably sounded stupid, but not half as silly as Alan felt at that moment.

For the second time in less than a week, he had let his emotions drive him to overstep the bounds of his relationship with Patrice. Had he learned nothing about rushing headlong into an emotional entanglement with a woman? Had the sobering outcome of his wild infatuation with Melissa left him no wiser than he had been as a first-year medical student, bedazzled by his beautiful, vivacious classmate? Had he forgotten the sobering lessons of an ill-matched marriage and the divorce that followed? Alan continued to castigate himself as he peeled the chenille spread off his bed and tested the rock-hard mattress.

At least Patrice didn't appear too put off by his lapse, only a little embarrassed. In fact, for a few seconds she had seemed to like it. A lot.

As he kicked off his shoes and climbed into bed, Alan studied the woman lying in bed only a few feet from him. Her back was turned to him, the ice-filled disposable shower cap balanced on her left shoulder. His eyes traveled from the bandage just visible beneath her bangs to the tangled dark locks curled over the cervical collar, and then along the silhouette of her exhausted body outlined beneath the sheet. It was hardly an image that usually stimulated male fantasies. Yet looking at Patrice evoked in Alan emotions stronger and more complex than any he had ever felt before. *Almost as if I were falling in love.*

Alan turned off the bedside lamp and then sank back onto the bed, digging his head into the lumpy pillow. "Goodnight, Patrice," he whispered. He listened for a while to her soft, even breathing before closing his eyes to join her in sleep.

JULIA CLUTCHED her arms, chafing the clammy skin beneath the thin silk dressing gown. The damp air rising from the bayou had a way of seeping through walls and clothes and flesh, as impervious to barriers as a ghost. Soon the nights would be warm and close, the air thick with the stultifying humidity of a Southern summer. For Julia, those were the worst nights of all, laden with memories that robbed her of any peace.

The old nightmares had come early this year, long before the remorseless heat had wilted the thick purple clusters of wisteria draped outside her bedroom window. The dreams had struck with such fury that Julia now dreaded the day's waning, hated the awful rite of retiring to her bedroom to pass the night, fitful and tormented, huddled in the armchair.

These days, she rarely risked climbing into the big four-poster. Sleep overtook her too readily there among the soft pillows and bolsters, leaving her easy prey for the monstrous dreams that followed. Propped in the chair, she dozed only in brief snatches, but that was preferable to a lengthier sojourn with the demons of her nightmares.

Julia closed her eyes. She pressed the lids with her fingers, digging into the sockets as if to punish the eyes that had recorded those dreadful images twenty-six years ago, preserved them with agonizing clarity. Those memories had transformed her mind into a madhouse, filled with screams and the violent blast of gunfire.

Julia shrank from the specter looming before her tightly closed eyes. Cowering in her chair, she watched the man slowly turn to reveal the mass of pulp and bone shard where a face should have been.

TWENTY-SIX YEARS EARLIER, something was about to happen. Young Alonzo, his face still smooth and boyish, could tell by the way the old man was drinking. Usually, he just drank steady, sitting on the front porch rocker with the bottle of corn mash cradled between his legs. By nightfall, he would either fall out or get loud and mean, busting up furniture and any of his kids unlucky enough to get in his way.

That afternoon, though, his drinking was different. Alonzo caught him taking a bottle out to the barn, looking nervous—like a hound dog that had stolen a piece of meat. Alonzo hid in the loft and watched his daddy nip at the bottle while he put things in his truck and then took them out again, pacing around but going nowhere.

His daddy finally went back to the house, and Alonzo started to climb down from his hiding place. When he saw his old man coming back across the yard, he got scared and hid himself real quick in the bed of the truck. He curled up under an old tarp and kept as still as a dead man. Alonzo listened hard, planning to jump out and run for it the next time his daddy left.

Instead, he heard the truck's engine sputter and grind. The old Ford bounced over the yard, slinging Alonzo around under the tarp like a sack of potatoes. When they hit the road, the truck picked up speed. He couldn't tell which way they were going, but his daddy hadn't driven too far before he slowed way down, like he was looking for something he was afraid he might miss.

The truck stopped, and a few minutes later the cab door slammed. The smell of rust and gasoline and moonshine under the tarp were starting to make Alonzo sick, but he waited a good long while before he dared make a move. He had just lifted the edge of the tarp when he heard a shriek that made his blood run cold.

All of a sudden, there was screaming all around, and he could hear a man panting, running toward the truck. Alonzo crouched back, too scared to do anything but stare through the narrow space between the tarp and the side of the truck bed. He saw his daddy's face, bleached as white as a sheet in the moonlight and shiny with sweat. His daddy climbed into the cab and just sat there for a second, breathing hard. Then Alonzo saw a woman coming up out of the dark, right before the whole night exploded in a blaze of light and spattered flesh.

Alonzo Finch awoke from his dream, bathed in sweat and trembling.

Chapter Eleven

Patrice winced, slowly lifting her sore arm as if she were operating a miniature crane. She checked her watch and was gratified to see that it was not quite seven o'clock. As battered as she had felt last night, she had feared she would sleep away half the day. With any luck, she could get washed up and dressed before Alan awoke. To that end, she carefully swung her legs over the side of the bed and stooped to retrieve the stirrup pants she had shinnied out of last night. She was tiptoeing to the bathroom when Alan rolled onto his back, yawning and stretching both arms over his head.

"Good morning. Did you sleep well?" Alan pushed up on his elbows, revealing a well-muscled bare chest. Apparently she had not been the only one to shed some excess clothing in the dark last night.

"Like a log. What about you?" Patrice tugged at the hem of her sweater that was showing a stubborn inclination to hike up to her butt.

"Not bad." Alan's slight smile added a maddening touch of ambiguity to the remark.

"I'm going to take a quick shower," Patrice announced before scurrying into the bathroom.

Patrice looked at herself in the mirror as she unwrapped a fresh bar of soap. Dressed in the big leopard-
skin-print sweater with her head perched on the cervical
collar like a jack-in-the-box, she tried to imagine how she
could possibly look less seductive. All the same, the
sooner they were fully clothed and out of the motel, the
better.

She still could hardly believe she had almost fallen into
a clinch with Alan the previous evening. She had convinced herself that she had a firm lid on her attraction to
him, only to discover the fundamental weakness of that
control. Last night she had pinpointed the problem: the
moment he touched her, her normal self-possession took
a dive.

What would Alan have done had she not evaded his
kiss? He hadn't impressed her as the kind of man who
took relationships lightly. On the other hand, in a motel
room with a willing woman... Patrice pulled up short.
Whatever the case might be, the Blue Bird Inn was not a
setting in which she wished to begin a relationship. In
fact, she would do well to purge the word *relationship*
from her vocabulary until she had closed Alan Lowndes's
case. Until then he was a client who had contracted her
professional services, period.

Patrice quickly peeled off the cervical collar, but her
sore arms and shoulders made wrestling the sweater over
her head hurt like hell. After considerable grimacing she
managed to undress and climb into the shower. The hot
water soothed her aching muscles, and by the time she
had dressed, shaken out her hair and arranged it over her
bandage, she was beginning to feel almost normal.

"All yours," Patrice announced cheerily as she returned to the room.

Mercifully Alan had pulled on his polo shirt in her absence. "Why don't you call a cab and tell them to be here in fifteen minutes?" he suggested. "I promise I'll be ready."

"The clock is running."

Patrice sank onto the bed and tugged the directory from the nightstand's shelf. When Alan emerged from his shower ten minutes later, she had ordered a taxi and reserved a Taurus sedan at Port Latanier's sole car-rental agency. Alan made a quick call to the hospital and determined that Dr. Hamilton's condition had remained stable over the night. When a horn honked outside the room, they collected the briefcase and key and then hurried to the curb.

"Good mornin'." The cabby who had delivered them to the Blue Bird Inn the previous evening grinned broadly as he unlatched the rear door of his taxi for them.

Patrice and Alan avoided looking at each other as they stopped by the motel office to return the key and pay for their phone calls. They managed to keep straight faces during the ride to Port Latanier. Once they had tipped the driver and sent him on his way, however, they indulged in a good laugh. If they could joke about the motel escapade, then things certainly hadn't gotten too far out of hand, Patrice reflected. Then, too, laughter helped defuse tension of every kind.

After picking up the rental car, Alan drove them to Madge and Jimmie's Café. Over a hearty breakfast of eggs, *grillades*, biscuits, orange juice and coffee, Patrice and Alan discussed the next logical move.

"I'm going to have another try at talking with Bernice Wood," Patrice declared.

"Julia isn't going to cotton to that idea," Alan warned, stretching his arm over the back of the booth.

Patrice raised an eyebrow as she took a sip of coffee. "Then I guess we'll just have to talk with her when Julia isn't around."

Before leaving the café, they ordered two large coffees to go and purchased a newspaper. Patrice drove the rental car to Julia's tree-shaded neighborhood. She cruised the block, evaluating the house from several angles before parking in the shadow of a mammoth live oak four doors away.

"We have a clear view of her driveway from here, but the street curves enough so that we don't stick out like a sore thumb," Patrice explained.

Alan looked impressed. "I've never participated in a surveillance operation before. Now what do we do?"

Patrice unlatched the seat belt and settled back comfortably, arms folded across her chest. "Wait."

By ten o'clock, they had finished the coffee and read the *Port Latanier Gazette* from cover to cover. By eleven, they had dispatched the newspaper's crossword and word jumble. At a quarter of twelve, Julia's black Mercedes sedan was still parked squarely in the driveway. Catching Alan rearranging his lanky frame for the third time in as many minutes, Patrice smiled.

"Feel free to take a nap, if you'd like. I can keep an eye on the place," she offered.

Alan heaved a bored sigh. "I might take you up on it." He broke off suddenly and grabbed Patrice's wrist. "Hey, look! There's Bernice Wood."

They both unconsciously leaned toward the dash and watched as the housekeeper walked down the driveway, checking the contents of her handbag. She halted beside the Mercedes and unlocked the door. When Bernice Wood climbed behind the wheel and backed the sedan

nto the street, Patrice and Alan turned to each other and
macked palms.

"Yes!" they both cried triumphantly.

Patrice cranked the engine. She waited until the
housekeeper had a half-block lead before following her.
Thanks to Port Latanier's abundance of stop signs, Pa-
rice had to move at a creep to avoid overtaking the
Mercedes. She was relieved when Bernice at last turned
onto the highway. When the Mercedes's turn signal
blinked, Patrice followed the black sedan onto the park-
ng lot of a small strip shopping center. She parked one
row away from the Mercedes. Patrice and Alan approached Bernice Wood as she was tugging a shopping
cart from the corral next to the handicapped-parking
spaces.

"Excuse me, Miss Lacourier." Patrice was elated when
the woman spun around in surprise. "That was your
maiden name, wasn't it?"

"Yes," the woman replied cautiously.

Seeing the wary expression growing on Bernice Wood's
smooth dark face, Patrice hastened to neutralize as much
suspicion as possible. "I'm Patrice Ribeau. We talked for
a few minutes at Mrs. Broussard's house yesterday, but
I don't believe I introduced myself."

Before taking Patrice's extended hand, Mrs. Wood
hesitated, but not long. Patrice was determined to inter-
pret that as a good sign, however feeble. She waited for
Alan to introduce himself before posing her first question.

"I'm trying to get some information about a baby who
was baptized at Saint Vincent de Paul in the summer of
1967."

"That was a long time ago." Bernice Wood glanced away, apparently seized with Port Latanier's peculiar form of twenty-six-year amnesia.

"You were the little girl's godmother, Mrs. Wood," Patrice chided. "Surely you haven't forgotten your own godchild."

Bernice Wood looked down at the leather purse she clutched tightly in both hands. "I remember," she murmured, scarcely above a whisper.

"Who was her mother?" Patrice asked, dropping her own voice.

The woman shook her head. "Please don't ask me that." Her dark eyes appealed for understanding. "I promised I'd never tell."

Alan placed a comforting hand on the housekeeper's arm. "Mrs. Wood, I know you hate the thought of violating someone's trust, but we desperately need your help. On Sunday my grandfather was bitten by a poisonous snake that was deliberately placed in his sun room. Yesterday, when Patrice and I were driving to the hospital to see Granddad, the brakes on her car failed without warning. We were both lucky to escape serious injury or worse." He paused, giving his plea a chance to work on Bernice Wood. "Whoever is trying to prevent us from learning the truth about that baby is willing to kill to keep the secret. My grandfather is lying in the intensive care unit right now because he knew too much. Considering what has happened in the past few days, no one who knows anything about that little girl's birth should feel safe. We've got to find out who's behind all this, Mrs. Wood."

Bernice Wood drew a deep, uneven breath, closing her eyes for a moment. "It was all so wrong, what they did

) that girl. Lord knows they meant well, but that still
idn't make it right.''

"Who were they, Mrs. Wood?" Patrice pleaded. She
tudied the housekeeper's fine-boned face, trying to
auge the storm of emotions reflected on it. Her heart
ank when the woman began to shake her head once
nore.

"Mr. Reed told me to burn everything, but I couldn't."
3ernice's voice cracked, and she bit her quivering lip.
'Putting those precious things into the fire, why, that
eemed almost like murder. I never said a word to any-
ne about it until this day, but I wrapped them up in a
ittle box and put it away where it'd be safe."

"Where did you hide the box?" Patrice posed the
question as gently as possible. Bernice Wood was exhib-
ting all the classic symptoms of a witness torn between
rreconcilable loyalties. Press her too vigorously, and the
;ates of her memory would slam shut for good.

For several moments, Mrs. Wood appeared lost in
hought, her wide brow lined with furrows. When she
traightened herself, she looked as if sheer will was all
hat kept her slender body from collapsing under its un-
earable burden.

"My husband was still alive back then. When we went
o his folks for Christmas, I took the box with me and hid
t at their family place over near Bienville. I hoped no one
would ever find it, that it'd just be there forever, like a
ittle memorial."

"As far as you know, none of the Woods ever stum-
led on it?" Patrice asked, but Bernice was already
packing away from them.

"I've told you all I can." Turning abruptly, Bernice
Wood shoved past the shopping cart and fled across the

parking lot. Patrice and Alan watched as she disappeared into the supermarket.

"I don't see much point in waiting for her to come out. I think we've gotten all we're going to get out of her," Alan commented, mirroring Patrice's thoughts.

Patrice impatiently shook back her sleeve to check her watch. "It's just a quarter to one. Let's pick up some lunch at Madge and Jimmie's and then head for Bienville."

Following Patrice's suggestion, they drove back through town and made a brief stop at the café to take out coffee and sandwiches to eat in the car. Fortunately, Bienville was located only ten miles from Port Latanier. The state highway ran directly through the town, dissecting its untidy collection of antebellum homes and vacation houses with the geometric precision of a surgeon's knife. When they spotted a convenience store, Alan pulled off the road.

Patrice bounded out of the car and headed for the pay phone. "Let's check the directory for Woods."

With Alan holding the directory open for her, Patrice deposited a quarter and then dialed the number listed for Wood, Emory C. A pleasant-sounding feminine voice answered.

"Hello, my name is Patrice Ribeau. I'm trying to find some relatives of a friend of mine, Bernice Wood. Would you happen to have the number for her mother- and father-in-law?"

"Sure. If you can hold on, I'll get it for you."

Patrice flashed Alan a thumbs-up while she held the phone. She popped the ballpoint and poised it over her notepad when the woman picked up again.

"That would be area code 318..."

"Three-one-eight?" Patrice interrupted. "You mean they're not here in Bienville anymore?"

The woman chuckled. "Oh, no. Uncle Paul and Aunt Betty have been living in Lake Charles for...oh, I don't know, must be nearly fifteen years now. After the bayou closed in on the old house, they just weren't much interested in starting out with a new place around here. I guess living in Bienville, they felt they'd always be reminded of the home they had to give up. You know how old folks can be. Anyway, here's their number."

Patrice noted the telephone number, just in case, and then thanked the woman for her help before hanging up.

"You don't look as happy as you did thirty seconds ago." Alan regarded her cautiously. He frowned when Patrice recounted her conversation with the senior Woods' niece. "Even if the bayou shifted enough to make the house uninhabitable, that doesn't necessarily mean that it's under water. These backwaters are full of deserted homesteads."

"How on earth would we go about getting to it?" Patrice was thinking aloud.

"Rent a boat." Alan sounded so matter-of-fact, either he knew what he was talking about or he had utterly lost his senses. "I've seen a bait shop on the outskirts of Port Latanier that also rents out boats. If they can direct people to the best fishing spots, then they can probably tell us how to get to an abandoned house."

"Okay, let's give it a try. I suppose I ought to phone Dad first and ask him to pick up Alex for me."

To that end, Patrice fished out her long-distance calling card and dialed Tony Lafon's number. He had turned on his answering machine, but that was probably just as well, she reflected. She had enough misgivings about navigating the bayou's shadowy recesses without having him raise any additional doubts in a personal conversation. After leaving a brief but reassuring message, Patrice thanked her father and hung up.

They got into the rental car and drove back toward Port Latanier. Patrice recognized the place Alan had in mind before he pointed it out. The shop itself, a small concrete-block building with a corrugated-tin lean-to jutting from one side, might easily have passed notice had it not been for the phalanx of signs surrounding it. From the looks of things, Finch's Bait and Tackle had taken full advantage of the promotional materials offered by the food, beverage, tobacco and fishing supply companies whose wares it stocked. As Alan had predicted, a hand-lettered sign proclaiming We Rent Boats was posted between advertisements touting Bud Light and Zebco reels. Alan parked next to a pickup truck with stickers of striking bass plastered on its rear window.

The inside of the shop smelled fishy but clean. Patrice and Alan joined a man wearing camouflage pants waiting near the cash register. Presently, a woman with lank brown hair walked through the door at the rear of the shop, carrying a minnow bucket. Patrice examined the assortment of fishing lures exhibited inside the glass display case while the woman rang up the other customer's order.

The man smiled as he dropped the change into one of his voluminous pants pockets. "Thanks, Billie. You have a nice day, now."

"You, too, Roy." Billie's tired voice sounded as if she would be doing well just to get through another day on her feet. Although she could not have been much older than Patrice, her face had a pinched, drawn look to it, as if she had seen plenty of trouble and expected more. She tucked a limp strand of hair behind her ear as she turned to Patrice and Alan. "Can I help you?"

"You rent boats, right? We need one with an outboard motor," Alan began. When Billie nodded, he went on. "Would you happen to know how to find the old Wood place? It's somewhere in the bayou between here and Bienville."

Billie pulled a pink photocopy from beneath the counter and placed it in front of Alan. Her knobby finger followed one of the broken lines weaving through the map's inlets and waterways. "You'll see part of the old road here." She tapped a thick, solid line drawn on the map. "The Woods lived somewhere around here. Far as I know, their house is one of the few left, so you should be able to find it without too much trouble."

Alan and Patrice thanked Billie for her help and then followed her through the rear door of the shop. After they had selected a boat with an outboard motor, Patrice fetched her briefcase from the car while Alan paid the deposit, checked the flotation vests and supervised the fueling operation. Billie saw them off from the dock.

"Y'all be careful." Billie's hand fluttered in a listless wave as Alan guided the boat away from shore.

"Don't worry," Patrice muttered under her breath, frowning as she jammed the briefcase under the seat.

When she looked up, Alan grinned and reached to chafe her wrist. "Relax." he told her.

Patrice managed a smile, although the feelings elicited by his finger's insistent pressure were anything but serene.

"I may be a rookie when it comes to detective work," Alan went on, "but I do know something about handling a boat in these waters. Granddad and I used to fish every Saturday in the summer when I was a kid. It's really beautiful out here, so still and peaceful."

Patrice leaned back, bracing her hands on the edge of the seat as she gazed up at the ethereal strands of moss wafting from the branches overhead. Alan was right, the bayou was a magnificent place, she reflected as they penetrated deeper into the marsh. Under happier circumstances, she would have enjoyed spending an afternoon exploring its meandering channels with him. Scanning the shoreline for the Woods' house, she spotted herons feeding in the shallows and a muskrat scurrying among the close trees. At one turn, an alligator slithered off the muddy bank to glide past the boat, as if to remind them that they were the outsiders here in this domain of nature.

True to Billie's prediction, the Woods' crumbling white clapboard house was impossible to overlook. The bayou had encroached so far on the surrounding land that the house at first appeared to be floating on the water. Alan piloted the boat as close to shore as the treacherous undergrowth would permit and then cut the motor. Jumping agilely along the network of exposed roots, he caught the mooring line Patrice tossed to him and dragged the boat up the bank.

For a few moments, they stood on the muddy bank, taking stock of the house. In its day, it must have been a lovely home, with a wide, shady veranda spanning it on three sides and fancy wooden scrollwork decorating the numerous arched windows. Fifteen years of neglect and punishing bayou moisture had exacted their toll, but the old house still retained a hint of its former grandeur.

"It's almost three o'clock. We'd better get started." Patrice spurred them into action.

As soon as they mounted the rotting front steps, they both realized the necessity of cautious exploration. Untrustworthy floorboards and ceilings near collapse forced them to proceed carefully. Further slowing their progress were the numerous pieces of furniture that had been left behind. Although Patrice doubted that Bernice would have selected something as impermanent as a bureau or a wardrobe as a repository for the box, she felt obligated to check every nook and cubbyhole in the house. Despite their diligence, however, their inspection of the house failed to uncover anything resembling the box Bernice had described.

"Unless it's plastered up inside one of the walls, it simply isn't here," Alan declared, dusting off soot he had dislodged shining the flashlight up the chimney.

Patrice reached to brush a cinder fleck from Alan's cheek, indulging herself in the brief but immensely pleasurable touch. "I'm inclined to agree," Patrice reluctantly admitted. "Maybe she hid it somewhere outside."

Alan groaned. "I suppose she could have buried it." He hopped off the edge of the veranda to peer underneath the house. "I'm willing to crawl under here if you think it's worthwhile," he volunteered.

"Before we start rolling around in the mud with spiders and snakes, let's eliminate the outbuildings. When we were in the kitchen, I noticed a shed behind those trees around back. I'd like to have a closer look at it."

Patrice led the way to the rear of the house, picking her way through the knee-deep weeds. She was thrashing through the vines and undergrowth when she suddenly pulled up short, startled by the scene opening before her. Far from a utilitarian shed, Patrice now realized that the

structure she had spotted from the kitchen window was
a marble mausoleum.

"It must be the family cemetery," Alan murmured
over her shoulder.

"You know, Alan, maybe *this* is where Bernice hid the
box." Patrice grabbed Alan's hand, suddenly excited by
the idea that had just occurred to her. "She talked with
such reverence about the things she'd wanted to preserve. Remember her saying that she hoped it would
simply be here forever, as a kind of memorial?"

Alan nodded slowly. "Got the flashlight?"

"Right here." Patrice slapped her pocket.

The door of the mausoleum was solid metal, without
benefit of a window. Patrice and Alan exchanged a dubious glance before seizing the heavy bar set in the door
and tugging against the rusted hinges. Inch by inch, the
door yielded to their pressure.

A moldy odor filled the dark chamber, the smell of age
and decay. When Patrice flicked on the flashlight, she
involuntarily gasped at the eyeless human skull captured
in the beam. She released an uneven breath, forcing herself to focus the light on the glass window revealing the
bones interred behind it.

"I wasn't prepared for that, either," Alan remarked
from behind her, giving her shoulder a comradely
squeeze.

Together, they stepped inside the mausoleum. With
deliberate patience, Patrice slowly guided the flashlight's beam along the rows of dirty glass windows. She
skimmed past a corner window and then refocused the
light for a closer examination. Patrice stepped closer to
the window and stooped to peer through the nearly
opaque glass. The chamber was empty. Or was it?

Patrice crouched and carefully ran her fingers along the window's corroded metal rim. She tested the lip of the window and then pried it open. Patrice channeled the light into the chamber.

"Look!" She steadied the light on a small metal box swaddled in cobwebs.

Patrice held the light while Alan reached into the chamber and removed the box. They both stared at it for a moment without speaking, unable to believe their good fortune.

"Let's bring it outside." Alan led the way out of the mausoleum.

In the daylight, Patrice could now see that the box had originally been designed to hold jewelry or the sundry personal knickknacks that accumulate on dressers. Dampness had caused the metal to oxidize, but the curling leaves and flowers etched into the tin were still visible beneath the dull blue-green cast. The lid opened with surprisingly little resistance.

A pair of pink satin baby shoes lay nestled against the box's mildewed blue-velvet lining. Patrice delicately shifted the shoes with one finger to examine the tiny silver locket, tarnished but still unmistakably fine. A folded piece of paper had been tucked beneath the shoes and locket. As she lifted the paper out of the box, Patrice realized that she had been holding her breath.

Patrice glanced at Alan before unfolding the piece of paper.

My dearest Beau,
The nights are getting warm now, but not so close and hot, I suspect, as those you must spend without me, far away in the jungle. Not an hour passes that I don't think of you and long for the day when we

can be together again, forever. In your last letter, you begged me not to feel lonely and to know that I am always in your thoughts and in your heart. I do miss you, my sweet love, so much it hurts, but I'm comforted that I mustn't wait for you alone. Soon there will be two of us living for the day when you come home. Please don't worry about me, about us. I don't care what anyone says. All that matters to me is loving you and being with you. My life would be nothing without you, Beau. Every night I pray for the day when you return to me and our little one. Know that I love you with all my heart.

Your Melanie.

"Melanie." Patrice repeated the name softly and then looked up at Alan. "This letter has to have been written by Melanie Reed, Alan, Leon's daughter who was murdered!"

"She must have written the letter not long before the baby was born," Alan concurred. "I wonder who Beau was?"

"I don't know, but when we get back to Port Latanier, I want to read everything about that murder that we can lay our hands on."

Patrice and Alan plowed through the underbrush, stopping at the house only long enough for Patrice to retrieve her briefcase and bag from the veranda. They hurried to the boat beached on the muddy bank. With Patrice seated in the bow, Alan shoved the boat away from shore and then climbed aboard. He started the motor and then let it idle, steering the craft around snags with an oar until they reached navigable water. The motor whined as Alan opened the throttle wider, propelling the boat as rapidly as the murky channel would safely permit.

"Yuck!" Patrice muttered, lifting her feet out of the small puddle collecting around them.

"Did I splash us with the oar?" Alan leaned to examine the brackish water spreading across the bottom of the boat.

"Either that or I tilted the boat when I climbed in."

Patrice heaved the briefcase onto her lap. When she looked down again, she swallowed slowly. No, it wasn't her imagination. At least a half inch of water had accumulated beneath the seat.

"Alan, I think we're taking on water." Patrice tried to keep her voice calm, but she was suddenly aware of the immense, uncharted bayou separating them from secure land.

Alan sized up the situation in an instant. "There must be a leak somewhere." He reached to plumb the water that now covered his shoes when he stood.

Patrice watched as he manipulated the rudder, turning the boat toward a dense brush island. "What are you doing?" she asked in a hoarse voice.

"I'm going to put into shore." Alan's jaw was set as he glanced down at the water sloshing around his feet. "At this rate we don't have any choice."

He was already reaching for the oar when a loud slap sounded from the thick marsh grass. Patrice gasped at the sight of an alligator crawling along the bank. "Oh, my God, it's coming this way!" she cried.

Alan jammed the oar against the trunk of a cypress and shoved the boat back into the channel. He opened the throttle and gunned the motor. The boat surged forward, churning a violent spray in its wake. Patrice could feel the water rising over her ankles, but her eyes remained fastened on the big reptile wriggling into the water.

"It's no use. We're starting to sink. We're going to have to swim for shore." When Patrice turned to face Alan, he shouted at her, "Go on!"

"What about you?" Patrice's lips felt almost too numb to form the words.

Alan gestured angrily. "Go on, I said!" He lifted the oar, hefting it in his hands as the alligator approached the boat.

Patrice glanced frantically about and then pushed off into the black water. She clung to the briefcase, thrusting it ahead of her, as she kicked toward shore. When she heard water thrash, she hesitated and turned. She froze, suspended in the water, unable to wrench her gaze from the alligator swimming directly toward the boat. The creature hissed, opening its jaws to reveal bristling rows of teeth. Alan swung the oar just as the alligator snapped. Patrice involuntarily closed her eyes, shuddering at the sickening crunch. When she looked again, she saw a broken oar floating beside the empty boat.

"Alan!" she gasped in a voice riddled with fear.

"What are you waiting for? Swim, for God's sake!"

Patrice glanced from the alligator cruising alongside the sinking boat to Alan, who was rapidly gaining on her with a powerful freestyle. She pivoted in the water and began to kick in earnest, not letting up until she had floundered onto land. She collapsed on the slimy bank as Alan slogged through the shallows to join her.

"For a second . . . I thought . . . the alligator . . ." Patrice spat out words between gulps of air.

"I gave him the oar to chew on." Alan sank down onto the riverbank beside her.

Patrice sat up, clutching the wet leather briefcase to her chest. "What about the boat?"

Alan only gestured toward the concentric circles slowly expanding across the empty stretch of water.

Chapter Twelve

Patrice stood up and drew a deep, calming breath. She scanned the pastel sky fading into the treetops like melting sherbert. "We should try to get back to the house. I don't think we have much chance of reaching civilization before dark, and I'm not interested in wandering around these backwaters all night." She emptied the water out of her shoulder bag and removed the sodden cervical collar, concentrating on practical tasks she could control to avoid thinking about the larger, less predictable obstacles facing them.

"You're right," Alan agreed. "Maybe we can find some matches in the house and build a fire." He was obviously trying to sound upbeat, and however unfounded his optimism might be, Patrice had no desire to challenge it.

They pushed through the bayou forest single file, stepping gingerly to avoid disturbing unseen creatures that might be lurking in the thick vegetation. For a time, the cypresses closed around them so densely that Patrice was afraid they had lost their way. Although she kept her fear to herself, she almost cried with relief when the big white house at last loomed into sight.

Alan trudged up the steps to the veranda ahead of Patrice. "I'll take a look in the kitchen and see if I can find any matches. Why don't you just have a seat out here..."

"And enjoy the sunset?" Patrice provided. Sinking down onto the top step, she looked up at Alan and grinned.

He reached to ruffle her wet hair and chuckled. "Something like that."

When Alan returned several minutes later, Patrice twisted around on the step. "Any luck?"

"There isn't a match in the house, I'm afraid, but I did find these in one of the wardrobes." Alan held up a bundle of folded sheets. "They smell like fermented gym shoes, but wrapping up in them is better than spending the night in wet clothes."

Patrice accepted one of the grayish white sheets that Alan held out to her. "This will teach us to make wisecracks about the Blue Bird Inn. We only *thought* we had it bad last night." She kicked off her soggy shoes and padded into the dark house. In the living room, she paused to point. "Ladies' changing room to the right, gentlemen's to the left."

As Alan retreated to the designated bedroom, Patrice stepped into the dining room. She peeled off the waterlogged sweater and stirrup pants. After wringing them out, she lapped her clothes over the single lyre-back chair remaining in the room. Her wet bra and panties felt like squid clinging to her skin, and she ripped the thin fabric in her haste to be rid of them.

After experimenting with various techniques for wrapping herself in the sheet, Patrice at last settled on a modified toga that left her legs bare below the knees and permitted free movement of her arms. If circumstances had contrived for Alan and her to spend yet another night together, she needed to preserve some semblance of formality, however symbolic.

When she returned to the living room, she found Alan standing at one of the windows with the ripped portion of a sheet knotted around his lower body bath-towel fashion. In the dwindling twilight, the sculpted muscles of his vee-shaped back reminded Patrice of those superbly lighted black-and-white photographs that celebrate the human body in its purest form. She caught herself when he turned, and immediately headed for the shoulder bag she had left by the fireplace.

Kneeling on the floor, Patrice examined its contents. "Well, I guess it was asking too much to hope that the leftover cupcake would make it." She held up the crumbled cellophane-wrapped remains of the previous night's feast. "The flashlight still works, though." Patrice demonstrated for Alan. When he sank onto the floor beside her, she sat back on her heels. Her eyes inadvertently drifted down the ladder of fine hair fanning over his taut midriff. She lifted her chin, forcing her eyes away from their dangerously fascinating preoccupation. "I don't know anything about boats, Alan, but it seems odd that ours would have sprung a leak just like that."

Alan's handsome face darkened. "They don't *just* spring leaks, any more than brakes on a new car *just* fail. I think someone followed us here and deliberately damaged the boat while we were crawling all over this house."

Without thinking, Patrice glanced at the door. *He could still be out there, waiting until dark.* She quickly suppressed the terrifying thought. Whoever sabotaged the boat had performed a hit-and-run maneuver, accomplishing his sinister mission as quickly as possible and then leaving the treacherous bayou waters and the alligators to finish the job.

As if he could see her disquieting thoughts reflected on her face, Alan slid a bare arm around Patrice's shoulders. "You know your dad. When you don't show up at home tonight, he'll be on the phone to every law-enforcement agency in Louisiana. That woman at the bait shop is going to wonder what happened to her boat, too. It isn't as if we'd vanished off the face of the earth." He gave her a little squeeze, pulling her into the crook of his arm for a moment.

The pressure of his strong arm around her filled Patrice with an almost irresistible urge to curl up inside his embrace, press her face against the solid plane of his chest, and simply feel close and safe and not alone. Instead, she smiled and pushed up from the floor. "I'll see what I can salvage from my briefcase while there's still some light."

Facing the wedge of faint light admitted through the door, Patrice opened the briefcase on the floor. Alan wandered out to the veranda, leaving her to peel apart wet papers and spread them on the floor to dry. By the time she had finished the tedious task, the house was almost pitch-dark.

Pulling the sheet around her shoulders, Patrice walked to the veranda rail and peered up at the star-sprinkled sky. Alan was seated on the steps, and he beckoned her to join him.

"Look at the vapor rising over the water." He pointed to the ghostly fog obscuring the line between water and air. "I remember one summer when Granddad and I had been fishing right before dusk. We hadn't paid much attention to the time, and when we started back to the dock, it was as if we were moving through a cloud. It was one of those little things that for some reason seem so important to share with someone." His smile looked wistful in the pale moonlight.

"You're very close to your grandfather, aren't you?" Patrice remarked softly.

Alan nodded. "We're all the family either of us has now that Mother is gone, too. He never said anything about it, but I think he was deeply disappointed when my marriage went down the tubes." He broke off so abruptly that Patrice guessed he had let the last revelation unintentionally slip.

"How long were you married?" Patrice asked, not looking directly at him.

"Two years, the length of an internship." Alan's brief laugh was rueful. "I don't have any hard feelings toward Melissa, and I hope to heaven she's kind enough not to harbor any for me. I've tried to rationalize why it didn't work out. The pressures and crazy hours of medical school. Two doctors making a bad match. Basic personality differences." He shook his head. "When I'm really honest with myself, I admit I was simply too young and dumb to know what a good marriage required. I leapt before I looked and then hadn't a clue what to do next."

"Do you now?" Patrice almost bit her tongue in a futile effort to check the question that had popped out of her subconscious without warning.

Alan studied his hands folded in front of him for what seemed a very long time. "I'd like to find out," he murmured in a voice barely audible above the droning hum of the cicadas.

When Alan looked up, his dark eyes shimmered with emotion, beckoning to Patrice in a way that made mere words pale by comparison. Locked in his sensuous gaze, she reached to stroke Alan's cheek. Her hand moved with deliberate slowness, savoring every nuance of texture, first the smooth skin drawn taut over his high cheekbones, then the pleasantly rough shadow of a beard covering his chin.

Alan turned his head slightly to plant a kiss inside her palm. Still nuzzling her hand, he encircled her waist and drew her closer to him. Patrice linked her hands behind his neck and leaned to meet his lips. As their mouths joined, she felt herself buffeted by a wave of emotions so powerful they threatened to demolish all the sane, reasoned, practical barriers she had erected between herself and Alan Lowndes. For an inexpressibly sweet moment, nothing mattered but the pressure of his lips, the feel of his warm, vibrant body pressed against hers, the passionate yearings drawing them together.

When Alan's hand skimmed the contour of her breast, outlined beneath the sheet, a white-hot ardor flared inside her. *I want to love him, to have him love me, not just physically but on every level possible between a man and a woman.* The enormity of the thought struck Patrice with such jolting intensity, she started.

"Don't be afraid of me," Alan murmured, his warm breath caressing her cheek.

Patrice pressed her face against his. "It isn't you I'm afraid of, Alan. It's me." Never before in her life had she made such an honest and painful admission.

Alan stroked her hair, fingering the tousled curls as if his fingers sought to memorize their silky texture. "I understand." His whisper was still husky with desire, but he loosened his hold on her.

Looking into Alan's passionate dark eyes, Patrice reached to take his hands and hold them tightly in front of her. "Please trust me, Alan. I just need some time."

Alan said nothing, but only nodded slowly. Patrice let his hands slide out of her grasp as she stood up. "Good night, Alan." Her voice broke, betraying the emotional war raging inside her. Without waiting for a reply, Patrice turned and fled into the dark house.

ALAN ROLLED ONTO his back, cushioning his head on his bent arm. He must have awakened a half-dozen times in the past few hours, twisting and turning on the floor in vain attempts to find a comfortable position. Although it was not quite two o'clock, he had reconciled himself to spending most of the night staring at the water-stained ceiling.

He shifted to look at Patrice, curled beneath a sheet in the opposite corner of the room. At least she appeared to be having more luck falling asleep than he was. Closing his eyes for a moment, Alan realized that more than the hard floor, the dank bed linen or the unfamiliar night sounds drifting through the windows, thinking about Patrice had deprived him of restful slumber.

Pushing aside the sheet, Alan rose as quietly as possible and tiptoed to the open window. He braced his palms on the sill and gazed across the dark bayou, following the glow of an alligator's eyes, two shining red dots floating through the moon-bleached vapor. *I've learned what it takes to make a relationship work. I was hurt once, badly, but I have the guts to try again. I want to try with you, Patrice.* Alan looked down at the weathered sill and listened to the unspoken words die within him.

He was turning back to the room when he noticed a brief movement from the corner of his eye. Frowning, Alan crouched by the window and squinted into the thick tangle of overgrown shrubbery skirting the veranda. The bayou was full of opossums, raccoons and any number of other night-foraging animals. In all likelihood, he had only spotted the trace of some nocturnal creature on its way to snuffle grubs from the damp soil under the house. Nonetheless, his logical explanation did nothing to quell the vague uneasiness gnawing at him as he knelt by the window with his eyes trained on the bushes.

Alan stiffened at the faint rustling sound beneath the veranda overhang. Holding his breath, he measured each step as he silently retrieved the flashlight lying beside Patrice's handbag and then walked to the door. He tested each floorboard in a painstaking catlike walk across the veranda.

Alan paused at the top of the steps. Tension had heightened his senses, making them alert to the slightest sound or motion. He studied the clump of bushes before slowly easing his way down the steps. Alan carefully reached to part the dense branches. He was about to switch on the flashlight when he caught a flash of reflected moonlight in his peripheral vision.

Alan wheeled and then lunged to one side, narrowly escaping the knife aimed at his midsection. He pushed away from the bushes and tried to gauge his attacker's next move. Dressed in dark clothes, his face smeared with camouflage paint, the man blended with the night, even at close range. Only the gleaming blade of his knife stood out with blood-chilling clarity.

The two men parried and feinted in a deadly game of bluff. When his assailant leapt at him again, Alan was ready. Smashing his forearm into the man's throat, he waited a split second for his opponent to reel back and then punched him squarely in the solar plexus. As the man fell to his knees in pain, he dropped the knife.

Alan dived for the knife, catching the man's hand just as it closed over the hilt. They rolled on the ground, grappling for possession of the knife. Although smaller than Alan, his opponent possessed an animal-like strength. His wiry limbs strained, resisting Alan's attempts to jar the knife from his grasp. With an explosive burst of force, he shoved Alan against one of the brick pilings supporting the veranda. Alan's head connected with the piling, releasing a shower of pain inside his skull. He winced, fighting dizziness as the knife inched closer to his throat. His blurred eyes were fixed on the blade quivering beside his face when a violent blast suddenly tore through the night air, followed by a shriek of pain.

Still unable to focus clearly, Alan saw his attacker fall backward, clutching his shoulder. Then the man stumbled to his feet and broke for the woods. Alan turned to see Patrice standing on the porch, the .22 still poised in her outstretched hands. She looked dazed as she slowly lowered the gun.

Seeing Alan weave slightly as he stood up, Patrice rushed down the steps. "Are you hurt?"

Alan rubbed the back of his head. "No, I was just stunned for a minute when I hit my head against the foundation. I would have been in big trouble, though, if you weren't such a good shot."

Patrice looked down at the gun cradled in her hand. She licked her lips, trying to regulate her uneven breathing. "Let's go inside."

Alan stooped to retrieve the hunting knife from the deep grass and then followed her. Patrice averted her eyes from the evil-looking blade as Alan tucked the knife behind the briefcase for safekeeping. She sank onto the floor, pulling her knees up under the sheet. Only when she felt Alan's arm slide around her shoulders did she realize that she was shaking.

"Hey, it's all right now," he whispered soothingly.

Alan's lips brushed her forehead. Then he pulled her close, rocking her gently in his arms.

"He could have killed you, Alan," Patrice whispered, choking on the awful words.

She pulled back enough to look up into his face. As Patrice lifted her hand to touch his cheek, her eyes began to sting. Letting the tears trickle unchecked down her face, she traced the outline of his jaw, his cheekbones, his forehead, reassuring herself with the warm, vital feel of him.

Without a word, Alan mirrored the movement of Patrice's hand. She felt his fingers follow the damp trails winding down her cheek to cup her chin. He tilted her face slightly, his eyes seeming to drink in the most minute details of her features as he leaned to cover her mouth with his.

Patrice closed her eyes and moved in rhythm with his kiss. She returned the soft caress of his lips. When his tongue probed, first lightly, then with a hot eagerness, she parted her lips to respond in kind. Patrice reached to capture his neck with her arms. Her fingers teased the warm skin at his nape before plunging into the thick hair. His head rolled to one side, reveling in the pleasure of her touch. When he reached up to clasp her hands, she opened her eyes.

Still holding her hands inside his, Alan kissed first her forehead, then the tip of her nose. His slightly parted lips drifted over her face, nuzzling the cleft of her throat before they planted a sweet trail of kisses along her collarbone.

Alan sat back and released her hands. Still holding her with his dark eyes, he loosed the sheet wrapped around her. When he bent to kiss the tops of her breasts, Patrice moaned softly, filled with an almost unbearable pleasure. With exquisite delicacy, Alan's finger separated the coarse fabric from the warm flesh beneath, peeling her sheet away from her breasts. His lips skimmed the curve of each breast, lingering for a delicious moment in her cleavage. Then his tongue began its magical work, caressing the skin until it tingled with sensation. Lips and tongue alternately plied her nipples, teasing them into rigid points.

Following her own yearnings, Patrice's hands wandered across his chest. She massaged the firm pectoral muscles, then skirted the tight midriff to glide around his waist and then up the smooth skin of his back. As she pulled him closer, the tips of her nipples grazed his chest, causing her to gasp at the delightful sensation.

Alan slid his arms around her and guided her gently onto her back. He kissed her throat, caressing her with his whisper. "I want you, Patrice. I want you so badly!"

Patrice covered his hands as they sculpted her hips to free them from the swathed sheet. Still working in unison, their hands relieved Alan of his makeshift clothing. When he bridged her body, Patrice sucked in her breath at the touch of his hard passion. She reached to stroke the silky skin, first lightly, then with a hunger that made him throb with desire.

"That feels so good," Alan murmured, a sensual smile playing on his lips. "Let me make you feel good, too."

Alan slowly began to move down the length of her, caressing her with his body. Every inch of Patrice's skin prickled with excitement as he tantalized first her breasts, then her stomach. When his lips lightly nibbled the inside of her thigh, she dug her fingers into his hair and gently pulled him up toward her. Her head sank back as the pulsing sensation welled inside her. She cried out, unable to contain the indescribable pleasure flooding her entire body.

She opened her eyes to look up into Alan's face. His dark eyes shone, deep and luminous as well-aged sherry, and for a moment Patrice imagined she saw herself reflected in their depths, just as he must see himself in her eyes, the two of them united as one. Patrice's body rose to meet the pressure of his thrusting hips. She felt a shudder pass through his body just as another passionate tremor seized her own.

Alan sank onto the floor beside her and pulled her against his body. Lacing her arms through his, Patrice locked them around her, snuggling deep into his embrace. She closed her eyes to welcome the repose settling over her sated body.

"I love you so much," she heard him whisper into the hair curling over her ear, just before she drifted off to sleep.

Chapter Thirteen

Patrice started, wrenched into consciousness by the sound of voices. Her heart racing, she sat up and gaped wildly around the shadowy room. When she heard footsteps outside the door, she pawed the floor, trying to remember where she had left the gun.

"Anybody home?" The question preceded a loud knock on the doorframe.

Patrice took a deep, steadying breath. If someone had come to murder them in the predawn darkness, he would hardly be polite enough to announce his arrival.

"What's that?" Alan asked groggily, pushing up on his elbows.

"Company." Patrice gathered the sheet around her just as a uniformed man ambled through the door. She scrambled to her feet, trying to collect her wits.

When the deputy caught sight of her, he removed his hat, looking at least as awkward as Patrice felt. "Clarence Bailiss, ma'am, deputy sheriff. And I'm hoping that you're Patrice Ribeau." When she nodded, he called over his shoulder. "We found 'em, Charlie!" Turning back to Patrice, the deputy regarded Alan and her cautiously. "Are you folks all right?"

"Now that you're here, we are," Alan replied. He quickly recapped the terrifying events of the previous evening, concluding with the knife attack. "When he ran for it, he left this behind." Alan stooped to retrieve the knife and hold it up for the deputy's inspection.

Deputy Bailiss whistled, scratching his temple with the tip of his thumbnail as he eyed the whetted ten-inch blade. "Do you think you could identify this fellow if you saw him again?"

Alan frowned for a moment. "I'm not sure. His face and hair were smeared with camouflage paint, and it was very dark. But at the very least, he has a bullet hole in his shoulder. That should give you something to go on."

"You say the lady here winged him?"

"She certainly did." Alan sounded unabashedly proud of the achievement.

The deputy gave Patrice another of those uncertain looks. "Well, you folks best get your clothes on, and we'll head back to town."

Tripping over the sheet trailing around her feet, Patrice hurried to the dining room. Thanks to the damp bayou air, her sweater and stirrup pants were as wet as when she had first removed them. Grimacing from the stiffness in her bruised shoulders, Patrice wriggled into the clammy clothes and then clawed the worst tangles from her hair. She was relieved that the search party had found them, but she felt strangely out of sorts, almost as if the deputies had intruded in a private domain known only to Alan and her. After sharing such intense intimacy with him, it seemed strange to be catapulted back into the real world so abruptly, like being awakened prematurely from a beautiful dream.

When Patrice returned to the front room, she heard Alan talking with the deputies outside the open window, re-creating his struggle with the assailant. She quickly gathered up the papers she had laid out to dry, shoveled them into her briefcase and then hurried to join the men.

"I'll get back out here today to see if we can find any evidence, but even if that fellow left a trail of blood, it's not going to do us any good once he got on the water again." Clarence Bailiss hitched his belt as he led the way to the motorboat tethered at the water's edge.

As soon as they had loaded into the boat, the deputy named Charlie took control of the throttle. They traveled at a faster clip than Alan and Patrice had dared, cutting a wide wake through the opaque green water. When they approached the dock at Finch's Bait and Tackle, the deputy cut the engine to a grumbling chug.

Billie was waiting for them in the rear doorway of the shop, a pilled navy blue sweater wrapped tightly around her thin torso. Her hollow dark eyes followed the party as they trudged up the wooden boardwalk. She looked upset, as if she had been fretting over the lost boat all night. When Alan stopped to apologize and offer to compensate her for the loss, however, she only tugged at the hem of her sweater.

"I'll be needin' to talk with my husband about it first," Billie explained.

"That's fine," Alan agreed. "You can always leave a message for me at the clinic."

When they were out of the woman's earshot, Deputy Bailiss shook his head. "You won't find a harder-working woman than Billie Finch. One thing's for sure, she deserves better than that sorry thing she's married to." He paused by the rental car, folding his arms across his husky chest. "If you don't mind, I'd like you folks to follow us down to the office so we can fill out a report." He shook his head and chuckled. "Sheriff Wade's going to be mighty happy to see you two, especially you, ma'am. Your daddy like to had a fit on the phone with him last night. I think Sheriff Wade half expected him to come down here and tear the parish apart if we didn't find you *tout de suite*."

Patrice bit her lip. She could easily imagine her father bullying and badgering the local authorities into action when she had failed to return home last night. Calling him was her priority. To that end, she headed for the pay phone as soon as they arrived at the sheriff's office.

"Hello!" Tony Lafon grabbed the phone on the second ring, a sure indicator that he had been hovering nearby.

"Hi, Dad, it's me."

"Where the hell have you been?" her father boomed. "My God, you had me worried sick," he went on without giving her a chance to vindicate herself. "I was just getting ready to take Alex to school and then head down there myself."

"You don't have to do that, Dad. Believe me, I'm fine." Patrice gave her father a brief account of the previous day's misadventures, omitting any reference to the terrifying assault on Alan. "I think I'm on the brink of a break in this case, but I won't know until I've had a chance to do some more research today."

"So you're not coming home right now?" Tony sounded disappointed and annoyed in equal proportions.

"I really need to pursue this lead. You know how these things are. You've got to stay on the trail while it's still hot," Patrice added, playing the card that never failed to trump her retired police-detective father.

"Yeah, well, just don't get yourself into any more ho water, okay?" her father conceded gruffly. "Is Alan wit you?"

"Uh-huh." Patrice glanced down the corridor, where Alan was drinking coffee and talking with the deputies.

"That's good," Tony declared. "Okay, girl, there' someone here who wants to talk with you. Take care o yourself," he added in parting.

"I will, Dad. I love you."

"I love you, too, honey."

"Hi, Mom!" Alex piped into the phone. "Where have you been?"

"Lost in the bayou. I went out in a boat that turnec out to be leaky. When it sank, I had to spend the night ir a deserted house out in the middle of nowhere."

"Wow!" Alex sounded duly impressed. "Was i haunted?"

"No, but it was scary enough for me. Did you anc Granddad behave yourselves without me?"

"We made nachos and watched *Star Trek*," Alex informed her, leaving her to make her own moral evaluation.

"Okay, Alex, I have to get back to work and you have to head for school. It may be late, but I promise I'll be home tonight. I love you, kiddo."

"Love you, too, Mom."

As the phone clicked in her ear, Patrice blew out a long sigh. Putting a harmless spin on yesterday's harrowing events for the benefit of her family had only reminded her of how narrowly she and Alan had escaped serious harm. As much as she wanted to wrap up her investigation successfully, Patrice was even more eager to free Alan and herself from the now-omnipresent shadow of fear.

"All quiet on the home front?" Alan asked as she joined him by the deputy's desk. When Patrice nodded, he gestured toward the phone. "I'm going to call the hospital and check on Granddad. Then I'll drive us to the house and we can get cleaned up."

"That sounds wonderful." As Alan jogged down the corridor to the phone, Patrice turned to Deputy Bailiss. "Do you know if the mechanic's report on my car has come in yet? Sheriff Wade was having the brakes checked for signs of possible tampering."

The deputy kept one eye fastened to the memo he was scanning. "I'm not sure, ma'am, but I'll ask the sheriff when he gets back. He's on a call over in Hampton."

"Okay, thanks. I'll catch him later." Patrice hitched up the shoulder-bag strap as Alan approached in the corridor. "How is your grandfather?"

Alan's smile lifted a measure of fatigue from his lean face. "I didn't get to talk with his doctor, but the supervising nurse said last night was the best he's had since he was admitted."

He reached to loop his arm over her shoulders and then quickly caught himself—not quick enough, however, for his intent to be wasted on Patrice. A gesture that had once been spontaneous and natural was now laden with significance. After last night, Alan was self-conscious about touching her, however casually. As they walked to the parking lot, the realization weighed on Patrice more heavily than common sense told her it should.

"A shower isn't going to do me much good unless I do something about these rotting clothes," Patrice warned, climbing into the rented Taurus. "There must be some place downtown where I can pick up a pair of jeans and a T-shirt."

Following Patrice's instructions, Alan drove down Main Street and angled the rental car into a parallel space near the Jeans Hut. He waited in the car while Patrice dashed into the store and selected a pair of Levi's and a black T-shirt with iridescent dinosaurs painted on it. Following the uneasy-looking clerk to the register, she snatched cotton panties, a bra and a pair of pink cotton socks off the racks, flung the whole mess onto the counter, and paid for it without trying anything on.

"That was quick," Alan commented as Patrice slid into the front seat of the car.

"I'm too anxious to get to the newspaper office to waste time shopping," Patrice told him.

During the short drive to Dr. Hamilton's house, Patrice pondered the love letter they had discovered among the baby things that Bernice Wood had so carefully preserved. She had little doubt now that Melanie Reed had been Anne-Marie's mother, the hush-hush adoption arranged by the ill-fated young woman's family to save face. But who was her beloved Beau and what role, if any, had he played in keeping his illegitimate daughter's birth secret? Patrice juggled the puzzling and still-disjointed factors in her mind as she followed Alan into the silent antebellum house.

"There should be plenty of fresh towels in the bath at the end of the hall," Alan told her on his way to the kitchen. "I'm going to put on a pot of coffee, and then I'll use the shower upstairs."

The bathroom was an old-fashioned, high-ceilinged room with a claw-footed tub deep enough to float an oil tanker. Patrice adjusted the tap and then quickly stripped off the damp sweater and pants. Under happier circumstances, she would have loved luxuriating in the steamy water for an hour or so, but she made do with a brisk, efficient scrubbing. Patrice wrapped herself in a towel and began removing the tags from her newly purchased clothes. After dressing and finger-combing her hair, she bundled her ruined clothes into the shopping bag and tidied the bath.

When she emerged into the hall, she heard water running upstairs. Patrice glanced up the wide staircase before continuing on to the kitchen. She rummaged through the cupboards, and by the time Alan appeared, had the breakfast nook table set and English muffins toasting. They fell on the cold cereal, muffins and coffee, devouring the meal in a manner more appropriately termed "refueling" than "eating." Leaving the dishes on the table, they hurried back to the rental car and headed straight for the town's business district.

Well, what had she expected? That Alan suggest a shower together followed by a leisurely champagne breakfast? Patrice upbraided herself as they cruised Main Street in search of a parking place. Perhaps he only seemed slightly distant because, like her, he was preoccupied with the serious business facing them. Patrice abruptly drew a curtain on her musing as Alan pulled into a slot across from the *Port Latanier Gazette*'s office.

"Need to have another look in the archives?" The freckle-faced office manager greeted them with the familiarity of a long-standing colleague.

"You guessed it." Patrice smiled, leading the way to the back room.

While the young man commandeered a couple of chairs for them, Alan and Patrice surveyed the microfilm storage cabinets.

"Can you remember when Melanie's murder took place?" Alan asked.

Patrice carefully slid open one of the wide, shallow drawers. "Sometime in the summer of 1967. I know I first ran across the headline when I was looking at the July birth announcements." She lifted three spools from the drawer. "This should get us started."

They huddled in front of the microfilm reader, both unconsciously leaning foward in their seats as Patrice scrolled through the columns. "Here it is," she murmured, twisting the focus knob.

"Debutante Slain In Burglary Attempt," Alan read the headline aloud in a low voice. "Then Melanie must have stumbled onto the intruder?"

"It looks that way." Patrice frowned, resting her chin on her hand as she began to read the newspaper account of the shocking tragedy.

According to the report, Melanie Reed had unexpectedly returned from a backpacking vacation in Austria to spend the remainder of the summer with her family. The night of the murder, Leon Reed had been out of town on business, leaving her and her sister, Julia, alone in the house. The sounds of a struggle had awakened Julia, who had been sleeping in an upstairs bedroom. She had rushed downstairs to find her sister lying strangled on the floor of her bedroom. Hearing the intruder in another part of the house, Julia had armed herself with one of Leon Reed's hunting rifles. In a blind panic, she had confronted the intruder and fatally shot him as he attempted to flee. The suspected murderer's name was being withheld, pending the sheriff department's investigation.

"Julia killed Melanie's murderer." Alan repeated the unexpected discovery that had left them both stunned. "I wonder if he could have been Beau. I know Melanie's letter talked about his being in the jungle, and I took that to mean Vietnam, but he could have been home on leave.''

"She never did mail that letter, either," Patrice concurred as she wound the microfilm. "Let's see." She advanced the film to the following day's coverage of the murder. "Here's his name. Orris Finch. Maybe Beau was a nickname," she suggested dubiously.

Alan shook his head. "He's described here as an alligator hunter with a history of heavy drinking and barroom brawls, not exactly the kind of guy you'd expect Leon Reed's daughter to fall for. And there's no mention of his having served in Vietnam. Of course, I suppose the jungle Melanie referred to in her letter could have been some swamp where he was trapping."

Patrice glanced at Alan and smiled. "You're starting to think like a detective. I'm inclined to agree with your initial impression, though. I somehow can't imagine a twenty-one-year-old debutante getting mixed up with a marginally employed ne'er-do-well twenty years her senior." She slumped back in the chair and folded her arms across her chest. "I wonder if the Finch of Finch's Bait and Tackle is related to Orris."

"It's worth trying to find out," Alan agreed. "Let's skim through the rest of these newspaper entries about Melanie and then drive out to the bait shop."

Despite the inherent drama of a society girl's murder in a small town, the *Port Latanier Gazette*'s coverage of the Melanie Reed case was short-lived. The sheriff's investigation confirmed what everyone assumed was a foregone conclusion, that Orris Finch, emboldened by drink, had attempted to burglarize the Reed household. When Melanie had stumbled on him at his work, he had panicked and strangled her. Julia's bullet had saved the state the expense of a trial that would have surely resulted in a conviction.

Patrice and Alan strayed from the front page to find Melanie's obituary. Reading the newspaper's description of the vivacious college senior's achievements and social activities, Patrice tried to imagine the real woman behind the golden-girl facade. Although she was careful to avoid succumbing to the *Gazette*'s dramatic coverage, Patrice's intuition stubbornly continued to link Melanie's hidden passion with her tragic death.

"Not a word about her having a child." Alan reached to underscore listed survivors with his finger. "Just Leon Reed and Mrs. Richard B. Broussard. That would be Julia, of course."

"Since the family went to such pains to conceal the baby's birth and shunt her to another home as quickly as possible, I would hardly expect them to trumpet the little girl's existence in the obit column. I don't believe that story about Melanie backpacking all over the Alps right before her death, either. That smacks of a convenient explanation for her absence during the months after her pregnancy started to show." Her shoulders sagged as she sighed. "Well, shall we try our luck at Finch's Bait and Tackle?"

Alan already had the car keys in his hand. As soon as they had returned the microfilm to its drawer, they thanked the friendly office manager and headed for the bait shop on the outskirts of town. A camper and an Isuzu Trooper were pulled up in front of the store, along with a snack-food distributor's step van. Patrice and Alan pretended to examine hip-wader boots and tackle boxes, waiting until the customers and the vendor had completed their business before approaching Billie.

"I haven't spoken with my husband about the boat yet," Billie announced, anticipating the reason for their visit. She twisted the hem of her sweater, her eyes automatically shifting to the open back door. "He's been out huntin', but I expect him back tonight."

"Actually, we didn't come to talk about the boat," Patrice told her. "We were wondering if you could tell us anything about Orris Finch."

Billie's gaunt face darkened. "What do you want to know about him?"

Patrice was a little startled by the steely edge that had surfaced in Billie's normally listless voice. "Who was he?" she asked, falling back on the obvious.

"The meanest man that ever lived." Billie's dark eyes were disconcerting when they stared straight at Patrice.

"Did he own this shop?"

Billie's brief laugh was full of contempt. "He never owned nothin'. The shop was Alonzo's doing, no thanks to his pa." Her lips tightened to a colorless straight line. "All Alonzo ever got from that old man was grief. And then he up and got himself killed, left them poor kids without a penny. I know there's folks who don't speak well of my husband, but what troubles Alonzo Finch has got, he can mostly blame on his pa." She lifted her chin slightly. "Alonzo knows how to fend for himself. I'd say he's done all right."

"I'm sure your husband has overcome a lot of hardship," Patrice assured her soothingly. Billie was starting to get defensive about her oft-criticized husband, the prelude, Patrice feared, to resisting any further questioning. If she hoped to learn anything about Billie's hated father-in-law, she needed to step lightly where Alonzo was concerned. "Did you know your husband at the time of his father's death?"

"Everybody knows everybody else around here. I'd seen him around, whenever he came to school and such like. After his old man was killed, they packed the kids off to foster homes. Alonzo didn't come back to Port Latanier till he was full grown." She looked down at the worn floor. "He should have never come back here."

"Why do you say that, Mrs. Finch?" Patrice asked gently.

A fearful look darkened the shadows of Billie's deep-set eyes, as if she was afraid she had already said too much. "'Cause of what happened here, what he seen." When she paused, Patrice stifled the urge to throw more questions at her, relying on her sense that Billie was about to open up. She was relieved when the woman went on. "That lady shot his pa, right in front of his eyes. That's a heavy burden for a child to bear, seeing his own kin die like that, I don't care how no-good and ornery he was. He still dreams about it."

"You're sure Alonzo saw his father killed?" Patrice probed.

Billie stiffened her neck, not taking her eyes off Patrice. "Leastways, that's what he told me once when he'd been drinking. I s'pose he could have just imagined it," she hedged. "You know the way kids sometimes think about something so much, they start to turn it around in their heads. Maybe he didn't see it after all," she concluded, obviously wishing she had not gone so far.

"I'd like to talk to your husband when he gets home."

Billie only stared at Patrice for a moment. "Like I said, I'm not sure when he'll be back."

"I'm certain he'll want to settle this business with the boat," Alan reminded her. "I'll feel better, too, when that's squared away. We'll see you later. Thanks."

"Alonzo saw his father killed," Patrice stated firmly s soon as they were a respectable distance from the shop.

Alan looked over the car at Patrice as he unlocked the oor. "Why do you suppose the newspaper reports made o mention of a witness?"

Patrice shrugged, sliding into the bucket seat. "Maybe Alonzo didn't tell anyone. From the sound of things, he asn't even been very candid with his own wife." She tared at the green wall of trees blurring past the window s they sped along the highway. "Maybe no one wanted im to tell," she said, almost to herself.

"You mean certain people pressured Alonzo to keep uiet because he knew about the baby?" Alan shifted his yes from the road to cut a quick glance at her.

"It's a possibility. Since Orris was already dead, the amily probably felt that justice had been served. At that oint, Alonzo's testimony would have accomplished only ne purpose, to embarrass the Reeds. I wonder how hey've kept him quiet all these years?"

"Money," Alan provided without hesitation. "My uess is that the bait shop was underwritten with Reed unds."

"And now that Leon is gone, the torch of protecting he family name has passed to Julia." Patrice twisted in er seat to face Alan. "Do you think she's behind these hreats against us?"

Alan frowned. "She's capable of constructing a voo-loo doll and dropping it in the mail, I suppose, but I an't imagine her squirming under your car to damage its rakes, and that certainly wasn't Julia who jumped me n the bayou last night. Even assuming that she would ire a thug to do the dirty work for her, I just can't be-ieve someone would take such drastic steps to cover up n illegitimate birth."

"Neither can I," Patrice admitted reluctantly. "Ther
has to be more at stake. If we could only find out wh
Beau was."

Alan halted at a stop sign. "I'm willing to dig into th
microfilm again," he volunteered. "But if you don
mind, I'd like to postpone helping you until tomorrow.
haven't seen Granddad for a couple of days now, and
want to catch his physician when he makes his rounds th
afternoon."

Patrice shoved back her sleeve to examine her watcl
"I'm ready to call it quits today, too. Why don't we driv
to the sheriff's office so I can check on my car? Then v
can stop at the rental agency and pick up another car fo
me to take back to New Orleans. You still haven't ha
your brakes checked, you know."

"Yes, ma'am." When Alan grinned, a trace of h
particularly endearing brand of warmth flickered in h
brown eyes.

Patrice quickly looked out the window. It was time t
call it quits, in more ways than one. After spending a
most two solid days with Alan, she could no longer re
on her emotions to retreat docilely to their cage at h
bidding. Then, too, she needed some time away from hi
to sort through her feelings. Patrice refused to doubt th
depth or sincerity of the powerful emotions that ha
drawn them into each other's arms last night, but she fe
strangely inept trying to adjust that relationship to th
sober light of day. Alan, too, was apparently havir
problems putting their intimacy into perspective, if h
strictly-business manner today was any indication. Pa
trice was so absorbed in thought that she did not at fir
realize that they were traveling along the street where Ju
lia Broussard lived.

They had passed the house when Patrice touched Alan's sleeve on impulse. "Why don't we try to talk with Bernice Wood again, Alan? She relented a bit when she heard about your grandfather's mishap. Maybe if we told her about that guy who attacked you with a knife, she would be willing to talk about Beau." When Alan only slowed the car, she persisted. "Come on. It's worth a chance. Julia's car is gone."

Alan eased the Taurus toward the curb. "Here goes nothing."

ALONZO HAD CALLED HER only once before, and that had been almost eighteen years ago. After their horrible pact was sealed, he had relied on Julia to initiate any extra contact, contenting himself with their scheduled rendezvous at the cemetery. When she had answered the phone today, she had known immediately that something was wrong. Alonzo had sounded frightened, and Julia had been too fraught with her own anxiety to take any pleasure in his distress. He had demanded they meet, without offering any explanation, and when she had agreed he had hung up.

Julia clasped her hands, trying to massage some blood into the cold fingers. Alonzo had balked at meeting at their usual place, insisting instead that she wait for him in an abandoned sharecropper's cabin near the parish line. She had dreaded the tryst all morning, but a strange calm had settled over her as she prepared to drive into the country. She had lived in fear of Alonzo long enough.

As she had planned, Julia arrived at the dilapidated cabin before Alonzo. After parking her car behind the shack, she collected her handbag and the manila envelope she had brought with her and walked to the rear of the car. Julia removed the tire iron from the Mercedes's trunk and then entered the cabin. She stationed herself by the window to wait.

Presently, an old pickup truck turned off the road, and after a few minutes a door slammed. Julia heard Alonzo limping across the porch's loose floorboards before she saw him. When he opened the door, she flinched in spite of her resolve. A dark red stain spread over the left shoulder of his shirt and down the sleeve, discoloring the fatigue green to a wet black. Sweat and oil mingled on his unshaven face, giving it an unhealthy sheen. His breathing had an irregular, labored sound to it.

"What happened to you?" Julia demanded in a rasping whisper.

"Goddamned bitch shot me." Alonzo lifted his hand from his shoulder and surveyed the bloody palm as if it belonged to someone else. "I was lucky, though. Bullet went clean through."

"Does anyone know about this?"

"That's all you care about, ain't it, Julia? Folks *knowin'*." Alonzo grinned, lips pulling back from his gums in an obscene leer. Then he winced in pain. "I can't go home. I already seen the law at the store this mornin', right after I snuck in and got my truck. I got no place to go."

"You expect me to help *you?*" Julia coldly regarded Alonzo as if he were a half-dead insect.

"I reckon you better." Alonzo's yellow eyes glowed with fever and malice. "'Cause if you don't, I got no choice but to turn myself in. And this time I'm gonna tell 'em everything."

"What do you want?" Julia asked through tight lips.

"Enough money to get me 'cross the country. Ain't nobody been killed, so I figure they won't think I'm worth comin' after."

"I thought you'd want money." Julia looked down at the manila envelope she held. "I can give you ten thousand dollars if you promise never to come back here again."

Alonzo's mouth twisted into another grin. "Ten thousand ain't much these days. Besides, you and me are friends. You might start missin' me after a while."

"Take it and get out of my sight!" Julia flung the envelope into the empty stone fireplace.

She watched Alonzo hobble across the room to retrieve it. Unable to restrain his greed, he opened the flap and pulled out a stack of bills bound with a rubber band. When he began to count, Julia reached for the tire iron she had laid beneath the window. Holding the iron behind her, she walked up behind Alonzo.

"It's all there," she murmured.

Julia lifted the tire iron and swung it with all her strength. A dizzying exhilaration surged through her as it connected with the back of Alonzo's skull. She stood over his inert body for a moment, panting in triumph.

Julia took a deep breath, steadying herself to complete her task. She avoided touching Alonzo as she stooped to retrieve the money. Stuffing it back into the envelope, she hurried to her car. Julia opened the trunk, returned the tire iron to its niche and then removed a red metal can. She circled the cabin, taking care to keep her shoes clean as she sloshed gasoline around the crumbling foundation. She checked to be sure she had collected everything she had brought with her before pulling a book of matches out of her handbag. When Julia tossed the lighted match into the gasoline-soaked weeds, the blaze erupted with a deafening whoosh.

She had lived in fear of Alonzo long enough. She would never have to fear him again.

Chapter Fourteen

Patrice lifted the thick brass ring and let it fall against the door-knocker plate. She listened for a moment before rapping with more force. When her efforts failed to yield a response, she leaned to peer through the leaded-glass panels flanking the doorframe on both sides. "There's a light on somewhere in the rear of the house."

"Why don't we walk around back and see if we can get an answer?" Alan suggested, gesturing toward the driveway.

As they followed the brick walk leading to the sun porch, the faint sound of gospel music drifted through one of the open windows. Patrice tapped on the sun room's glass door and waited for results. When she tested the door handle, she found it unlocked.

"Shall we?"

Alan gave her an uncertain look. "Isn't this what's termed 'breaking and entering' in legal circles?"

"No breaking, just entering." Patrice jiggled the door handle to support her point. She pushed the door open and entered the sun room, with Alan bringing up the rear. Patrice hesitated on the threshold and peeked into the formal dining room. "Mrs. Broussard?" Even if they had barged into the house with reasonable certainty that Julia was gone, it didn't hurt to be on the safe side.

Bernice Wood appeared in the interior doorway with a bundle of neatly folded table linen in her arms. "Good Lord, you gave me a fright!"

"I'm sorry," Patrice apologized. "We knocked at the front door, but we were afraid that no one had heard us."

"My hearing isn't what it used to be," the housekeeper apologized. "I wasn't expecting anyone while Mrs. Broussard was out, so I turned the radio up a little louder than usual while I was ironing. I'm afraid I don't know when Mrs. Broussard will be back."

"Oh, that doesn't matter," Patrice fibbed. "We really stopped by to see you."

Bernice's kind face grew solemn, but she said nothing, in part, Patrice imagined, because she was too polite to order them out of the house.

"We don't wish to hound you, Mrs. Wood," Alan spoke up. "And we're very grateful for the help you've already given us. We found the box you placed in the mausoleum."

Bernice Wood stood so still that for a moment Patrice feared she had quit breathing. "Then you know now," she said simply.

"Not everything we need to know," Alan went on quietly. "Someone followed us into the bayou and damaged our boat while we were searching for the box. We didn't realize anything was wrong until we started back to Port Latanier. We barely made it to land before the boat sank. Later that night while we were stranded in the bayou, a man attacked me with a knife. Fortunately, Patrice frightened him off before he could accomplish his purpose, but I have no doubt he intended to kill both of us."

The housekeeper clutched the linen to her chest, bracing herself with one hand against the doorframe. "I don't know who's doing these terrible things, Dr. Lowndes. I swear I don't!"

Mrs. Wood looked so stricken, Patrice place a comforting hand on her elbow. She gently guided the housekeeper to the dining table and eased her into one of the chairs. Patrice drew up a chair and seated herself facing her. She covered Mrs. Wood's tightly clasped hands with her own. "I know talking about all of this is very upsetting for you, Mrs. Wood, but I'm scared." Given Bernice Wood's demonstrated sensitivity to both Leon Reed and his daughter, Patrice guessed a personal appeal would carry more weight with her than any investigative probing. "Please help us."

The housekeeper looked down at their joined hands and sighed. "I'll tell you about Miss Melanie, but I swear I don't know who would try to hurt you," she repeated.

Bernice Wood straightened herself and took a deep breath. "Mr. Reed was just beside himself when Miss Melanie told him she was expecting a child. Nothing like that had ever happened in the Reed family, at least, not in his time. And she wasn't the least bit ashamed. I think that bothered him as much as anything. As headstrong as that girl was, I don't know how he managed to keep her penned up in the house after she started to show. To tell you the truth, I think Miss Melanie thought that going along with her father was the best way to get her way in the end. And she was bound and determined to keep that baby, kept telling me how her Beau was going to come back from Vietnam and marry her someday. That poor child!" She broke off to cover her eyes with her hand.

Patrice and Alan waited, giving Bernice Wood a chance to recover her composure. She wiped the moisture from her cheek with the back of her hand before going on. "'Course, she never lived to see Beau again." Her voice cracked. "I think Mr. Reed somehow felt like Miss Melanie's death was a punishment to him, for trying to take her child away from her. Not many kind words had passed in that family for a long time, and then suddenly Miss Melanie was gone, and none of them could make it up to her. Mr. Reed asked me to witness the little baby's baptism, since I'd been taking care of her. Then one day he put her in the bassinet and just drove off with her. I never did see that sweet child again." Bernice shook her head, staring at the polished tabletop as if the wrenching separation had happened only yesterday.

"How did Julia feel about all of this?" Patrice asked.

When Bernice looked up at her, Patrice was startled by the reproach in her eyes. "Why, I suppose how any woman would feel and then some."

Patrice frowned in puzzlement. "I'm afraid I don't quite understand what you mean."

"She just couldn't face the thought that she might lose Beau, I guess, but she said some awfully hurtful things to her sister, things I'm sure she didn't mean."

"Julia was in love with Beau, too?"

Bernice shook her head with sad, slow finality. "Not just that, Ms. Ribeau. She was married to him." She looked off. "I remember her screaming and crying, saying she'd see them both dead before she'd give Beau up. You know, Ms. Ribeau, my mother always told me never to say something you don't mean, no matter how angry you are, because it just might come true and then you've got to live with yourself. I think that's why Mrs. Broussard seems so bitter now. Her poor sister is dead, and her husband never made it back from Vietnam."

At the sound of a car turning onto the driveway, Alan nudged Patrice's elbow. "I think we'd better be going now. You have that appointment in New Orleans, remember?"

Patrice cut a nervous glance toward the driveway. "I'm glad you reminded me." As she stood up, she stooped to clasp Bernice Wood's hands once more. "Thank you so much, Mrs. Wood. Please don't bother to get up. We can find our way out."

The housekeeper nodded. Fortunately, she seemed oblivious to her employer's return. Grabbing Alan's hand, Patrice headed for the hall just as the Mercedes's engine fell silent.

"Let's see if we can sneak out the back," she whispered.

Alan nodded as they flattened themselves against the wall. They could hear Bernice's surprised voice as Julia marched into the dining room. Holding their breath, they tiptoed across the kitchen's waxed floor to the door. As luck would have it, the solid door was standing open, freeing them from dealing with any troublesome noisy hinges. Alan unhooked the screen door and held it open.

"Let's move it!" Tension had roughened his whisper to a harsh rasp.

They crouched, keeping their heads below window level as they slunk along the side of the house. They had reached the corner when a cold voice behind them froze them in their tracks.

"Going so soon?"

Patrice took a deep breath and slowly pulled herself erect. Julia had caught them in their little caper, but she couldn't very well call the police and have them arrested for talking with her housekeeper.

"As a matter of fact, we were," Patrice began. Her voice died when she caught sight of the gun that Julia clutched in her hand.

"Come on. Get in the car." Julia looked so incongruous gesturing with the gun, jerking it like a mobster in a 1940s movie, that Patrice would have giggled had the situation not been deadly serious.

"Wait a minute, Julia! This is crazy." Alan balked, but he kept a respectful eye on the gun pointed at them.

Julia ignored his argument. "Open the trunk and get in." She was trying to sound calm, but her voice was unnaturally tight, betraying her tension.

Keep her talking. Buy some time. She's at least as nervous as you. Patrice tried to calm herself and keep a handle on her wits. "I don't know what you intend to do, Julia, but you're not going to get away with it. We've been dealing with the police so much, they're going to come looking for us the moment I don't show up at my dad's house this afternoon."

Julia snorted a brief laugh. "Save your breath. Those fools never questioned why Melanie was killed, and I think it highly unlikely they'll connect your disappearance with me, either."

Patrice felt all the color slowly drain from her face. Julia had engineered Melanie's murder in an insane attempt to keep her husband! The thought was so shocking that for a moment Patrice's mind blanked to everything else. The gun Julia held brought her back to reality. "You're wrong, Julia," she countered.

"The police know where we are right now." Alan joined in the gambit. "Sheriff Wade's expecting Patrice to show up at his office for questioning at four. If she doesn't—"

"You're lying!" Julia shouted.

Patrice flinched as Julia's hand grasped for a better hold on the gun. More often than she liked to think, people were killed when guns accidentally went off in some hothead's hand. Julia was a desperate, cold-blooded woman, but she was definitely not comfortable handling a gun. She held it with a finicky grip, as if she disliked sullying her hands with something capable of spraying guts and brains all over the place.

"I mean it. Open that trunk and get in." Julia's finger twitched on the trigger.

When she saw Julia's eyes widen, Patrice closed her own. *Please, God, don't let this be the end. Please let me see Alex and my father again.* When she dared to look, she discovered that Julia had shifted the gun to point at the shrubs bordering the driveway.

"What are you doing here?" Julia's voice sounded as if she had seen a ghost.

Based on appearance, the man who had just stepped through the bushes could well be a specter from the spirit world. Wild yellow eyes stared out of a grizzled face blanched the color of cold oatmeal. His thatch of greasy hair was matted with blood. Shapeless clothes clung to his gaunt frame like rags hung out to dry. When Patrice noticed the blood seeping through his left sleeve, she realized with a jolt where their paths had previously crossed.

"You thought you'd seen the last of me, didn't you, Julia? But I come back for you." The man's grin was pure evil.

"Another step and I'll shoot you, Alonzo. I swear I will!" Julia shook the gun, her rigid arms stretched out in front of her.

"Come on now, Julia. What would the neighbors think? I thought you'd learned to be more careful,"

Alonzo chided. "Remember, you done that once, blew my daddy away without botherin' to see if anyone was watchin'. It never occurred to you that one of his kids might be hidin' in the back of that truck. So you just walked up to him as bold as you please, thanked my poor ol' stupid swamp-rat daddy for takin' care of your sister, and while he was shakin' and wonderin' how he'd ever been fool enough to get tangled up with you, you just took his head clean off." Alonzo paused and lifted the sawed-off shotgun he had carried concealed in the folds of his ill-fitting khakis. "Just like I'm gonna take yours off."

"Alonzo, don't!" Patrice shouted. "She's not worth spending the rest of your life in the pen."

Unlike Julia, whose eyes were darting wildly among the three of them, Alonzo kept his frightening yellow gaze trained straight on Julia. "My life ain't worth nothin' anyway." He braced the shotgun against his shoulder, grimacing as he used his bad arm for a prop.

"No!" Alan yelled.

Julia swung, distracted by his cry. Taking advantage of her confusion, Alan lunged and knocked her off her feet. He rolled to one side just as Alonzo fired. Shot sprayed the driveway and scattered in every direction.

"Look out!" Patrice screamed, but Julia had already recovered her pistol.

Scrambling to her feet, she leveled the gun at Alonzo. He struggled to hoist the shotgun again, but his disabled arm was working against him. Julia fired a wild shot that ricocheted off the gutter downspout. The second time, luck was on her side. Alonzo reeled back into the shrubs just as Bernice Wood appeared in the sun room doorway.

When Julia saw the housekeeper staring in disbelief at the scene unfolding on the driveway, she froze for a split second, enough time for Patrice to act. She tackled Julia from the side, grabbing her wrist with both hands and wrenching it behind her back. Julia cried out in pain and dropped the gun. As Patrice dived for the pistol, Julia grabbed Alonzo's shotgun and pointed it at them.

"Don't anyone move," Julia warned.

She backed toward the Mercedes, fanning the shotgun in front of her. Her free hand shook as she grappled with the door. Just as she wrenched the door open, a car screeched to a halt at the end of the driveway. Julia wheeled to see Sheriff Wade stepping out of his cruiser, and in her surprise, dropped the shotgun.

"Get your hands up and keep 'em up!" the sheriff ordered, holding his pistol steady. His eyes fixed on Julia, he crouched to retrieve the shotgun. Sheriff Wade surveyed the driveway, his gaze traveling slowly from Julia to Alonzo, huddled, clutching both bleeding arms, to Patrice and Alan. "Someone's got a *whole* lot of explaining to do."

ChapterFifteen

"Thanks." Patrice gave the deputy a grateful smile as she accepted the cup of coffee he handed her. She emptied a packet of sugar into the dark brew and swished the stir stick in a little circle, pleased that her hands could perform at least those simple tasks without shaking. She jumped up, almost upsetting the coffee, when Sheriff Wade ambled into the room. "Is he going to be all right?"

"Why don't you ask him yourself?" The sheriff stepped aside, nodding toward Alan, who hung back in the doorway.

Alan smiled, gesturing sheepishly toward the white bandage taped around his right forearm. "I just got a little nick from some stray shotgun pellets. The emergency room doctor insisted that my arm would be as good as new long after you were still feeling aches and pains from your accident."

Patrice looked unimpressed. "You could have been seriously hurt, you know," she reminded him severely.

"So could you," Alan retorted.

"Hey, will you folks hold the fussin'?" Sheriff Wade interrupted. When they fell silent, he sighed. "That's better." He surveyed his cluttered desk. "I guess I just need to have y'all sign your statements and then you can be on your way."

Patrice scanned the typed copy of her account of the afternoon's events. When she had placed her signature at the bottom of the second page, she handed the form back to the sheriff. "We both owe you a big thank-you for staying on top of things. If you hadn't showed up this afternoon, I don't know what Julia might have done."

"She's a real sick woman, but to be honest, I would never have suspected she was behind all this business," Sheriff Wade confessed. "When we realized that someone had fooled with the brake line on your car, I just knew I needed to keep an eye on you. And you." He glanced over Patrice's shoulder at Alan.

"Is Alonzo going to make it?" Alan asked.

Sheriff Wade nodded wearily. "That kind is hard to kill. When they hauled him into the emergency room, he was still ranting about getting even with Julia. I expect he will, in court. He's so eager to nail her, he kept fighting those painkillers, tryin' to tell me stuff before his tongue got too thick. 'Course, Alonzo was willing to go along with Julia and try to stop your investigation when he thought the truth coming out would undercut his own blackmail game. He just soured on her when she tried to kill him. Can't say I blame him." The sheriff chuckled. He sobered instantly when he heard a booming male voice approaching in the corridor.

"I'm not interested in procedures, son. I'm here to get my girl." Tony Lafon dismissed the deputy tagging helplessly behind him as he strode into Sheriff Wade's office. His face wore a higher color than usual, and his mouth was set in a strained line.

Patrice rushed to reassure her father. "I'm just fine, Dad," she began, but when she noticed the moisture cading in the corner of his eyes, her voice caught. Putting her arms around him, she hugged him tightly.

Tony Lafon patted her back. "Let's go home, baby. I promised Alex we'd grill some hamburgers after we picked him up from basketball practice. When I didn't hear from you this afternoon, I figured I'd better come down and get you so I wouldn't have to break my word." His voice was husky, betraying the profound emotion hiding beneath that homey statement. He cleared his throat, releasing his hold on Patrice to offer his hand to Sheriff Wade. "Thank you, Sheriff. I appreciate your staying on top of things." He turned to Alan. "And thank you for—" he hesitated "—for taking care of my girl."

Alan looked slightly embarrassed. "She did a pretty good job of taking care of me a lot of the time."

Tony looked from Alan to Patrice as if he couldn't quite decide what to make of them. "Well, the important thing is that you're both still in one piece."

As her father started for the door, Patrice gently slid her hand free of his clasp and turned to Alan. The afternoon had been so emotionally draining, she had not yet had time to recover her equilibrium, much less to think of what she wanted to say to Alan now that the investigation was completed. Relieved as she was to have resolved the troublesome case, she was acutely aware that she no longer had a specific reason to see Alan tomorrow, or any day, for that matter.

"I guess you'll be staying in Port Latanier tonight." Patrice almost cringed at the bland statement she had just uttered.

Alan nodded. "I'm going to hang around town until they take Granddad out of intensive care. When I was in

the hospital this afternoon, I did manage to check o
him, and he's doing remarkably well.''

"That's wonderful," Patrice said.

She swallowed, trying to find a way to translate he
complicated feelings into words. The simplest—and mos
authentic—expression would have been to put her arm
around Alan and hold him as close as she could for
long, long time. *But I'm too cowardly to do that, even i
I didn't have an audience.*

As if he had an inkling of her inner turmoil, Ala
looked down and then reached for Patrice's hand. "Tak
care of yourself, okay? I'll be in touch." His hand tight
ened around hers with such force she almost winced
When he released it, Patrice let it hang in the air for
moment. "I think your dad's getting impatient."

Patrice forced a smile. "I'm used to that by now." Sh
stepped toward the door, where her father stood chat
ting with the deputy. "Oh, and Alan." She hesitated. *
care about you. I want you to care about me. I love you*
The words raged inside her in vain. "Thanks for you
help."

Turning on her heel, Patrice dashed to the door to joi
her father. As they walked down the corridor to the exit
she looked back to see Alan standing in the doorway. Hi
lips moved in some last whispered farewell, the meanin
of which Patrice could only guess.

"I'M SO GLAD you caught me before I left for the hospi
tal this afternoon." Anne-Marie Bergier smiled as sh
sank onto the sofa beside Patrice. Just as quickly, sh
moved to stand up again. "Can I offer you some cof
fee?"

"No, thanks. I promised not to take up a lot of your time, and I'm going to keep my word. I just had something of yours that I wanted to give you."

Anne-Marie's gaze followed Patrice's to the briefcase resting beside the coffee table. "I was going to phone you and ask for an invoice," she apologized. "I know you put a lot of time into my investigation before I decided to drop it."

Patrice shook her head as she reached for the briefcase. "You don't owe me anything, Anne-Marie." When the young woman opened her mouth to protest, Patrice placed a quieting hand on her slim arm. "At the very least, I'm working on evening the balance for all the kind things you've done for Alex and me." She lifted the briefcase onto the coffee table and unfastened the latches. "This is yours." Patrice removed the etched metal box and placed it on Anne-Marie's lap.

Anne-Marie looked from the box to Patrice and back again, too surprised to speak.

"Go on. Open it." Patrice encouraged her.

Anne-Marie delicately lifted the tiny hook securing the box's lid. When she opened it, a palette of the most complex emotions washed over her young face. Her finger trembled slightly as it traced the narrow pink ribbon coiled around the tiny baby slippers. With a care approaching reverence, she lifted the locket out of the box and stretched it across her open palm.

"They're yours, Anne-Marie. Someone who loved you very much chose them for you a long time ago. She wasn't able to care for you and see you grow up the way she would have liked, but it wasn't for want of love. I think she would be happy to know you had these things now." Seeing the tears beginning to trickle down Anne-Marie's face, Patrice felt a constricting tightness seize her own throat. "There's a letter in the box that you can read later, when you're alone. I think she would have wanted you to have it, too."

"Thank you, Patrice." Anne-Marie brushed her wet face and then reached to put her arms around her "Thank you so much." She sat back, holding on to Patrice's hand. "You know, when I first asked you to look for my birth mother, I don't think I really had a clear idea of what I expected to find. Most of the time, I told myself I was simply curious to know what she looked like where she lived, things like that. But deep down inside—" she pressed her midriff with one small fist "—I knew it was something more." She paused, her fine dark brows knitting in concentration. "Peace. That was what I was looking for. Peace."

Patrice gave her friend a warm hug. "I hope you've found it."

Anne-Marie smiled through her tears. "I have, Patrice, and you helped me."

The memory of the intensely emotional experience she had shared with Anne-Marie lingered with Patrice long after she had left the young nurse's apartment and returned to her office that afternoon. Compared to the precious legacy that Bernice Wood had preserved for Anne-Marie, the dry-dust data that Patrice had originally hoped to uncover about her birth mother—name, date and place of birth, Social Security number and so on—now seemed pitifully inconsequential. But then, investigations seldom developed in quite the way one expected at the outset.

As Patrice rummaged through the paper littering her desk, she did not have to look far to find concrete reminders of another case that had evolved in a radically different fashion than she had first anticipated. Sinking

own into her desk chair, Patrice stared at the receipts she
ad accumulated on behalf of Alan Lowndes.

Only a day had passed since she had last talked with
im, but it might as well have been an eternity. If any-
hing, their brief phone conversations had left her feel-
ng even more confused and disconnected than a
omplete silence would have. After exchanging polite in-
uiries about Dr. Hamilton's condition and Alex's gen-
ral welfare, they never seemed to know what to talk
bout. Maybe the phone was to blame, but until circum-
tances permitted a face-to-face meeting, it was the best
hey could do.

"I love you, Alan, and I want our relationship to go
n." Uttered in the privacy of her own office, the words
eemed simple enough. Patrice stared across the room,
rying to visualize Alan somewhere between the book-
ase and the potted ferns withering on the Parsons table.
Maybe if she practiced a bit, she would find the gump-
ion to move beyond the dress-rehearsal stage. But then,
vhy should she be the one to take the big risk? If Alan
oved her, why couldn't he simply pick up the phone and
ay so? If he loved her...

Patrice sighed as she pulled out a blank balance sheet,
rying to make herself feel cool and businesslike. The receipt on top of the pile sported a clip-art drawing of a
bluebird to which some budding artist had added a free-
hand nightcap. In an effort to pass both of them off as
Mr. and Mrs. Suburbia, Alan had paid the motel bill. She
needed to deduct the amount from the final tally.

What about all the junk food they had eaten that
night? And the ice? Alan had sprung for those things,
too. Should she estimate the amount and take it off his
bill, as well? It was impossible to consider all the silly,
petty issues raised by their joint venture and not think

about the unresolved relationship now hanging in the balance.

The car-rental receipt was scarcely legible, thanks to its dousing in the bayou. At the reminder of that last night they had spent together, Patrice leaned back in her chair and closed her eyes, surrendering for a moment to the magical memories drifting through her mind. She let out a deep breath and shoved her chair forward, cutting short the reverie that threatened to consume the remainder of the afternoon.

Patrice was adding up billable hours on the calculator when the door buzzer sounded. Striking the total key as she stood up, she hurried out to the front office and opened the door. She gaped, her mouth falling open when she found Alan Lowndes standing in the corridor.

"May I come in?"

Patrice took a fumbling step backward. "Yeah, sure. As long as you don't have any voodoo dolls with you," she added. Caught as she was, her best bet was to rely on humor to keep things light until she got her bearings. "I was just working on your account," she went on, leading the way to her office.

"Great. That's why I stopped by."

Patrice's back was turned to Alan, allowing her to indulge in a wince. With monumental personal matters between them remaining unsettled, could he possibly have popped in on her today only to conduct a cut-and-dried business transaction? Well, whatever he had in mind, she had no intention of letting him out of the office until she, at least, had her say.

Patrice wheeled and gave Alan a coolly appraising look. "If you've got a few minutes, I'll check my figures before I print out an invoice."

"I'm in no hurry."

Patrice could feel his dark eyes on her as she rounded the desk, and she avoided looking at him. Curling the calculator tape over her hand, she studied the figures. "You know, I'm really in a quandary about the number of hours I should bill you. You helped with so much of the footwork." She took a deep breath, fortifying herself to look up into those melting dark eyes. "How would it be if I added up all the time and then divided it in half?"

"You mean an even split, right down the middle?"

"Uh-huh. That way I don't have to pay you for your assistance and then bill you back," Patrice quipped.

"I have an even better idea." Alan reached to pluck the calculator tape from her unsuspecting hand and rip it in two. "Why don't we simply set up an open account?"

Patrice frowned at the ruined tape. She hated paperwork, and the thought of having to reconstruct all those numbers did not sit well with her. "Look, Alan, I don't pretend to be up on the latest accounting techniques, but I'm afraid I don't have the faintest idea what you're talking about."

"A partnership." When she continued to stare dumbly at him, Alan stood and placed both hands flat on her desk. "Damn it, will you help me out with this?" he blurted. He gave her a look of pure exasperation. "You know good and well what I'm talking about."

Patrice suppressed a smile. "A good detective never jumps to conclusions," she reminded him.

Without further ado, Alan rounded the desk and pulled Patrice into his arms and planted a heart-stopping kiss on her lips. Stepping back slightly, he held Patrice at arm's length. "Have I made myself clear?"

Patrice swallowed hard, waiting for her pulse to subside. "I think I'm catching on."

Alan's face grew serious. "I'm sorry I haven't done a very good job of telling you how I feel up to now. To be honest, I don't think I recognized the symptoms at first. I kept trying to make excuses for wanting to be around you all the time, worrying about you when I wasn't. Now that the investigation is finished, all my excuses have gone out the window. I'm left with only one reason. I love you, Patrice, and I want to spend the rest of my life showing you that I do." When Patrice locked her hands around Alan's neck, he grinned. "Do you think you can stand that?"

"If you can stand having a woman who loves you so much it makes her crazy." She touched the tip of her nose to his.

"Is our account settled, then?" Alan's lips lightly brushed hers as he formed the words.

Patrice caressed his mouth with her smile. "Case closed."

HARLEQUIN®
I N T R I G U E®

HARLEQUIN INTRIGUE INVITES YOU TO

A HALLOWEEN QUARTET

Celebrate All Hallows' Eve with four couples who battle things that go bump in the night—and emotions that have a life of their own. Ghastly ghouls and midnight trysts abound in these four Halloween romances from your favorite Intrigue authors.

#249 MUSIC OF THE MIST by Laura Pender
#250 HAUNTED by Patricia Rosemoor
#251 MIDNIGHT MASQUE by Jenna Ryan
#252 FRIGHT NIGHT by Linda Stevens

For the scare—and the love—of a lifetime, be sure to read all four. Available now.

Relive the romance...
Harlequin®is proud to bring you

A new collection of three complete novels every month. By the most requested authors, featuring the most requested themes.

Available in October:

DREAMSCAPE

They're falling under a spell!
But is it love—or magic?

Three complete novels in one special collection:

GHOST OF A CHANCE by Jayne Ann Krentz
BEWITCHING HOUR by Anne Stuart
REMEMBER ME by Bobby Hutchinson

Available wherever Harlequin books are sold.

1993 Keepsake

CHRISTMAS

Stories

Capture the spirit and romance of Christmas with KEEPSAKE CHRISTMAS STORIES, a collection of three stories by favorite historical authors. The perfect Christmas gift!

Don't miss these heartwarming stories, available in November wherever Harlequin books are sold:

ONCE UPON A CHRISTMAS by Curtiss Ann Matlock
A FAIRYTALE SEASON by Marianne Willman
TIDINGS OF JOY by Victoria Pade

ADD A TOUCH OF ROMANCE TO YOUR HOLIDAY SEASON WITH KEEPSAKE CHRISTMAS STORIES!

HX93

Fifty red-blooded, white-hot, true-blue hunks
from every State in the Union!

Look for MEN MADE IN AMERICA! Written by some
of our most poplar authors, these stories feature fifty of
the strongest, sexiest men, each from a different state in
the union!

Two titles available every other month at your favorite
retail outlet.

In November, look for:

STRAIGHT FROM THE HEART by Barbara Delinsky
(Connecticut)
AUTHOR'S CHOICE by Elizabeth August (Delaware)

In January, look for:

DREAM COME TRUE by Ann Major (Florida)
WAY OF THE WILLOW by Linda Shaw (Georgia)

You won't be able to resist MEN MADE IN AMERICA!

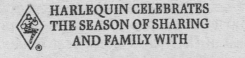

HARLEQUIN CELEBRATES
THE SEASON OF SHARING
AND FAMILY WITH

Friends, Families,
Lovers

Harlequin introduces the latest member in its family of
seasonal collections. Following in the footsteps of the popular
My Valentine, Just Married and *Harlequin Historical Christmas
Stories,* we are proud to present FRIENDS, FAMILIES,
LOVERS. A collection of three new contemporary romance
stories about America at its best, about welcoming others into
the circle of love.... Stories to warm your heart ...

By three leading romance authors:

> **KATHLEEN EAGLE**
> **SANDRA KITT**
> **RUTH JEAN DALE**

> Available in October, wherever
> Harlequin books are sold.